THE PROMISE KEEPER

CONVENIENT WOMEN COLLECTION BOOK TWO

DELPHINE WOODS

PEPPER POT PUBLISHING

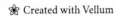 Created with Vellum

INSPIRED BY

A wise old owl lived in an oak
The more he saw the less he spoke
The less he spoke the more he heard.
Why can't we all be like that wise old bird?

PROLOGUE

She blinks, takes in the darkness. Her lids are as sharp as crushed glass over her eyeballs. Tears swamp but do not soothe. She feels the clumps of her own hair laced across the pillow as she rolls her head to one side, unable to lift it, unable to sit up, unable to stand, no matter how hard she might try.

Her body clenches involuntarily. Her muscles bunch, spasm. Her stomach heaves again. Her arse pushes, but she is dried out.

The convulsion ends. Still, the sickness remains. Liquid swims in her mouth. Stale. Foul. The stench of her. God! She would shudder at the sight of herself if her mind were clear, but it is not. It is as if someone has taken hold of her brain and is squeezing it, crushing it into confusion, blinding her with agony.

Slow ... she is slowing down. Every movement is hard.

She tries to breathe but she has not the energy. Breathe ... breathe ... but what is the use? It will be better this way.

She closes her eyes. She is slipping away. The pain and the fear are all slipping away.

CHAPTER 1

 anuary 1869

'How long before we arrive?' Liz says and swallows down the taste of bile. The journey is longer than she had been expecting. The air is too clear out here, everything so green. It makes her head feel light upon her neck.

'Not long now,' Mary says as each tremble of the carriage makes her cheeks wobble.

'Not a good day to begin a honeymoon, I'm afraid, my dear.' Tom pulls his collar closer to his throat and fiddles with the delicate ends of his moustache.

'I don't mind,' Mary says, her fingertips brushing his knee. 'I cannot wait for you to see Floreat. It is such a beautiful house. Do you know it means flourish?'

'Yes, dear.' Tom meets Liz's gaze, raises an eyebrow. 'You told me before.'

The carriage rumbles on. Liz rearranges her skirts, shifts

her backside to try to find some feeling in it, and when she looks up, Mary's eyes are locked in the distance. Liz cranes her neck to see; they are approaching a tiny church, surrounded by headstones and two towering yew trees. Near the entrance gate, a large tomb stands.

Mary sighs. 'I wish they could see me now.'

'Would you like to stop?' Tom says.

Mary shakes her head and rests her gaze on the velvet cushion beside Liz.

As the church fades into the distance, two birds fly by the window. Liz wonders where the crows are heading and if their fate is as uncertain as hers. She looks at Tom, at his sharp cheekbones, his full lips, his hair, his eyebrows, his lashes, his moustache, all as jet and shiny as the crow's feathers. Where is he taking her? Where is she blindly following him?

'Are you well, sister?' he says.

Liz rolls her shoulders back, hears the creak of her spine. 'Just a little stiff.'

Mary grasps her arm. 'You will have a bath tonight, Elizabeth. I have given Bet instructions to prepare one for you before the wedding dinner. I thought this cold would not suit you, you are too skinny. We must feed her up, mustn't we, Tom?'

Liz smiles and hopes it reaches her eyes.

'I do hope Bet has prepared some beef. And sugared plums. We must have sugared plums for our wedding night. And cake! Of course, how could I forget the cake?'

'I'm sure Bet knows you well enough, dear. It shall all be taken care of.'

Mary giggles, a sound too infantile for a woman of her years, then she gasps.

They have reached a stone wall beset with an iron gate which has been opened for their arrival. At the end of the lengthy, gravelled path sits a grand house. Strong sunlight, rough winds, and slanting rain have carved the golden stone into a patchwork of brown and grey stains streaking from the roof and window panes. The windows are small and dark. Apexes and chimneys stretch into the sky. Liz is sure that the manor is the size of at least ten omnibuses. So big, so looming; she is sure it will eat her up.

Above the door, an archway is engraved with the word Floreat.

Mary claps her hands. 'Home at last.'

FLOREAT. Mary's childhood home, her father's domain, is now hers.

She sees the little white fleck in the middle of the 'o' in the house name. She smells the peat, the muck, the sea. She is already rushing for the doorway when she realises that she has forgotten her husband.

Husband.

It is a strange word, one she thought she would never associate with herself, but now, almost into her third decade of life, she has, finally, found love.

She regards him as he dismounts from the carriage. In his wedding suit of fine black wool, silk top hat, and vivid white waistcoat, Tom is the most handsome man she has ever known.

He smiles at her and turns to help his sister. Elizabeth's small feet kick out the hems of her emerald silk dress as she descends the carriage steps. The breeze lifts a strand of her silver-blonde hair, and she brushes it from her cheek as she beholds the house with wide eyes, the same shade of glassy green as her brother's. She is beautiful. Too beautiful.

'Ma'am,' Bet coughs from behind Mary. 'Welcome home.'

Mary smiles at her old maid, pleased to see that Bet's

usually creased face has softened at the sight of her mistress in ivory satin.

'I have prepared tea in the drawing room, ma'am. Dinner will be served at seven.'

Mary is about to follow her maid into the house when Tom speaks.

'Excuse me, Wife, but where do you think you are going?'

Tom leaps to her side, scoops her into his arms, and carries her over the threshold. The closeness of him, his smell of orange blossom, his whiskers that tickle her cheek as she presses against him, make her impatient for their wedding night.

WITH DAYLIGHT ALMOST GONE, several dozen candles brandish the cavernous entrance hall in a buttery glow. Animal heads stare down at Liz from the walls amidst sooty oil paintings and gilded mirrors which multiply their reflections.

Tom places Mary on her feet. 'Now, how about you show us around our home?'

Liz would like nothing more than to retreat to her private room. Her new shoes are too tight and she yearns to kick them off, to feel cool wood on the soles of her feet. She longs to close her eyes so that she can sink into her dreams, forget the horror of today, and imagine herself somewhere filled with sunshine. But Mary is too proud to let Liz slip away, and Liz is too polite to leave without her sister-in-law's consent.

'Through here is the snug.' Mary opens the door to their left and wafts Liz and Tom inside. A musty smell permeates the room, and two well-worn and sagging armchairs sit in the middle, invitingly. 'Daddy and I used to read in here in the wintertime before … well, before he became too ill. And through here,' Mary continues into another room, 'is the library proper.'

Books of all sizes, leather bound and traced with golden letters, adorn three walls. A large fireplace, made from marble, dominates the place.

'I'm sure you will find much to occupy yourself within here, darling,' Mary says to Tom, who peruses the shelves. 'Come along now, you can look tomorrow. This is the music room.'

Liz hesitates. A grand piano crouches in the corner, covered with a sheet, as if in sleep. If Liz were to touch it, she is sure it would bite her.

'Do you play, Elizabeth?'

'Not very well.'

'I hate the damned thing.' Mary's lips turn down at the edges, she shudders. 'Many an unhappy hour I have sat trying to make sense of it. Use it if you like.'

'I'm sure I will have no need.' Liz skirts the edge of the room, putting distance between herself and the piano, as Mary heads into the drawing room where a monstrous fire rages. Fleshy lilies sit statuesque in ornate vases, oozing a nose-tickling stench, and a silver tea set is laid out on a mahogany table between the settees.

'Let us have some tea and then we ladies must make ourselves beautiful.'

'You are already beautiful.' Tom takes Mary's hand before it reaches the teapot and holds it to his lips.

Liz finds her reflection in the window so she does not have to watch Tom's affection. The bones in her neck stick out like rail-road lines, her lips are pursed tight, and the shadows in the hollows of her cheeks are too black. She must relax and breathe. This is what she wanted, after all; this is what she agreed to. She must do nothing but sit and be quiet and follow Tom's lead. It will be over soon enough, if only they stick to the plan.

She straightens her spine and forces herself to smile.

'That door leads to the smoking room.' Mary gestures with a nod to the far end of the room as she pours hot liquid into delicate china cups. 'Then past there is the study. Daddy never liked me to go in there. You can explore for yourself, Tom. I'm sure there are many things you would like to change.'

The briefest of smiles flits across Tom's face.

'It is a beautiful house,' Liz says before Mary notices him.

'Thank you, Elizabeth, I am glad you like it. I hope we shall all be very happy here.'

NOW THE LADIES HAVE GONE, the drawing room is quiet but for the grandfather clock in the corner, ticking like a lullaby. The tea has left a sour taste in Tom's mouth, and he walks to the fire, spits into it, and watches the sizzle.

His reflection looks very well within the gold framed mirror atop the mantelpiece. The clothes suit him, as he knew they would, and the house is far grander than he imagined; he has done better than they could have expected.

But, what must Liz make of it all? He imagines her in the bath upstairs, naked. Will she be able to stomach it? Perhaps he has pushed her too far too soon, but he can't dwell on that now. It is too late, they are here.

He shies away from the mirror and stalks to the study.

With no lamps lit, his candle flickers in the gloom. Amidst the covered furniture, he finds a desk. He peels back the sheet to find a pen and ink pot. The pen gleams golden in the light, and the engraving on it comes through clearly; George Buchanan.

'Nice to finally meet you, sir,' Tom whispers and smiles at his silliness.

He tries the drawers. They are locked, but he can guess where the keys are hidden.

The painting above the fireplace is of a young man, an old man, and an ethereal woman playing a harp. The painted inscription reads *fugit irreparable tempus*, something about time passing irreversibly, Tom discerns from the Latin he can remember. It is a good painting, it is apt. He smiles as he finds the key to the desk secured behind the painting's frame, and winks at the old man who stares back at him.

Papers lie like dead leaves in the first few drawers, all of no importance, but in the very bottom drawer, black, title-less books are neatly stacked. Tom slips one out from its place, opens it, and finds it is George's diary. All of them are George's diaries; a wealth of knowledge.

He sits back and takes his time to read them.

IT IS UNDOUBTEDLY the largest chamber Liz has ever had. The floorboards are hidden with thick woollen rugs, the four-poster bed has covers of fine silk, and oil paintings of virginal women line the walls.

A bath steams before the grate; the scent of lavender pervades the air. It is a luxury to have a bath in the privacy of one's room, without having to worry about the residue from those who have gone in before.

She unfastens the hooks of her dress and slips off her clothes. In just her chemise and drawers, the coldness of the room presses upon her, so she tiptoes to the fire. For someone so used to being exposed, she doesn't like the idea of it. Glancing around, she knows the eyes of the virgins watch and judge her, and she feels the ghosts of Floreat peek out from the shadows. She peels the chemise over her head timidly, her body curled inwards to keep her breasts covered, and then the door clicks. She tries to shield herself, but it is too late.

Turning, she finds Bet at the door, mouth gaping, too shocked to remember her manners. The firelight has shown Liz's back, has illuminated all too clearly the silver scars that crest her skin in thick, sluggish lines; a sight which can never be forgotten.

Liz holds the chemise to her chest. Bet stands half-hidden behind the door, her hand twists the knob back and forth, back and forth, and the metal squeaks and shudders. The air between them could snap.

'Wanted to know if you needed any help,' Bet stutters.

The squeak of the metal grinds louder.

'Stop that,' Liz says.

Bet's hand stills. The old woman's eyes trail down Liz's body, taking her all in, searching for other stains, as if Liz is a slab of rotting meat.

'You may go now,' Liz says.

Bet drags her eyes away, turns, and gently closes the door. Liz listens to the soft pads of the maid's feet retreating, and only when all is silent does she release the breath she has been holding. She closes her eyes and imagines lapping blue water and beating hot sun until her pulse slows.

Her bath is ruined, but she is so chilled that she slides into it anyway, and winces as the heat sears her skin.

'TIGHTER.'

Bet pulls harder on the strings of Mary's corset. Mary has washed and perfumed herself and wears a new dress of sky-blue silk. She likes the colour, believing it sits well against her chestnut hair and brown eyes.

'Tighter.'

'Ma'am, I fear it is tight enough.' Bet frowns at her mistress's waist.

It is small enough, she supposes, although not as small as her new sister's, which is barely the size of Mary's thigh. She will begin tighter lacing henceforth.

'Ma'am, I …' Bet is flushed as she brings over a necklace.

'What is it?'

Bet fiddles with the clasp and the cold diamonds tickle and scratch at Mary's collarbones.

'Put the necklace down, Bet, and tell me what is wrong.'

'Ma'am, are you sure about Mr Oliver? And Miss Oliver.'

Mary sighs. Her maid, who is almost fifty years old, is of the same opinion as her aunt – the classes should not mix. Deep down, Mary feels the same, but … Tom is Tom.

Mary motions at the necklace again and turns her back on her maid. 'I do not want to hear it, Bet. Mr Oliver and I are married. Happily.'

Bet finally fixes the clasp and retrieves the matching earrings.

'His sister is somewhat of a burden, I agree, but I believe she is of a fragile nature. What kind of a wife would I be to turn away my husband's sister when she is in need?'

Bet nods, but the twist of her mouth remains.

'May I ask,' Bet says, 'what Miss Oliver did for a living?'

'She was a dressmaker for a while, I believe.'

The space between Bet's eyebrows creases, and her mouth opens to speak again.

'That is enough, Bet. It is no concern of yours what either of the Olivers were doing before they came here. All you need to know is that I am in love with Mr Oliver, and we shall all live here, as a family. If you do not like it, you can go back to Aunt Emily and I shall find myself a new maid.'

Mary strides into the drawing room to find Tom and Elizabeth together near the fire, heads bowed in conversation which ends on her arrival.

'My darling, you look divine.' Tom strolls towards her and kisses her on the cheek.

Elizabeth wears the magenta dress that Mary bought her as a welcome gift. The colour makes her look anaemic. 'Elizabeth, that dress is a marvel on you.'

The gong bellows and the three of them make their way to the dining room.

Mary smirks as her husband and sister-in-law stare in awe at the grandeur of the room. Vibrant burgundy walls are bedecked with glittering gold lamps, gilded mirrors, and floor length, silk curtains. Two chandeliers hang from the ceiling and cast shards of sparkling light around the room. A polished table, which seats no less than fourteen people, heaves with a display of glittering glassware and bouquets of white hellebores.

'What a marvellous room.' Tom takes his place at the head of the table, flanked by Mary to his right and Elizabeth to his left.

'Bet has outdone herself,' Mary says, with a fleeting feeling of guilt, and smiles at Bet as the woman emerges from the inner door and hobbles between the guests. Her guilt does not last long, though, for Bet smacks into the back of Elizabeth's chair as she pours the white wine.

'I must apologise for my maid,' Mary says, once the woman has left. 'She can be quite bullish at times.'

'I have been thinking,' Tom says, 'that we must employ new staff. This house is too big for one maid and one hired cook who walks in from the village.'

'I agree. This house was full of servants before daddy died, but you see, there was no point in keeping them on while I was in the city.' Mary sips her wine. 'I shall begin interviews this week.'

'But darling, I do not want to trouble you with the task of finding staff. Liz and I can take care of it.'

It is a preposterous idea, but she must be patient with Tom; he does not understand how such households operate. 'Don't be silly. I am the lady of the house. I shall organise the staff.'

Tom lays his napkin across his lap, and when he looks up, he is smiling. 'My dear, you are quite right, of course. Now, let's eat.'

THE DINNER HAS LEFT Liz with an uncomfortable lump in her stomach. Too much suet pudding and too much wine. She has not drunk so much in a while, and her head feels fuzzy as she climbs the stairs with heavy legs.

She enters her cold room. The fire in the grate is nothing but a tiny patch of orange embers surrounded by shrivelled, grey ash. The bathtub has been removed, as has the towel. There is no evidence of what passed only a few hours earlier.

She removes her dress too hastily and tears one of the seams. It is for the best – she has never liked the colour purple. It reminds her of toes almost falling off, of stinking old men, of dead babies.

With a sigh, she lets out the laces on her corset. She prods her stomach gently. It is still sore inside, but she likes to feel the ache, she wants to know the pain is not just in her mind.

The candle beside her flickers and casts dancing shadows upon the walls as she slips into bed. She will not look around; it is best to close her eyes and tuck her chin under the quilt and dream of sunshine and summer. She will not think of how alone she is, stuck in a strange room at the end of a mansion where the silence is suffocating.

Indeed, isn't this what she has longed for? A room all to herself without fear of being disturbed? No one will come to her here. There will be no tap on the door, no footsteps flitting along the corridor outside, no noises at all. The only other living creatures are together in another room at the other end of the landing; no matter how much she may long for him, Tom must be with his wife tonight.

She blows out the candle and tries to sleep. In the silence, she realises that she would prefer to hear the familiar muffles of passion than nothing at all.

TOM GUIDES his wife to her chamber like a blind woman. Inside, a decanter of wine and two glasses have been set on the bedside table, and the fire has been stoked. The room is stifling.

'How efficient Bet is.' He removes his hand from his wife's waist to pour their drinks. 'Come and sit, my dear.' Tom pats the bed before him, and Mary does as she is told. 'Let's toast. To us!'

'To us.' Mary clinks her glass against his and downs the drink in one. Her head is level with his navel, and she glances towards his trousers. He takes her empty hand and kisses the top of it as the wine's fiery tendrils bite at his nausea. He should have drunk more at dinner.

'I have been looking forward to this night.' He kisses the inside of her palm and hears her gasp. Bringing her to her feet again, he begins to unfasten her dress, stooping to run his lips across her neck as he does so. He sees the movements of her chest, the rapid rise and fall of her breasts, and has to close his eyes.

'You are a marvel.' His breath traces her décolletage. He pulls at the corset laces so that she sways with his strength. 'This is too tight. It is no good for you, my love.'

'I like it tight.'

'I fear Bet is doing you harm,' he says, as the corset falls to the ground. In the same moment her stomach churns, and her cheeks flare scarlet. 'I think it is time that Bet, perhaps, went back to your aunt?'

He turns her around to face him. The outline of her body is clear beneath her thin cotton undergarments. He pulls her towards him so that her breasts press against his silk waistcoat.

'I hope I did not offend you earlier when we spoke about finding new staff?'

Mary licks her lips, swallows, and shakes her head as Tom presses her against one of the bedposts.

'I only thought that Liz may like something to do.' His thumb trails across her collarbone. 'I thought it might make her feel more useful.' His fingers trace the side of her breast. 'But of course, if you would prefer to do it all?'

'She can do it,' Mary says.

His right hand begins its journey down her body, bumping over the ridge of her drawers until he finds the start of her thigh. 'I would not want to put you out, my love. I only thought it might be nice for Liz.'

'She can do it!'

He grins, and without allowing himself a second thought, he thrusts his fingers between her legs and kisses her. Her glass crashes on the floor.

CHAPTER 2

*M*ary wakes with a crick in her neck. The pillow was too hard, too high, and now there is a dull throb behind her eyebrows. She throws off the bed covers and feels the chill of the January morning. Pulling her body up, she is suddenly struck by an unpleasant heat between her legs, an unusual sting, as if the skin has been ripped.

She is now a woman.

She turns, smiling, but finds the space beside her empty; Tom has gone. She did not hear him wake or dress or leave. Disappointed, she looks about the room, wondering if he might be hiding somewhere, but she is alone. The only proof of their liaison is the empty tumbler and the empty glasses, which have stains of wine like droplets of dried blood upon them. The headache is not only from the pillow.

She yawns, clicks her neck, puts her bare feet on the rug, and makes her way to the window. She has not bothered to look at the clock, and so it comes as a shock when sunlight slams into her eyes as she parts the curtains.

Furious, she runs for the lever and yanks the bell.

16

'Ma'am.' Bet curtseys as she pants and wipes her forehead.

'What time is it, Bet?'

Bet's eyes flick towards the clock. 'Just after half-past nine, ma'am,' she says as if her mistress might have suffered a blow to the head.

'Why have you not woken me?'

'I was told to let you sleep. Mr Oliver's sister said you might be tired after …'

'Yes, yes.' Mary swats the air and looks out of the window so she does not have to see her maid's stupid face. It is a glorious morning, with silver frost glistening over the fields, the sky a clear, pale blue, and the sun like a spot of water-colour paint on the horizon. 'But you do not take your orders from Elizabeth. You take them from me.' She faces her maid again. 'Go and fetch me water to wash with.'

Mary inspects the bed sheets once Bet has gone. A few pink spots lie halfway down. With her fingers, she checks herself, wondering if there is any blood on her, but she finds nothing out of the ordinary. The sheet, then, is her trophy. She will instruct Bet to remove it, wrap it up, and store it in the base of her trunk.

'Find my riding dress,' Mary says when Bet returns with a tray containing a washbowl, a jug, some fine cloth, a towel, and the slop bucket. 'I shall show Tom the estate this morning.'

Bet clears her throat. 'Mr Oliver and his sister have already gone, ma'am.' Bet picks at the cuff of her dress infuriatingly. The habits of a maid! Mary watches the fabric tighten and release, tighten and release. Any moment now it will tear.

'Stop that!'

Bet's hands fall to her sides.

Mary inhales slowly, rolls her head from side to side.

When she speaks again, she has control of herself. 'Gone where?'

'They have taken the horses and gone exploring, so they called it.'

'When was this?'

'Eight o'clock.'

Why would Tom not wait for her? It is her house, her estate – he does not have the right to explore without her.

She stalks back to the window. From this angle, she can just see the deep blue line of the sea almost two miles away. There are no horses or riders in the parkland. Her glance shifts towards the woods, of which she can only see a part, but again, all appears still.

'I told them you would most likely wish to show them around, but they didn't listen to me.'

'And why should they?' Mary prowls towards Bet, then fixes her attention on her reflection in the looking glass. 'He is the man of the house now, you would do well to remember that.'

Bet presses her lips together, shakes her head ever so slightly. Mary chooses to ignore her stubbornness.

'Tom wouldn't have wanted to disturb me, that is all.' She will not spoil her first day as a wife with anything so lowly as anger. She forces a smile. 'Bring my pink dress and my pearls. There is a new bottle of scent I brought back from London in one of the trunks. Find it.' She will make herself pretty for Tom's return, and she will hold her tongue as wives are supposed to do, knowing that it is only his ignorance to blame for his insensitivity.

'Would you like some breakfast, ma'am?'

Mary dips the cloth in the bowl of water then pats her neck. 'Have the others eaten?'

'Yes. They had eggs, ham, and toast before they left.'

'I will not have breakfast,' she says and soaks the cloth again. She brings it to her collarbones this time and flinches from the soreness there. She will have bruises from last night. The memory of Tom's kisses makes her cheeks flush, and she closes her eyes so she might remember his naked flesh against hers, his urgency, the swell of pleasure cresting through her body.

'Ma'am, you must eat.'

'Do not tell me what to do!' Mary throws the cloth at her maid, hating the interruption of her thoughts. She tries to return to them, but the heat of passion has turned into the heat of rage, and she cannot claw her way back.

She pinches the bridge of her nose as Bet trembles and picks up the cloth from the floor. Such a meek, snivelling woman. The sight of her is already grating. Tom was right – Bet does not belong here.

'It is time you returned to Aunt Emily, Bet. I believe it is for the best. The country does not suit you.'

THE CLOCK HAD CHIMED twelve by the time Liz and Tom had returned home. Liz had been sweating ever so slightly, and her hands had been stiff from holding the reins. It had been the first time she had ever ridden a horse. Once out of sight of the house, Tom had helped her to sit straddling the creature, which had been much more comfortable, and they had even managed a gentle trot at one point. Now, her thighs ache, her neck is stiff, and she is ravenous. After a brief clean-up, Tom and Liz find Mary in the library.

'Good morning, my darling wife.' Tom strides into the room, bounding over to Mary, who lounges in a chair near the window with a book in her hands. She does not look up as Tom kisses her forehead.

'Good afternoon.'

Tom laughs. 'My, my, you're quite right. I didn't know we had been gone so long.'

He pours himself a small glass of sherry and falls into one of the sofas.

Liz, with more decorum, and because of the increasing pain of her leg muscles, perches on the edge of the opposite sofa.

'Is everything well, sister?'

'Why did you tell Bet to let me sleep?'

Liz takes a moment. It seems such a long time ago since she instructed Bet to leave Mary alone.

'Liz just thought you may be tired, Mary. That is all. She did not mean to upset you.'

'But I wanted to show you around.'

'My dear, you need your rest. It is a tiring business, being a wife.' Tom winks at her, mischief animating his features. Mary's cheeks flare pink as she smiles back at him.

'I hope I have not offended you, sister?' Liz says, distracting Mary from her husband; she cannot stand the sight of them like that. She would rather them bicker, but Tom will not let that happen, not yet.

'Oh no, not at all. You must be hungry after your ride. Lunch is in the dining room, and I have informed Bet that she will be returning to Aunt Emily's before the week is out.'

Tom nods, suddenly serious. He pats his thighs, brings himself to his feet, drains the last of his sherry. 'I think it is for the best. I fear she is past the demands of such a large house and a growing family. And our new staff begin tomorrow anyway.'

Mary's smile falls. 'What new staff?'

'Liz and I have been to the village this morning, and while there we thought we might as well have a look about for people. We have acquired a new manservant, a hall and stable boy, two maids,' he lists them on his fingers, 'a cook-come-housekeeper, and a lady's maid. Six new staff. Not bad for a morning's work.'

'But what about references?' Mary leans forward in her chair, frowning. 'Are they reliable? Trustworthy? Are they any good?'

'Well, they are local folk,' Tom says. 'The manservant and stable boy are father and son. The father helped us out when we had a little trouble this morning. I found him a very respectable sort of chap. Mr Chipman!' Tom clicks his fingers in the air. 'That's his name. Will is his son. I asked if they had regular work, Chipman said only sometimes, so I offered them permanent positions. They start the day after tomorrow, as do the maids, who are neighbours of Mr Chipman and only thirteen years old. They are a great strain on their mother. It was service or the workhouse. I thought you would be only too glad to help such unfortunates?'

'Well ...' She averts her gaze to the floor. 'Yes, of course. But, do they,' she clears her throat, 'do they know what they are doing?'

'I believe, with a little training, they shall be excellent. And it's not like you will have to see them, my dear. They shall be below stairs.'

Not waiting for further comment, Tom continues:

'Mrs Beacham shall be the cook and housekeeper. I have not met her, but word has it that she is employed in Cornwall and is deeply unhappy. Her family lives here. Mr Chipman introduced me to her brother, who is a fisherman and he was telling me all about her and the scoundrels for whom she works. Dastardly lot. She hasn't been paid for weeks. So, I said, with a reference and an interview with my wife, we would definitely consider her if she could start as soon as possible. I am to send post to them this afternoon. Is that all right, darling?'

His speech has left Mary baffled, which, Liz knows, was

his intention all along. She watches Mary struggle to put her argument across.

'I should like to see her before we take her on.'

'Oh, of course. And then we have Anne, the new lady's maid.' Tom claps his hands. 'Lunch! I am starving.'

Liz rises from her seat and follows Tom, who makes his way to the door, until Mary speaks.

'Who is Anne?'

Tom takes a long breath and faces his wife. 'A very nice young girl. She has little experience, but her mother was a lady's maid and has taught her well, so I believe. She even understands some French!'

'No references?'

Tom sighs. 'I thought she would be a good investment. We can train her up to suit us.'

Mary's leg twitches under her skirts. The material quivers.

'What is she like?'

Tom saunters to his wife's side and helps her out of her chair. 'You'll like her,' he whispers in her ear and guides her towards the door, then winks at Liz. 'She's biddable.'

At six o'clock the three of them sit down for dinner of mulligatawny soup followed by roast beef and vegetables picked from the garden, finished with damson pudding. All very heavy, again, but at least there was no fruit cake. Yesterday, Tom had to follow each mouthful with a swig of wine, just so the damned stuff would go down.

Now, the ladies have withdrawn. Tom has come to the library, where he nurses a large brandy.

He assesses the day, and yesterday, and indeed the last few months which have led up to this moment. He feels unaccountably tired. Perhaps it is the relief that all has worked out how he has planned. But he cannot relax, not just yet, there is still plenty to do.

Anne was a brilliant idea. A small girl of maybe sixteen years, full figured, with curly red hair and invisible eyelashes. When they knocked on Anne's door, she had swooned over him within seconds.

Her sickly mother had been chained to the stove for warmth. Her father, thank God, had been out; fathers can be tricky when it comes to daughters. So, Tom had offered Anne the position of lady's maid there and then, and with tears in her eyes, Anne's mother had accepted, glad to see her daughter going into a respectful position.

Tom chuckles into his glass.

It is nearing midnight now. He will soon have to retire to bed, although he would rather stay on the sofa and sleep here, with the fire crackling, without the nuisance of explaining to Mary that he will sleep alone tonight. Yet, he knows he must broach the subject.

He slips into the drawing room.

The pulse in Liz's neck is illuminated by the fire as she reads her book. Her breathing is steady as her eyes flick over the lines on the page, but the raising of her eyebrow tells him she knows he watches her.

Mary nibbles her lower lip, and her brow furrows as she reads the novel held too close to her face.

'What are you reading, my love?' Tom says.

Mary jumps, then laughs at herself. 'Ruth. By Elizabeth Gaskell.'

'I know it.'

'It is one of my favourites.'

'Well then, I would not want to disturb you. I am for bed.'

Mary closes the book and is standing in a moment. 'I have read it a hundred times. It can wait.' She joins his side.

They ascend the stairs. Mary's excitement pulsates

through the air, and the distance to her chamber shortens at an alarming rate; he must think of something quickly. He clings to the bannister, gasps, winces.

'Tom?' Mary's hand presses hotly into his shoulder. 'Are you well?'

He brings his fingers to his brows, and his breath gushes out of him. 'A migraine coming, I think. Too much brandy.'

He squints up at her, paints a pained smile onto his face, and continues up the stairs unsteadily. Mary takes hold of his arm to aid him, and together they stop outside Mary's door, where the silence grows.

He slumps against the wall. 'I would like to come in–'

'I would like that too.' She edges closer, wets her lips.

Tom leans in and accepts her kiss, but breaks away with a cry, and cradles his head.

'You should rest, Tom.'

'But I–'

She strokes his cheek. 'We have plenty of time. Tonight you need sleep. Would you like me to bring you anything?'

Tom shakes his head, moans for effect.

'Very well,' she says, and he hears the disappointment in her voice. She is still so close that he only needs to move forward a little to brush his lips against her cheek.

'Goodnight, my dear.'

'Goodnight, Tom.' With one last embrace, she whispers feverishly, 'I will dream of tomorrow night.' She slips into her room and gently closes the door.

Yes, Tom thinks, as he trudges to his own chamber and pours himself a large glass of whiskey: there is always tomorrow.

ANNE WEARS her best dress and has brushed her hair three times, applying oil and wax to it in an effort to calm the frizziness. She has washed her face meticulously, scrubbed her hands clear of any grime, and now she smells of nothing but carbolic. She grins at the sight of her bright white skin in the stained and cracked hand mirror.

She does not think too much about her mother or her three siblings who she must leave behind. After all, her ma was all too happy for her to be going. She has been teaching her little sister, Grace, how to do all the house-work anyway. Her brother, Eddie, already works the farm with her father, and now Paul is six he can start earning as a crow scarer.

Yes, her family will be just fine without her.

And, in all honesty, she does not believe she would have turned down the position even if they weren't, when it was offered by the most handsome man she has ever seen.

'You best be getting off,' her mother, Gwen, says, bringing her out of her trance.

'Yes, Ma. You sure you'll be all right?'

'I'll be fine. Just do as I've told you and make me proud. Following in your ma's footsteps,' Gwen says, and her smile makes her eyes twinkle. 'I don't suppose Miss Buchanan would remember me.'

'It's Mrs Oliver now.'

'Yes, I suppose it is. No need to mention me anyway.'

The worst thing about this position is working for Mrs Oliver. Anne remembers seeing the dumpy, spoilt woman riding through the village occasionally with her father. She never even looked at Gwen, who had been a loyal maid to Mrs Buchanan until the time of the woman's death, after which, Mr Buchanan simply got rid of Gwen. It seemed that Mary did not want her mother's cast-offs.

'Just do as you're told and be polite, remember they are your betters.'

Anne tuts to herself.

'Come here.' Gwen opens her arms for an embrace. 'You're a good girl. We'll miss you.'

'I'll be coming back to see you.' Anne can feel tears brimming, but then her mother starts coughing, and Anne must fetch some water.

Once Gwen has recovered, Anne straightens her clothes and puts on her bonnet.

'Right. I'll go.'

There are no more tears. Anne does not look over her shoulder as she leaves their squat little cottage with smoke already billowing from its chimney. She glances around the village, waves to Mr Marsh, the butcher, who has three pheasants hanging from his hand, smells the scent of baking bread from Mr Cole's shop. She watches the fishing boats leaving the harbour.

But she has no time for sentiment; her feet can't carry her fast enough to Mr Oliver's study.

A KNOCK on the door forces Tom to close the diary and hide it away.

'Come in.'

Bet strides in, her mouth set in a twisted line, her face as wrinkled as an old pear. 'Anne Witmore, sir.'

Tom smiles at Anne, baring his teeth, and flicks his wrist at Bet so that she leaves.

'Good morning, Anne. How are you?'

'Very well, sir.' She blushes. Her eyes flit to the floor.

'Good.' He looks her over, taking his time. Her skin shines, the apples of her cheeks glow, her lips are bitten red. Her fingers flutter as she clasps her hands before her waist. 'Come and sit down.'

Anne tiptoes to the chair opposite his own. The tang of

soap floats in the air as she sits, and still, her eyes will not meet his.

'This used to be George Buchanan's study. I might redecorate. What do you think?'

'I … I don't know, sir. I think it is quite nice.'

'Mmh. I think I will take down that painting.' He points behind her. 'Rather a macabre feel about it, wouldn't you say?'

Anne swivels in her chair to look. Stubborn curls, as bright as saffron, fall out of her bun and tickle her freckled neck.

'It is a bit unnerving, sir.' Finally, her gaze meets his.

He spreads his lips into a smile. 'Exactly what I thought.'

Anne lifts her fingers to her cheek before quickly returning them to her lap. He likes to see her nervous, but it would be better to ease her, so he ceases his teasing.

'Now, let's talk about you, Anne. Tell me a little about yourself.'

'Well … my father is a farmer.'

'Yes, Mr Witmore farms part of my estate, I believe. Crops mainly, and cares for the cattle.'

'Yes, sir. He does love his job, sir.'

'And your mother?'

'She just does the odd bits, as much as she can. She's a wonderful seamstress, sir,' Anne says, and she beams as she talks of her mother. 'If ever you need anything mending, my ma is the woman.'

'I will keep that in mind, Anne. Mr Chipman said she had previous lady's maid experience?'

Anne's smile falters. 'Yes, she did, sir, before the accident.'

'Her leg?'

'Oh, no, sir. Mrs Buchanan's accident, when she drowned.'

Her words stun him. They tumble over in his mind, again

and again. After a moment, he laughs, uncertainly. 'Sorry – your mother was lady's maid to Victoria Buchanan?'

Anne nods.

'I did not even know Mrs Buchanan had drowned.'

'Oh, gosh!' Red blots Anne's skin from her ears to her nose. 'I'm so sorry, sir. I should never have said it. Ma told me not to mention it.'

'Hush.' Tom reaches forward as if he would calm her with his touch. Anne freezes. His hand hovers halfway across the desk. 'Do not worry yourself, Anne. You were quite right to tell me. Perhaps you could tell me how Mrs Buchanan came to such an end?'

'I believe, from what Ma has told me, that Miss Buchanan – that is, Mrs Oliver now – got into some trouble in the lake. Mrs Buchanan thought she were drowning, so she ran into the water. Next thing is, Miss Buchanan's running inside, screaming, saying her ma's in the water. By the time everyone got out there, Mrs Buchanan were dead.'

How had he not discovered this? How had he not been informed? The idea unsettles him; he must know everything about his wife if his plan is to succeed.

'What a dreadful thing for Mary,' he chokes, and the shock must be evident in his face.

'Oh, gosh! I did not mean to upset you, Mr Oliver. I shouldn't have said anything. Me and my silly mouth!'

'You said she drowned in the lake?' Tom interrupts her hysterics. 'Where is it? I have not seen it.'

'Mr Buchanan got it filled in afterwards. It was on the other side of the woods.'

They sit quietly for a moment. Tom picks at the corner of leather on the desk, recovers himself. 'Sorry – we were talking about your mother. When did she lose her leg, if you don't mind my asking?'

'When our Paul were two years old. Accident with a cart. The horse bolted, ran her over. Miracle she survived.'

'Yes.' He stretches out of the chair and saunters to the window. It is grey today, and the sea is not visible through the low-hanging cloud. An altogether depressing vista. 'It is a cruel world.'

'But she is proud of me now, sir.'

'Then you will not want to let her down, will you?'

'I will do my very best, sir.'

'Good.' He smacks his palms together and grins at her. 'Bet will show you how things work around here. She will be leaving on the morning train on Saturday.'

'And then I shall be in charge?'

'Mrs Beacham – when she arrives – shall be the house-keeper, but you will not have to answer to her. I shall have my manservant, but again, you won't have too much to do with him. Your responsibility is to my wife and sister. And I shall require you occasionally, if that's all right with you? Just some basic errand running, things like that. You shall report to me regularly. Do you think you will be able to manage?'

'Yes, sir, most definitely.'

'Then you shall make me a happy man.' He extends his arm for a handshake and Anne rises to meet him. Her skin is hot and damp. 'Welcome to your new home, Anne.'

'I DO NOT LIKE HER,' Mary says, over a forkful of pheasant.

'Who, dear?' Tom saws at his own breast of meat.

'Anne.'

Liz has given up with the bird, it is too tough and over-cooked. Instead, she nibbles on a roast potato. 'I think she is nice.'

'She was far too rough with me while arranging my hair this evening.'

'I found her very gentle.' Liz meets Mary's flash of anger with a smile. Already, Mary's spoilt petulance is grinding on her nerves. She is struggling to contain herself as more hours pass in the woman's dreadful company.

'Really, the problem is with Bet,' Tom says. 'What has she done to this meal? It is as tough as leather.'

'She is not a cook,' Mary says. 'Maud, who you are also so fond of, has taken the evening off. Bet did not know until four o'clock this afternoon that she would be away.'

'I let her go,' Liz says.

'Why?'

'I went to the kitchen after luncheon to have a look around. Maud was all in a bother.' She recalls Maud sitting at the kitchen table, plucking out the pheasant feathers, yawning widely. The poor woman had been worked to the bone, barely able to keep her eyelids open. 'Her husband has the influenza. I told her she could have the evening off.'

Mary's head twists from Liz to Tom, and she croaks out a laugh. 'And you did not think to tell Bet?'

'I could not find her,' Liz lies.

The door opens and Anne appears. 'Beg your pardon. I've just come to see if I should clear the plates.'

'Can you not see we have not finished? Stupid girl.'

'Take the plates, Anne.' Tom leans back in his chair, prods the crockery away from him in disgust. 'This meat is inedible.'

Mary is like a fish; her mouth hangs open, and she gasps for breath as Anne works her way around the table. With a quick curtsey, Anne leaves. Mary's chair screeches along the floor as she stands, pulling at the tablecloth so that her glass of wine teeters precariously. Liz steadies it. Mary makes her way to the door.

'Are you not staying for the spotted dick, my dear?' Tom says, his eyes on Liz, his smile evident in his words. Liz stares at him, stunned by his boldness. It is a dangerous game he is playing, one he should take seriously, but despite her concerns, she is relieved to see his true self coming through.

'I have no appetite.' Mary stalks out of the room and slams the door behind her.

Tom chuckles. Liz's lips lift upwards.

'Be careful, Tom.'

'Oh, come on, Liz!' His fingertips interlace through hers, setting them alight. He tickles her palm, teasing out the laugh that is bubbling in her throat. In a moment, she is lost in laughter, her eyes watering with it and how good it feels, but then Anne enters. Tom draws his fingers into his lap, and Liz feels the absence of them keenly.

'Is Mrs Oliver all right, sir?'

'Didn't fancy the spotted dick.' Tom gasps with laughter as confusion colours Anne's face.

Liz brushes the tears from her cheeks, the joke now getting old, and glares at Tom. 'She's fine, Anne.' The girl's innocence serves to remind Liz of the lack of her own; she pities them both. 'You can get the pudding now.'

Anne leaves the room.

Taking his napkin, Tom wipes his eyes and grins at the look of admonition on Liz's face.

'Get too close to the fire, Tom, and you shall get burnt.'

'Isn't it nice to laugh, though?'

There is an ache in her stomach, but yes, it was nice to feel the pressure lift for an instant, for there to be light in the perpetual gloom of life at Floreat.

'I haven't seen you smile for so long.'

They used to laugh all the time when they were little, before … But this is not the time for sentimentality, and there will be no chance of joy if they do not sort their problems now. 'What about Anne?' she says. 'Mary has not taken to her.'

'I like her. She will do us good.'

She studies him. 'What have you got planned for her?' No one in Tom's life is ever useless.

Before he can answer, Anne returns with a steaming pudding on a silver tray. A knife sits beside the suet.

'Do you like it here, Anne?'

'Yes, sir. It is a beautiful house.' She cuts the pudding, scooping it on to the plate before serving it to her master.

'And do you like us?'

For an instant, the girl meets his gaze, and her breath catches in her throat. 'Yes, sir.'

'Mary is ...' Tom begins, his eyes roaming over Anne's face, 'she is troubled at times. You will tell me what she does. It is for her own sake, do you understand? You must tell me everything, Anne.'

'Of course, sir.' Anne dips low, backs slowly out of the room. Tom watches her go before he turns to Liz.

'I see,' she says.

CHAPTER 3

*M*ary sits at her bedroom window, surveying her land. It is a breezy morning. She can see the trees swaying, can make out the white breakers on the surface of the sea in the distance. Three pheasants, two females and one male, strut along the gardens below her window, pecking at nothing. The male's feathers glisten in the sunlight, his blue-black neck shines like oil. It reminds her of Tom.

She has passed another fruitless night, alone and angry. She did not bother to go to the drawing room yesterday evening, having no desire to see Elizabeth again, and even less desire to try to make conversation with her after their ruckus at dinner.

Mary had heard her; she had heard them both, laughing at her while she stood with her back against the dining room door, wondering if Tom might follow her out, offer her an apology and a night of love-making. He never did.

In her chamber, she had also waited. She had brushed her hair a hundred times until it looked like treacle. She had known, when the clock had finally struck midnight, that Tom would not be joining her.

And for the first time since girlhood, she had let a man bring tears to her eyes. She had never given her father the satisfaction of seeing her emotions; even when he had died she had refused to cry over him, sure that he would be watching from somewhere up above. Then, over nothing more than a silly argument about a stupid maid, she had found herself crying because her husband had not agreed with her! She was ashamed of herself. It would not happen again.

After all, she was right – Anne was a lady's maid, and as such, Mary would decide whether she was appropriate or not. She had settled to carry out a series of tests for the girl to determine if she was suitable, starting with breakfast.

At seven o'clock, Mary had rung the bell. Anne had arrived within a few minutes, fresh-faced and neat – she had obviously been awake for a while. Mary had ordered a breakfast of one boiled egg and one slice of toast, with a pot of tea, to be brought as quickly as possible. Sure enough, Anne had returned within half an hour with the tray of breakfast, and the toast was still hot.

'Did Bet cook this?' Mary had asked, as she cracked the egg to find the yolk golden and soft, just how she likes it.

'No, ma'am, I did it. I know how to boil an egg.'

She had not cared for the girl's tone. She had turned her nose up at the food. 'The yolk is too runny.'

'Sorry ma'am,' Anne had said, though she hadn't sounded like she was sorry at all. 'I shall cook it longer next time.'

'Is Elizabeth dressed yet?' Mary says as Anne finishes lacing her corset.

'No, ma'am. I said I would help her once I have seen to you.'

'Are you able to manage here, do you think? It is a lot to do for such a young girl, looking after two ladies. I could easily find another maid for myself or for Elizabeth.'

'No, ma'am, don't you worry.'

'I'm not worried,' Mary says.

Anne clears her throat and swallows before she continues. 'Mr Oliver says I am to be a lady's maid to you both because he is trying to be eco ... ecnom ...'

'Economical,' Mary says, appalled. 'Never speak of that again.'

Why would Tom say such a thing? Mary seethes as she glances about the room, noticing, for the first time, the shabbiness of things. When was the last time she had ordered new bed sheets? The chair by the window has been there since she can remember. The jewels in her drawers are her mother's, grandmother's, great-grandmother's – she can remember the women wearing them at Christmas celebrations. It is what she loves about Floreat; the way it holds her childhood in its soft, weathered hands. Everything preserved safely, her lineage clear to all.

'Mr Oliver has no need to be economical, Anne, I can assure you. He probably just said that to you to make you feel better, though Lord knows why.'

She averts her gaze from the sorry state of her tattered crinoline, too round and unfashionable now, as Anne finishes dressing her. She sits before the mirror and feels the lumps in the stool cushion under her backside with a flurry of humiliation, as Anne begins styling her hair. In the glass, she examines the girl.

Anne's brow crinkles in concentration as she tries to command the unwieldy pins. She is a similar shape to Mary; short, and with a fleshiness about her that makes her look like a little pig sometimes, but when her face is not screwed up, her youth makes her pretty.

Mary brings her focus upon her own reflection. With sourness, she notices the dark rings beneath her eyes, the blueness on either side of the bridge of her nose, the shrivelled appearance of her grey-pink lips. Worn and aged, like Floreat.

She must stop crying, stop shouting, stop pursing her lips, or else she will look twenty years older than her husband rather than ten, and it will be even harder to get into bed with him.

'They didn't like me leaving,' Mrs Beacham says, smirking. 'Not without any warning, like that.'

The day before yesterday, Tom sent her a letter saying she had a position here as head cook and housekeeper, a significant rise in her station, if she could arrive as soon as possible. She was on the train the very next day.

'Not right, though, is it?' she says. 'I've even been sharing a bed, what with them having to sell mine for the money. There was no way I was going to get paid this year. I'm afraid I haven't got a reference.'

'Not a problem.' Tom steeples his fingers, rests his elbows on the desk, smiles. 'You come on the recommendation of the local people, and I think we should look after our own around here.'

'Very kind of you, sir.' She touches a hand to her eye.

'I shall call for Mrs Oliver now. She would like to meet you, interview you, so to speak. There is no need to worry her with references. I will tell her I received a telegram with a positive account of you.'

'Very kind, sir.'

'My wife,' he lowers his voice, 'is more traditional than

myself. I believe in progress. Money is needed in this day and age.'

Mrs Beacham's lips press together, her chin wobbles for an instant. This wrinkled woman, with mousy hair streaked grey, with fingers freckled with old burns, is indebted to him.

The door blasts open. Mary. Her quick strides have left her with pink cheeks and messy hair.

'Darling,' Tom says to fill the silence. 'You must be able to hear through walls – I was just going to call for you. This is Mrs Beacham, the cook from Cornwall that I was telling you about.'

Mrs Beacham rises from her seat and curtseys low. 'A pleasure to meet you, ma'am.'

Mary ignores her and directs her glare at Tom. He stands, smiles, nods at Mrs Beacham, and brushes past his wife. Mary closes the door so they are alone in the corridor, and speaks in a rushed whisper.

'Why did you tell Anne that we needed to be economical?'

He turns to her, wondering if he will find rage upon her features. Instead, there is worry. He takes her hands, cradles them in his, and barely meets her eyes. 'I was hoping I might keep it from you. It seems that your father ... he might not have been quite so clever with money after all.'

Mary gasps. Her grip tightens.

'Don't worry, my dear. It is nothing that being a little frugal over the next few months won't cure.'

'Is it bad?'

'Not at all,' Tom says, hoping she hears his tremor. 'As I say, we shall just have to be careful for the time being. I shall sort it all out. Do not trouble yourself.'

Her grip loosens. He strokes her hot cheek with the back of his finger and brings his lips against hers. When he pulls away, he can hear the quickening of her breath.

'Now, go and see Mrs Beacham. I will be waiting to know what you think of her.'

ANNE LEAVES Miss Oliver in her room and skips down the back stairs, her black boots clipping on the bare stone. Muffled sounds permeate the corridor; scratches and thumps of objects being moved and put down; voices of men and women; the scuffling of shoes. In the kitchen, she finds a woman older than her mother and at least two heads taller than herself, dressed in a black uniform. The woman is ordering little Clair about, telling her where to put the meat that's just been delivered, to fill the kettle, to peel the potatoes.

'Mrs Beacham,' the large woman says once she notices Anne standing by the door. 'Housekeeper and Cook.'

'Miss Witmore.' Anne pretends an air of confidence. 'Lady's maid.'

'Nice to meet you, Miss Witmore. Is there anything I can do for you?'

'Where is Cate?'

It takes Mrs Beacham a moment to comprehend who Anne speaks of. 'Oh, yes. I've sent her to the wash house. There is a pile of laundry that Bet has not seen to.'

'The fires were not lit this morning either. I thought you should know.'

'I shall have this house running ship shape in no time, Miss Witmore. You have no need to trouble yourself over fires and dusting, I can assure you. Clair and Cate shall be under my strict supervision.'

Anne nods and forces a smile. 'I'm sure the place will be much more efficient under your control. Where is Bet?'

'Haven't seen her. I gather she'll be gone soon enough.'

'This Saturday. Mr Oliver told me.'

Mrs Beacham chops the head off a partridge. 'Yes, he told me as well.'

Anne hates her.

'Right.' Anne smooths her dress, and without another word from Mrs Beacham, she leaves.

Loud crashes are coming from the butler's room, as if suitcases are bashing into the furniture. She creeps towards the door, knocks, although it is not her place to do so; she has always been too curious. She holds her breath as she waits.

A boy, with dull brown eyes and dull brown hair, emerges. It takes her a moment to realise it is her old child-hood friend grinning back at her.

'Anne!' Will's lips part in a wide smile which shows multiple missing teeth. 'Da told me you were here. Lady's maid! You'm doing well. Good to see you.'

Anne returns a smile the best she can. 'And you, Will. What are you doing here though? Should you be in here?' She cranes her neck, hoping to get a better view of the room and who else is inside it.

'I'm the new hall and stable boy. Da's the manservant. Seems we've all got to muck in together, not how I thought such a grand house would be, but–'

'Mr Oliver is doing his best.'

'Never said he weren't,' Will says, cut short, and he kicks at the skirting board.

'You should be grateful you have a position at all, you and your father, since you have no experience or training.'

'I know.' Will twists from side to side like a child, and she remembers the times they would play on the beach pretending to be a courting couple, or pirates finding lost treasure. The games stopped after Gwen's accident. There was no more time for pretending after that.

'Yes. Well, you've always had a way with horses,' she says,

guilt stirring in her chest. Finally, she rewards him with a smile. 'And your da's a good man. He helped me get here, I know.'

They stand awkwardly for a few moments until the back door swings open and a gust of icy air blows at them. Will's father, Mr Chipman, staggers into the house, a few small leather bags under his arms, his bulbous nose red from the cold.

'You two catching up?' he says.

'I didn't know you would be here. Will was just telling me about it.'

Mr Chipman strides past the youngsters and into the room and places his bags down with a sigh. 'Mr Oliver has done us a great deal of good, hasn't he, Will?'

'But what about your wife?' Anne says. 'And your daughters?'

'Staying at home. With our wages, and without our mouths to feed, well,' he says and laughs as he takes off his cap, 'they'll be living like ladies themselves.'

'And you're in the butler's room?'

'I know.' Mr Chipman shakes his head, unable to believe his luck. 'Will and I shall be sharing it. Mr Oliver says we might as well have our beds down here, keep you ladies separate upstairs.'

Small mercies, she thinks. 'Well, I hope you'll be happy here.'

'I will, Anne, now I know you're here,' Will says.

Anne dips ever so slightly, then trots for the back stairs. With each step, she knows that Will is watching her.

LATER, after another quiet hour in his own company in the comfort of the library, Tom makes for his chamber. He longs for the softness of his bed; indeed, it is one of his favourite things since moving here, into this new world of wealth. His pillow is of finest down, and his silk sheets are seductively smooth – they soothe him into a deep sleep. He does not wish to share it with Mary at all.

Yet, as his feet find the first step on the grand, sweeping staircase, he hears the click of the door and the heavy fall of her footsteps. By the time he has reached the landing, she is close behind him.

'Tom.' She is panting from hastening up the stairs.

'Darling, I did not hear you come.'

'I thought you might join me.'

His stomach sinks. How should he broach it tonight? How many more nights will he have to find excuses until she might finally grow tired and leave him alone?

'Not tonight.' He leans against the wall. 'I have drunk too much.'

Mary's mouth forms into its recognisable pout. 'We are newly married.'

'Tomorrow,' he promises and turns for his room.

'Am I not ...?' she begins but is too scared to finish.

'It is nothing to do with you.' How could he possibly tell her that the very thought of her naked body writhing underneath him makes him want to heave? 'I am simply tired.'

'This is not how I thought marriage would be.' Mary's voice is gratingly thin. 'I should be with you. Why won't you just come with me?' Her reddened face appears before him. The sight of her, the tang of her stale breath, makes him flinch.

'I am tired,' he says, between clenched teeth.

'That is not good enough! A wife should lay with her husband.'

'A wife should do what her husband tells her to!'

She recoils as if he has slapped her.

'Now.' He inhales, and the air splinters down his throat.

41

He smooths his hair, forces the scowl off his face. 'Go to bed and get some sleep. I will see you in the morning.'

After a moment, she does as she is told.

THE BELL RINGS FURIOUSLY. Anne, who has just sat down to eat her supper of cold leftovers, races upstairs.

She crashes into Mary's bedroom to find it utterly calm. The candles flicker and paint the wall murals golden. Mary sits at a chair facing away from Anne, entirely still, and, at first, seemingly relaxed.

Once the floor stops spinning and she manages to steady her breathing, Anne hears strange noises coming from her mistress. 'Ma'am? You rang the bell?'

Anne waits by the door. With her eyes adjusted to the dim room, she notices Mary's bare hands, which hang by her sides, are clenched into fists so that the skin on her knuckles is stretched pure white.

'Can I help you with anything, ma'am?'

'Undress me.' Mary's voice is low and rough, like rocks scraping against bricks.

'Yes, ma'am.'

Mary unfolds herself from the chair and rises with difficulty to her feet. She keeps her back to Anne, who begins unfastening her clothes. Anne's fingers have never felt so stiff. She works as best she can, with Mary's peculiar breathing reverberating around her.

At last, Mary must turn so that Anne can continue. Slowly, Anne sees Mary's face. It is as white as Mr Oliver's starched shirts, yet her eyes glow red like cherries. The dress slips away, leaving her in her undergarments, revealing red marks on her chest and neck, some with faint spots of blood where the skin has broken.

'Oh, God!'

Anne is so shocked that she does not notice the clawing hand that slams against her cheek. It knocks her off her feet. She lies upon the rug, holds her stinging skin, and stares up at her mistress.

'Do not look at me like that!' Mary screams. Her whole body shakes, and her teeth rattle as she grips and pulls at her hair.

It is as if a demon towers above Anne, and she runs. She runs all the way back downstairs, tears streaming from her eyes until she collides with Will.

'Anne! What's wrong?'

Anne cannot talk, her voice is held in terror, and she clings to Will.

'Come on, come in here.' He guides her into his father's room.

'What on earth's the matter?' Mr Chipman says. 'Sit her down, Will.'

'Mrs Oliver...' Anne groans between gulps of air and tears.

'What's happened? Is she ill? Speak, Anne!'

His forcefulness rouses her. Anne sniffs back her mucus, wipes her eyes, and flinches when she catches her sore cheek with her sleeve.

'What's that?' Will says and turns her chin so her face is to the light. 'Did she hit you?'

'She is mad,' Anne whispers.

'Why did she hit you?' Mr Chipman says.

'I saw the marks. Marks what she's done to herself. It were awful!' Anne's head throbs now, and her neck aches from the weight of it. 'She were breathing like ... like something demented.'

Mr Chipman sighs, and his eyes dart nervously between his son and Anne. 'Go to bed and get some rest. And don't tell anyone about this.'

'What?' Will reels on his father. 'This ain't right! Mrs Oliver can't get away with this.'

'Mrs Oliver can get away with as much as she likes, son, and don't you forget it. If you want to stay here, stay earning, you keep that mouth shut, do you hear me?'

Will shrinks back. He nods once, short and sharp.

'I hate her,' Anne says, holding her cheek.

'That's enough of that.' Mr Chipman checks the other side of the door to see if anyone has heard their conversation. 'You're doing well here, Anne, don't go spoiling it.'

Anne meets his gaze. She rises from the seat, takes her hand away from her face, and straightens her skirt. All she had hoped for was a little pity, a little understanding; she did not need chiding. She will not be humiliated a second time. 'It's Miss Witmore, to you.'

She stomps out of the room, promising that Mr Oliver will know everything by nine o'clock tomorrow morning.

CHAPTER 4

*M*arch 1869

IT IS SNOWING. From Liz's bedroom window, white, like a thick blanket of bleached lamb's wool, shrouds the landscape. It is as if they have been cocooned inside a spider's web and cannot escape.

She thought she would like it here. She thought the fresh air would suit her well. Before, she had dreamed of seeing blue skies and open fields – they were such rarities in London. That time that Tom had taken her to Hampstead Heath, the vastness of the sky had frightened her for a moment, for she thought she might fall into it, be consumed by it. The lumps of cloud had appeared close enough to touch, and she had reached out her hand, hoping to feel the softness of them, but she had felt nothing but the breeze.

It's beautiful, she had whispered.

Even now, she can feel Tom's arm around her waist, firm

and reassuring, his cheek against hers as they look into the deep blue.

We'll have it all, he had whispered back.

But, on days like this, it is like she is trapped by the expanse of land, like she had been trapped by the narrow streets and squat terraces of the city.

The silence, too, seems to play tricks on her. At night she cannot sleep, for when no sounds come from the house, they come from her mind instead. After two months here, things are only getting worse.

Tom assures her it will be different soon. Once the spring arrives, the place will come alive, so he says. He tells her of drooping bluebells, of buzzing bees, of bleating baby lambs.

Spring seems a long way away.

So, she passes her time in her chamber, away from the intimidating library with its vast selection of books, which she has no desire to read, and no certainty that she'd be able to understand. The drawing room is a bore too, and she does not know where Mary is. She has not the energy nor the inclination to roam around the house with the possibility of unexpectedly meeting her sister-in-law, who is growing more restless by the hour.

But, Liz cannot lay idle for long today. Aunt Emily is due to visit tomorrow, and preparations for her arrival must be made. Everything must be perfect. Mr Chipman must be corrected on his stoop. The maids must make sure there is not one speck of dust anywhere, even in their own rooms. Anne must learn to speak properly, without her accent.

Thinking of Anne, Liz rings the bell to summon her. She enters within minutes.

'Anne, I have need of some company. I wondered if you might like to join me?'

Anne's skips to the seat opposite Liz. 'What an horrible day, miss. Can't stand the snow, me, no good for anyone.'

'Horrible.'

'Yes.'

'No, I meant, horrible.' Liz stresses the word. 'It has an H at the beginning of it. Remember what Mary was telling you about pronunciation?'

'Yes, miss. Sorry, miss.'

'I have no desire for you to change anything, Anne. But I'm afraid I'm not the lady of the house.'

'I wish you were,' Anne says under her breath.

'How has Mary been lately?'

Anne's face sours, but she does not complain. 'Fine.'

'Tom told me about your bruises. May I see?'

Nervously, Anne unfastens the buttons on her left sleeve and rolls it up. There, lie four purple marks, like fat slugs.

'What was her reasoning?'

Anne breathes deep. Liz can feel her reluctance, but she will get it out of her eventually.

'Tom said it was something to do with water?'

'She said it weren't warm enough for her to wash with.'

'I am so sorry, Anne.' She has seen the wounds on the girl and heard the tales from Tom's lips. Anne has been hit with a hairbrush, clawed at, slapped. And it is always Tom she goes to when she is hurt.

'You know, sometimes I hear Mary when she is alone.' Liz leans forward, lowers her voice. 'She talks to herself. Do you know anything about that?'

Anne licks her lips, peeks back at the door. She continues in a whisper. 'I know she shouts and cries. I hears her, as I'm bringing up the tray. Sometimes, she stops when I go inside, and she stares at me as if it is me who is–'

Anne stops herself short of saying the word. *Mad.* Aren't they all, Liz thinks?

'I've told Mr Oliver all of this, miss. I do feel ever so sorry for him, she ain't an easy wife.'

Liz does not like the look in Anne's eyes when she speaks of Tom, but she is glad that Anne is witness to these fits of Mary's. It will prove useful.

'Tom is a good husband.'

'I know, miss. Cannot fault him,' Anne says and deflates as if she has been punctured.

'I know what will cheer you. Your dresses, they are not ugly, but I have some beautiful old garments that I think would suit you marvellously. I would like you to have them. They are in the wardrobe, on the left-hand side.' Liz instructs Anne to find them. 'There they are, those two at the far end.'

Anne takes out two dresses, one is white cotton trimmed with green, the other is a deep red gown.

'The white one is for summer, but the other should do you for now. I'm sure you can tailor it to your size, make it more fashionable for today. It is a few years old. I wore it with a crinoline. They are the only dresses I brought with me from ...'

'They are beautiful, miss.' Anne examines the clothes in awe.

She might not be so happy if she knew what Liz was doing the last time she was in them.

'They served me well. Go and try them on. You have my permission to alter them this afternoon. If Mary asks for you, tell her I have set you a task to alter my dress and get one of the twins to deal with her. It's no lie, after all.' Liz winks at Anne.

With a giggle, Anne scoops up the dresses, curtseys low, and runs from the room, leaving Liz to look out of the window once more.

TOM IS ROOTED in his thoughts, sat in old George's chair. He had said he would throw it away, not liking to sit in a dead man's place, but he has grown fond of the worn-out leather, the comfortable dip in the seat from years of heaviness placed upon it, the way it feels throne-like in the small room. He has taken to leaning back in it and lifting his feet onto the desk while looking out at sea, although today the sea has vanished.

He has already done his morning duty of looking busy. What did George do, holed up in here for days on end? There is only so much paperwork one can pretend to care about.

The study door opens, and Liz enters. She strolls towards him, strokes the polished mahogany desk, then sits on it. 'Where is Mary?'

Tom shakes his head. He doesn't know and doesn't care. 'The library?'

He returns his gaze to the white canvas of the window and sees Liz in the reflection on the glass. He watches her watching him.

'She is getting worse.'

'I know.' He can't help his smile.

A frustrated sigh escapes Liz's lips. 'She must not be upset for her aunt's visit. Emily must think all is well or else—'

'Yes, yes.' Tom knows that Liz is right, although he wishes she weren't.

'You must bed her.'

He meets Liz's gaze in the glass. 'Do you want me to bed her?'

Liz's reflection vanishes like a fly on the water's surface, and she paces towards the fire. He chuckles.

'Stop laughing at me!'

The tears in her eyes sober him. He joins her side, takes her forehead to his chest. 'I'm sorry.'

He shouldn't rile her, not here. He only does it so she might smile, might be reminded of how things used to be between them when they could tease and tickle each other openly, but it is not fair to her while they are stuck here, playing pretend roles. He pulls her closer, inhaling her, feeling her bird-like frame against his own solidity.

'I will see that she is better for tomorrow.'

'I hate it here,' Liz says, and he knows why. He too has come to think of the place as nothing more than a waiting room, a big, grand, waiting room that feels more and more like a gaol each day.

'Remember Venice?' he says, swaying their two bodies together like babes in a cradle. He recalls the time he took her to see the great oil paintings in the National Gallery, remembering how Liz stood for what seemed like hours, staring at the clear skies, the blue rivers, the romantic gondolas. 'We will get there soon.'

Liz lifts her head. Her eyes look up at him through her wet, ashy lashes. He wipes away the tear on her cheekbone.

'Promise?'

'Promise.'

ANNE HAS GONE to her room to make the alterations to the dresses she has been given, not before telling Cate – or was it Clair? She can never remember which is which – that she must see to Mary this afternoon.

She has tried on the gowns, noting a little nervously that Miss Oliver is smaller than herself, for the fabric is stretched around her middle and across her bust. She has let out the seams and re-stitched them as best she can, but really, she quite likes the way the red satin strains across her breasts.

She takes the hem higher, for Miss Oliver is several inches taller than Anne, and as she does so, she notices a small singed area. She sniffs it and smells smoke. Perhaps an ember flicked from the fire and Miss Oliver saw to it quickly before it made a corpse of her. Anne shudders at the thought.

Now, with the hem seen to, she dresses in her new outfit and prances downstairs, hoping to show herself off to the twins and Mrs Beacham. She does not have the chance to reach the kitchen, though, as Will is upon her in the hallway.

'Anne.' His eyes roam over her body. 'You look lovely.'

'Miss Witmore, Will. You must call me, Miss Witmore. How many times must I tell you?'

'Sorry, it's just you've been Anne to me all my life.'

'Yes, well. We were younger then, weren't we?'

His gaze rests on her chest. She folds her arms in front of herself and turns for the back stairs.

'I was thinking.' Will lunges into her path. 'Perhaps you'd like to go for a walk, sometime, with me?'

'It is snowing, Will, I have no want to go out in this weather.' She steps around him. He blocks her again.

'All right, not now, but perhaps when the snow has gone, maybe I could walk you home on a Sunday?'

He is like a fly, pestering around her. If she could, she would swat him. 'I like to walk on my own.'

'Well ...' Will begins to fidget, his forehead creases.

'Will, you are the hall boy. I am a lady's maid. I must be getting on.'

She leaves him shuffling his feet, and stomps upstairs to change into her old clothes.

LIZ HEARS the carriage before she sees it. Since lunch, she has been curled up in one of the comfortable old chairs in the snug with the fire blazing. She had wondered whether Aunt Emily would make the visit, as treacherous as it must be in the snow, but it seems the train lines have been cleared and a few inches of slush on the lanes is no problem for a well-bred stallion.

So now, Liz sits. Her book is open but face down on the

table, hinting that she has been immersed in the lines of Wordsworth when really her eyes only skimmed the words.

She can just about hear the opening of the front door.

She must go to the drawing room. Mary told her before that they should all be assembled there, with the afternoon tea ready and waiting, for her aunt would be exhausted and shivering by the time she arrived. For somebody she cannot stand, Mary is making a tremendous effort to impress her aunt.

Liz hauls herself from the warmth of her chair and makes her way to the drawing room where she finds Tom languid on one of the sofas, sherry in hand, and Mary pacing before the fireplace.

'There you are! Where have you been? She's here, you know.'

Liz holds Mary's shoulders still. 'Everything will be fine, Mary, you must stop worrying. You are a beautiful wife.'

With Liz's touch, Mary takes a full breath of air. Now calm, Mary does, indeed, look rather beautiful. Her blue day dress, Liz admits begrudgingly, really does suit her, highlighting the glossy darkness of her hair. Despite the worry in her eyes, Mary appears remarkably fresh, her skin clear with only a soft pink blush in her cheeks.

Liz cannot say the same about herself.

The door opens. All three face Mr Chipman as he introduces Aunt Emily.

She has seen her only once before, yet even so, Liz is somewhat shocked by the woman's appearance. Emily is a remarkably thin woman compared to her niece. If Liz did not know they were relatives, she would not guess that they shared any kind of blood-line at all. Emily's hair is pure grey and parted sharply in the centre, sleeking down over her ears in the fashion of the fifties – it does not suit her long face. Her dress is black, as it was at the wedding, and Liz does not know if she wears the colour out of mourning for her husband or Prince Albert; both died in the same year.

'So nice to see you.' Mary stands on tiptoes to kiss her aunt's cheek. 'How was your journey?'

'Cold.' Emily stalks to the fireplace.

'Lovely to see you, Aunt.' Tom gets to his feet and swaggers towards Emily, arms outstretched. The old woman is still and unsmiling as Tom kisses her. 'You know my sister, Elizabeth.'

'We met at the wedding,' Emily says, with a look that pins Liz to the spot.

Emily twists round to face the fire and holds her hands towards the flames. Tom smirks at Liz, and for one dreadful moment, Liz thinks he might laugh, but then he slaps his hands together, cracking the silence.

'Right then, Mary, where is this tea? I'm parched.'

It was a long night last night. Mrs Beacham had prepared a mountain of food, all rich and creamy, sweet and sugar-laden. The conversation was stilted, the atmosphere thick with unsaid words and incorrect manners. And after all that hard work with Emily, Tom had to bring Mary to his bed-chamber as well.

He was full of food and drowsy with wine, but he did it. He unfastened Mary's clothes, laid her naked, panting body upon the bed and watched as she opened her legs for him. It had been a struggle to get going, but he had closed his eyes as he had fallen upon her, his face in the space above her collar-bone, her hair tickling his forehead, and he had imagined that she was someone else. When she had moaned, he had placed a hand over her mouth, his excuse being that Emily would hear them.

It had done the job. Mary is as happy as a lamb again this

morning and has taken breakfast with an air of glee that her aunt has not failed to notice. Liz, meanwhile, sits quietly, picking at the shell of her boiled egg until Emily chides her for it.

'Why don't you play the piano for us, sister?' Mary says.

Liz's eyes widen in panic. 'I don't feel too well this morning.' Tom can see her scrambling for an excuse. 'The food was a little too much for me last night. I think I may go to my room if you would not think me rude?'

Whether Aunt Emily thinks her rude or not, Mary accepts the plea and lets Liz go, saying Liz must play tonight after dinner instead, for Aunt Emily loves to hear a jolly tune. It takes all of Tom's strength not to scoff at that.

THE SNOW IS FINALLY MELTING. Only patches of it lie about, like icebergs in the ocean. There is a thin layer of cloud which will have burned out by lunchtime. Perhaps Mary could take her aunt out in the carriage this afternoon, show her around the village, give her the opportunity to throw stones at poor children, a pastime Tom believes would suit them both well.

There is a knock at the door.

'Aunt.' Tom welcomes Emily into the study and gestures for her to take a seat opposite him.

'I see you have made yourself comfortable,' she says as she sits.

She smells old, like the first signs of decay have already set in. The scent reminds him of the reverend's house back in the city, but he pushes the memory away quickly; he must be on his guard around Emily.

'My father loved this room.' She gazes about herself, unfazed. 'He would never have believed someone like you would be sitting in his chair.'

Tom does not rise to the bait. 'How can I help you?'

'Why did you marry Mary?'

He swallows, smiles. Women like Emily can smell fear. 'She loves me. And I love her.'

'Why?' She is like a hawk, hovering before she dives in for the kill. 'I can't understand.'

'There was something about her ...' His collar is too tight, his neck too hot. 'A look. Sad, I thought. I saw her coming towards me, I noticed her above all the others. She looked so dreadfully sad until she saw me, and then she smiled. I thought I could help her.'

'She was perfectly happy.'

'Was she really?' Even Emily cannot think her niece was happy in London, with her. His brutal honesty makes Emily's grey cheeks flush ever so slightly. The woman sniffs, not one to be defeated.

'Is she what you were hoping for?'

He stutters, trying to read her. 'I'm sorry?'

'I warned you of her madness.'

'She seems content to me.'

'Yes, I agree. Today Mary is happy. But she will have days when she is not, when a blackness shadows her. It is a living nightmare when she is like that. I wonder what you shall do then?'

Tom clenches his jaw.

Aunt Emily smiles, coldly. 'You have seen that side of her already.'

'She has high passions,' Tom admits. 'Sometimes, I think she is a little too wild for me.'

'She is unwomanly. But perhaps that is what attracted you? The fact that you must put her in her place, tame her, like men do.'

'I ... She is ...'

'Yes, she is your better,' Emily takes his words. 'Lord

knows why she chose you of all people, but she was always too stubborn to be reasoned with. And you must live with that. You are a man who knows his station in life and cannot believe his luck. Well, neither can I. But, I believe, for some reason that I cannot fathom, you do think a lot of her. So, you must do your duty by her. Be a man. Make her a woman.'

'I do not wish to control my wife.'

'Mary must set an example. You must set an example. I warned you of this before, do not say I did not warn you! Her father was too weak to deal with her, too soft at heart. A man is no good to anyone like that.' She rolls her eyes.

'If she continues her mood swings, call Doctor Jameson. You remember I told you about him at the wedding? He knows what medicine suits her. But you must make sure she takes it. She is strong-willed, but she must be controlled.'

'I will take care of her, Emily, I will do all I can.'

Emily rises, wincing at some pain that she will not admit to.

'I do not like you, Mr Oliver,' she says between pursed lips. 'But you know that already. I shall not be returning to visit. Though I do not like my niece, I do care for her. She is my brother's daughter; she carries my blood in her veins.'

Emily staggers to the door and takes one final look at the study. She sighs, shakes her head. 'I shall be leaving in the morning, you shall be pleased to hear.'

As they sip their wine, the clock ticking ever forward in the silence, Liz begins to think she may not have to play. Perhaps Mary has forgotten or just cannot bear the idea of entering the music room. Perhaps Liz can just stay until she has finished her drink, feign exhaustion, then retire early.

Liz yawns. 'I think I shall go to bed.'

'But you can't.' Mary rouses herself from her sleepiness, sits straighter in her chair. 'You must play for us.'

'I think everyone is quite tired.'

Tom crouches over a book on the table and props his head up with his arm. Emily reclines on the sofa, her small sherry glass teetering in her hand, her breath too loud and slow to be fully conscious.

'Aunt Emily.' Mary prods her aunt until the woman grunts awake. The sherry spills onto her dark bodice, but she does not notice. 'You would like to hear Elizabeth play the piano, wouldn't you? She says she is for bed otherwise.'

'Oh, yes.' Emily drags herself upright. 'Play. The music soothes me for sleep. If you're any good, that is. If you are like Mary, I should prefer silence.' Her eyes, which had been drowsy moments before, are now beady once again.

'Not much good, are you, sister?' Tom says, rallying himself to his feet. 'I'm sure it would not settle your nerves at all, Aunt. Much better to retire, I should think.'

'Tom, what a thing to say about your sister!' Liz is sure there is the sound of a smile in Mary's words. 'You said you played, Elizabeth?'

'Yes but ...' Liz clears her throat, sips her sherry. 'Not very well, Tom is right.'

'Nonsense. You are too modest.'

'You have long fingers,' Emily says. 'Good pianists always have long fingers. I was excellent in my youth, but then, I have a sharp brain also.'

Liz lets the insult pass. She would rather be known as a dunce if it meant she did not have to play.

'That's it, I'm afraid.' Tom walks towards Liz. 'Never managed to get the hang of it, have you, sister?' He tweaks her under the chin. She smiles up at him, playing along.

'You shall play,' Mary says, her jealousy so rigid in the air that Liz thinks she could touch it.

There is no way out now.

Like a woman to the scaffold, Liz leads the way to the music room. It is spotless and aired, not like the last time she was in here. The lid is already raised on the piano.

They take to their chairs. Emily sits like a tutor waiting to hear her protégé perform. Tom's gaze is buried in the rug on the floor. Mary sits between Emily and Tom, smirking, her eyes shrewd, her brows raised in expectation.

Liz sits at the stool. She glances at the keys, like a set of black and white bones laid ceremoniously before her. Touching one with her finger, she finds it just as she remembers – cool and hard, like a whip. She struggles for breath; her lacing is too tight, and her corset crushes her ribs.

Tobacco, brandy, and sweat pollute the air. Laughter rumbles, low and growling, high and breathy. Glasses tinkle, skirts rustle. She tastes the sourness of a foreign object in her mouth, the dryness of cheap wine. She feels a clawing hand at her shoulder squeezing harder and harder until Liz's fingers find the keys, and she begins.

She does not know what she plays. She has forgotten the title of it, for the act of playing it a thousand times and more has rendered it nameless. Sweat trickles between her small breasts and seeps onto her stomach, her stomach which throbs constantly. She sees her fingers work like milling machines, too fast to understand.

She plays for as long as it takes. She cannot stop even though she wants to. The notes must flow, the memories must unfold, the sickness must come.

And finally, her fingers slow, dying as they press the final key.

Now she waits.

She waits for the uproar. She waits for the demand for more. She waits for the spectators to place their bids. She waits to be taken, like a circus lion to the ring, to do what she is forced to do.

But the uproar does not come.

She lifts her gaze and finds two female faces staring back at her, mouths hanging open, smirks lost to shock. In the green oasis of Tom's eyes, there are tears.

Liz stands. She would bow, but she reminds herself that there is no need to do so anymore.

'I said she had good fingers.' Emily's voice echoes in the silence.

'Yes.' Mary swallows. 'I don't know what all the fuss was about. You are a good pianist.'

'Exceptional,' Emily says.

Mary stands. 'I am ready for bed now. Come, Tom.'

Mary stalks out of the room, followed by her aunt. Tom rises, quickly wipes his eyes, and touches Liz on the back.

'It's all right now,' he whispers to her, then leaves.

Alone, Liz looks about her and waits for the ghosts of her memories to show themselves again, to swirl out from behind the curtains and pull her back to the past. But they do not. She is free, she tells herself. And with that, she slams the piano lid shut.

 pril 1869

SINCE AUNT EMILY'S VISIT, Tom has been to Mary's bedroom only three times. It is usual, Mary tries to reason with herself, that husbands should only avail themselves once a week. She has read booklets about it. Yes, Tom is quite the gentleman. It is almost like he has read the pamphlets himself. But Mary is not satisfied. She dreams of him when she is awake. She dreams of his solid, young body as if carved by Michelangelo himself. Once a week is not enough.

The day is stretching. The cold and snow have turned to mild wetness. The landscape is drab and dreary, and Mary has nothing with which to occupy herself.

At times like this, she likes to think of her days in London to remind herself how lucky she is to be at Floreat. She thinks of the calls she had to make with her aunt, of how the old ladies looked at her with pity for she was an orphan and spinster. She hated the way those old ladies' daughters smirked at her, revelling in their superior marital status. She hated how her aunt would remind her that she must marry or else she would be burdened with city-life forever and would never see her beloved Floreat again. Her childhood home would go to some French landowning relative whom she had never met in her life.

She thinks of those horrid afternoons, those hideous faces, and she smiles. How those faces fell when news came of her marriage to Tom, of all people!

She replays their meeting. It is one of her favourite pastimes to remember the steam on her face, the bustling crowd, the way the fog had seemed to lift and the people to vanish as she saw Tom standing before her in a halo of light.

Or, at least, that is how she remembers it. The details are becoming hazy now. Who was the first to speak? How did she come to find such a fresh-faced young man beside her, asking if he could help her in any way?

It is a struggle to find a connection with Tom these days. He is distant, not quite so adept at listening as he once was, not quite so keen to spend his spare time with her. Perhaps it is because of her moods. She is terrible when in a rage, but she cannot help herself. If he would only spend more time with her, then she would not get in such moods in the first place.

There is a gentle tap at her door. She calls for the person to enter.

Tom creeps inside, smiling. How she loves that smile! She can never resist the urge to return it with one of her own.

'You look well, my dear. I am glad to see you feeling better now.'

'I was well this morning.' Why must he ruin things? She turns away from him petulantly. 'Anne has obviously been telling lies about me again.'

'She did not say anything.' Tom strokes the top of her arm

and comes before her. 'I saw the bruise on the girl's cheek-bone. Anne did not like to mention it, but I made her.'

'Well.' Mary sips her cold tea. 'I have told her to be gentler with the brush. That girl does not learn.'

She would continue, but Tom has stopped listening to her; she can tell by the vacancy in his eyes, even though he nods as if he cares.

'What do you want?'

'You have a visitor,' he says.

She is not expecting anyone. 'Who is it?'

'Doctor Jameson.'

The name makes ice form in the pit of her stomach. 'I have no need to see him.'

'He is to examine you, darling. I called him. It won't take long.'

Before she has time to object, Tom kisses her quickly and exits, leaving the door open and revealing Doctor Jameson who has been standing there all along.

It is a pleasant afternoon spent in the company of Anne, embroidering. Liz has never had much time for the art of embroidery before – she thought it inconsequential, useless, leading to nothing but a pretty square of material. Now, it fills the spare hours.

Anne is excellent with a needle. Her short, podgy fingers work quickly and elegantly, and she is already on her second pattern before Liz has finished her first.

'You have talent.' Liz gestures at Anne's stitching of a butterfly.

'Thank you, miss.'

'Why a butterfly?'

Anne shrugs, waits a moment, then decides. 'Spring is coming. And they're pretty.'

'Have you ever seen one leave its cocoon?'

'No, miss. What's it like?'

Liz recalls the butterflies she saw in the zoo, with wings soft and flat, and bodies which looked as if they had been squashed underfoot. 'Grotesque to begin with. It takes time for them to emerge. It looks painful at the start, but then, with time, they dry out. Their wings harden, they take their shape, and then it is hard to believe they were ever ugly.'

'Da tells me they come from caterpillars.' Anne's stitching has slowed. She manages to thread without looking at her hands.

'That's right. Lowly little caterpillars, and then they transform themselves.'

'God's miracle.'

Liz bites her tongue. Of course, the girl is devout and why shouldn't she be? She has not yet had reason to question His existence like Liz has.

'Yes.' Liz takes to her embroidery again. Her lines are not so neat, but she will persist.

'Miss, if you don't mind me asking, what were it that you did, before? Only I heard you ...'

Liz stops stitching.

'Begging your pardon, miss. I didn't mean to be rude.'

'I was a seamstress.' She pokes the needle through the material, and the point only narrowly avoids her skin. Really, she should have said a different job at the start of all of this, she should have considered her lie more carefully. It is evident that she has no skill, but Anne is too careful now to question further. 'I took in piece work, to pass the time. Once my brother was settled, I went to live with him and cared for the house.'

Silence returns.

Liz pushes the needle, trying to get the right angle for the curve of the dogwood flower. This time, she jabs too fast, and the tip stabs under her nail. She gasps as drops of blood drip onto the material, seeping into the delicate petals.

Anne rushes for some spare cotton, drops to her knees before Liz, and bandages the finger. With each turn of the material, Liz can feel her pulse throbbing, the flesh warm, itchy, and sore.

'I was only good with dresses.'

Anne ties a small, neat knot into the makeshift bandage. 'No matter, miss. I think your dogwood were going well.'

Liz smiles her thanks. 'Is it hard for the rest of them? The staff, I mean. Knowing that Tom and I are ... Well, we are not like Mary.'

'No, miss.' Anne shakes her head, her stray curls springing about her neck. 'Well, maybe some found it a little odd, at first. Bet certainly didn't like it. I never had any problems though, you know that!'

'What do they say now?'

'Everyone thinks you're both wonderful, miss. Not a bad word to say about either of you.'

'And about Mary? What do they say about her?'

'Everyone is very happy here.'

'Are you happy with Mary?'

Anne flushes, licks her lips as if her mouth is suddenly dry. 'Yes, of course–'

'I know, Anne.' Liz squeezes her arm. 'I am only teasing you. I understand Mary is not the easiest.'

Still, Anne does not trust Liz as she trusts Tom. Liz had hoped the girl would confide in her by now, tell her all of Mary's secrets, tell her how much she loathes her mistress. Yet, it is still Tom she runs to, and Liz does not like their growing intimacy.

'You know, you can tell me anything, Anne. You can be honest. We are alike, you and me; more so than Mary and me. We should stick together, don't you think?'

'I suppose so, miss.'

'I should like us to be friends.'

Anne regards her, uncertainly. Perhaps Liz has gone too far. Ordinarily, mistresses should not be so close to their staff, but nothing about this situation is ordinary. Liz waits, smile fixed, hoping she has not ruined everything.

'I would like that too, miss.'

Liz sighs. 'Good.' She rests back in her chair and watches Anne finish embroidering.

'There.' Anne lifts it up so Liz can see. 'A beautiful butterfly for you.'

THE LIGHT IS FADING. Tom pulls the lever to summon Chipman.

'Light the lamps for me, would you? I can't see a thing.'

'Anything else I can do for you, sir?' Chipman's suit is pressed and clean, his hair is slicked back. He has even managed to fix his stoop. He is almost a completely different man to the one Tom met in the village months ago.

'Sit with me.'

Chipman hesitates but eventually perches on the seat opposite Tom.

'I am worried, Chipman.' Tom plays with the leather on the desk, lifts his gaze to the window and observes the inky-blueness of the sky, before seeing their two reflections in the glass, like yellow waxworks.

'Sir?'

'I am worried about Mary. She has not been herself for a while now. She is violent. I presume you have seen Anne?'

'Anne is ... she is not always ... What I am trying to say, sir, is that perhaps Mrs Oliver, being the mistress of the house, has cause to be how she is with Anne.'

'Are you saying that Anne is dishonest?' Is that perspiration he can detect on Chipman's brow? 'I believe it was you who recommended her to me, Chipman.'

'Yes, sir, I did. And I am not calling her a liar, only she is wilful. Perhaps it is not always the best thing for a maid to be.'

'Are you saying I should let her go?'

'No, sir! Forgive me, sir. What I am trying to say is ... I am only trying to think the best of Mrs Oliver. I am sure she is a most kind woman.'

Tom would laugh if he thought it would not upset this naive fool of a man. 'Thank you, Chipman. My wife is indeed a very kind woman. It is only these rages she is occasionally burdened with. Perhaps I should speak to Anne?'

'I could speak to her, sir, no need to trouble yourself. Only I am not sure she would listen to me.'

'You are the manservant here, Chipman. I should hope Anne does not think herself above you.'

'She is civil with me. It is not something I can quite put my finger on ...' Chipman searches for the words. 'It's as if she thinks herself special. She's very cold with Will.'

Will. Fifteen years of age, tall. His gangly limbs have started to fill out, from what Tom has seen of him when he has ordered a horse to be readied.

'Will is doing well. My boots are always sparkling.' Tom lifts his feet off the floor and taps his boots together in mid-air. 'Does he like Anne?'

'They've been friends since they were kiddies.'

'But does he like her?'

Chipman's cheeks redden. 'It is not proper for ... that sort of thing to go on between staff, sir. It will pass.'

Tom chuckles. 'I do not forbid a man love. I think it rather pleasant for Will to be taken with the girl.'

'Anne thinks herself above him.' Chipman wipes the beads of sweat from his brow with the back of his hand.

'She is young. Young girls do not always see what is best for them.' Tom looks out of the window again. The blueness has been submerged by black, and the clouds have left no room for the stars. 'Leave it with me, Chipman. Now, I should like you to see how Doctor Jameson is getting on and have Will ready his horse and our carriage. Will can drive him home. I should not like to see the man ride his horse in the dark.'

'Sir,' Chipman says half an hour later, as he steps aside to let Doctor Jameson enter the study.

The doctor is short and thin, his clothes are sharp and tight. He does not smile as he comes, and Tom notices the marks on his cheeks, like tiny craters in his grey skin. He reminds Tom of the spindly Pied Piper from old storybooks.

'Take a seat, doctor. Whiskey?'

'Thank you.'

Tom reaches for the decanter and pours two high measures. 'Water?'

'No.'

Tom pushes the drink at the doctor, then leans back in his chair. He puts his own glass under his nose to smell the smokiness of the liquor, rich and clawing at the back of his throat. He sips it and lets it slip around his mouth, like liquid fire, smarting and stinging and soothing different parts of his tongue, before swallowing it.

The doctor holds the glass to the firelight then drinks. 'An excellent Scotch.'

'So?' Tom says. 'How is my wife?'

Jameson takes another sip. 'She is not mad if that is what you were hoping.'

Tom stills. The remark catches him off guard, and there is a smirk of triumph on the doctor's face. Tom will not let his anger rule him. This is a smart man who sits before him; he must be cautious. 'Her aunt told me about her condition. I need to know if it has returned.'

'What do you know of her condition?' He emphasises the word, mocking Tom.

'She cannot control her emotions.'

Jameson nods, examines his whiskey again, then gulps down the last drop. He puts the tumbler on the table and stares at the decanter. Tom refills his glass.

'Have you ever been to the Highlands?'

'No. How is my wife?'

'I remember when everyone thought the Scots savages,' Jameson says. 'I was quite frightened when my father took me with him one summer for a visit. Alas, there were no savages, only little gnats that sucked the blood out of us.'

Tom taps his glass to his teeth. The doctor's sharp eyes flick at him.

'I don't suppose you would have had the time to visit the place. Or the money, before.'

'Perhaps I shall go with my wife this summer.' Tom returns the doctor's bitter smile. 'If she is well enough?'

'Quite well.'

'She is not ill, like before?'

'I understand you went to Rugby, Mr Oliver?'

'I don't see what that has to do with anything.'

'What did you make of your time there?'

Tom recalls the march to Reverend Oliver's house when he was twelve years old, the man's forced signature, how Liz had cried endlessly when she was told that Tom was leaving. He had wept silently into his pillow that first night until he learnt that crying was useless. Was weakness.

He blinks the memory away, pulls himself back into the present. 'Not much.'

'The grandson of a clergyman? I suspect it was rather hard for you there.'

'I was as good as any of them.'

The doctor grins. 'Why didn't you go to university afterwards?'

'I had to leave. What has this got to do with my wife?'

'Oh, nothing.' The doctor rolls the whiskey around the glass with excellent control. 'I just like to know who I'm dealing with.'

'Are you satisfied?'

'What made you leave?'

'My grandfather died when I was sixteen. My grandmother soon after him. Rugby is not a charity.'

'No inheritance?'

'I was found a position in the railway.'

'Mmh. A bit of a drop down the ladder though.'

Tom laughs, hollowly. How he would like to smack the doctor! His fists, hidden behind the desk in his lap, clench. He imagines it for one blissful moment; the crack of bone against bone, the blood spurting from Jameson's split lip, the shock on the man's face. But he must only imagine it. He inhales, slides his shoulders back, forces himself to relax. After all, it is Tom who owns Floreat, and it is Tom who pays this man's wages.

'I did not need Reverend Oliver's money.'

'Of course not. You met Mary soon afterwards.'

Tom grinds his teeth. 'Yes. And now I am asking you again, Doctor, is my wife ill?'

'No.'

'She is violent. She has bruised her lady's maid and drawn blood.'

'Because the maid is unlearned, so I gather. I should point out, Mr Oliver, seeing as this is all new to you, that it is not unusual for ladies to be strict with their staff.'

Tom wishes he had not instructed Chipman to sort the carriage for Jameson's ride home. He hopes the wheel gets stuck in a bog.

'I would, however,' Jameson says, 'err on the side of caution. She should take plenty of rest.'

'Nothing to worry about?'

'Nothing to worry about at all. In fact, it seems marriage has done her some good.' Jameson downs his last drop of whiskey and motions at the bottle again. Tom pours him a half measure. 'I propose a toast. You have something to celebrate, Mr Oliver. Your wife is not mad. Your wife is pregnant.'

Jameson knocks the liquid back in one, keeping his eyes on Tom, who reaches for his glass and copies the doctor. He hopes his shock is not too apparent, but it would appear that it is, for the doctor continues smugly.

'Pregnancy does wonders for women. It settles the womb. Her rages will soon disappear once she has a child to focus her attention upon. Even the maid won't have to dodge her blows.'

'Good.' Tom clears his throat. 'That is good news.' He cannot stand another minute in this man's company. He rises and strides to the door without meeting Jameson's eyes. 'Chipman has prepared a carriage for you.'

'No need for that, I would have managed just fine.'

'Nonsense. I'm actually rather surprised that you don't have your own carriage, Doctor.' Tom motions Jameson towards the door. 'I'd have thought a man like yourself would have a whole fleet.'

Jameson laughs and unfurls out of the warmth of the chair. 'Your wife needs rest,' he says, inches from Tom's face. 'Don't bed her.'

'Very well.' Tom does not try for a handshake. 'Goodnight, doctor.'

LIZ IS NOT hungry enough for dinner. Her finger is still sore where the needle wounded her, but she likes to press it, to feel the pressure beneath her nail, to see the cut open and bleed again. She has on her dark crimson gown this evening, and Anne wears the red hand-me-down; standing in front of the mirror, from a distance, they could almost be twins, but when they come closer to the glass, they look nothing alike at all.

'You are beautiful tonight, miss.'

'Thank you, Anne.' Liz's stomach growls.

'You're hungry, miss?'

'I am.' Liz laughs, but it rings hollow. She is nervous. Tom told her of the doctor visiting, but so far, she has not managed to catch him to find out what the doctor said.

The gong rings.

'Have you seen to Mary?'

'Yes, miss. I went to her just after the doctor left her.'

'And? How is she?'

Anne hesitates. Another test of trust. Liz waits until finally, Anne says, 'She were crying, miss.'

'Do you know why?'

'No.'

Sickness stirs in Liz's guts, a dread that she cannot under-stand. She lifts her gloves from the dressing table. The silk is like slime as she slides it over her damp skin. 'Thank you, Anne. You may go now.'

Her stomach gurgles again. She notices the butterfly embroidery next to her perfume bottles. Staring hard, she sees the insect flutter away from its stitches. She follows it around the room until it disappears behind the curtain of her bed. She searches for it, tearing the material. She must find it before it finds her ...

But it is too late. Out of the darkness, it collides into her mouth and burrows down into her body.

She can feel its wings tickling her lungs as it creeps around underneath her ribs, its antennae pricking her bloody flesh. She grips her neck when she feels it crawling upwards again.

She will squash it dead.

She wrings her throat, but the antennae stab the back of her tongue. She squeezes and squeezes, but the butterfly grows stronger. Her mouth opens, but she cannot get her breath.

If she were to look in the mirror, she would find the mighty head of the butterfly stuck in her throat, its wings stretching out through her lips, its black eyes staring back at her.

Then it escapes. She doubles over, purging herself, and finally, she can breathe again.

She gulps air like someone saved from the sea. She wipes her wet face with her glove to find that the white silk is now brown. There is a pool of vomit on the floor.

Glancing quickly at the embroidery, she sees the butterfly has returned to its home. She flips the cotton over and covers it with one of her shawls – she will burn it later.

She leaves the room and descends the stairs on shaking legs. She breathes in deeply, exhales slowly, until she can no longer feel her pulse throbbing in her temples.

The door to the dining room is open. Mary and Tom are already at their places. Mary greets her with a broad smile, the tears long evaporated. Tom does not look at Liz.

'Sorry, I am late,' Liz croaks, then takes her wine glass and drinks. The alcohol burns as she swallows.

'No trouble, sister.'

Liz jumps as Mary's hand reaches across the table and squeezes her own.

'We have some news, don't we, Tom?'

Tom looks up. His smile is one she has seen so often, but it has never been used on her before. 'Yes.' Suddenly, he frowns. 'What has happened to your neck?'

Liz touches the flesh on her throat and winces. 'I ... it is nothing. Your news?'

'We are having a baby.' Mary's eyes appear black in the dimness of the dining room, like the eyes of the butterfly. Liz gazes into them, falling into their darkness … It cannot be. She cannot have heard Mary correctly.

'I said,' Mary's laughter cracks in the silence, 'we are having a baby. You shall be an auntie.'

Liz tries to swallow, but she has no saliva. She eases her hand free of Mary's and takes another gulp of wine.

'Congratulations,' Liz whispers, the word breaking in the middle.

'Doctor Jameson says I might have been pregnant for a month. It is still early yet, but I am so excited.'

'Congratulations, Tom.' Liz hopes her sourness is not heard by Mary. 'I am afraid that I am unwell.'

Mary's hand touches her stomach. 'What's wrong?'

'Sickness. So, I shan't stay for dinner. I wouldn't have come down at all if I had known.'

She pushes her chair back herself, for Chipman has not had time to apprehend her movements, and it screeches against the floorboards. She makes her way to the door.

'Shall I bring your dinner to your room?' Tom's voice is a desperate plea. Good, she thinks, let him suffer.

'No. I should like to be alone.'

CHAPTER 6

*J*uly 1869

IT IS A GLORIOUS DAY. The sun is keen, but the cool breeze brushes against Anne's face and smells as lovely as perfume. A warbler perches amongst the pink and yellow heather and sings, tilting his dainty head from side to side and puffing out his throat and crown. She stops for a moment to watch him, his body no bigger than her thumb, enjoying his pompous cries, before he vanishes in a feathery blur.

'What you laughing at?'

She turns to find Will's freckled face smiling at her. Why must he always ruin everything? She lifts her chin and glares at him before striding on.

'Thought I could keep you company.' Will is out of breath, but he trots alongside her, easily matching her pace. 'I'm going to see my ma, as well.'

Anne walks quicker, and dampness builds in her

armpits. All day, she has felt his eyes on her; on the way to church; during the service; even while singing the hymns. It had made her all too aware of the way her lips moved with each word, of how she lowered her head in prayer, of how her mouth opened to receive the wafer. If only it had been Mr Oliver watching her! She would not have minded that at all.

'Beautiful day, ain't it?'

She frowns at the blaze from the sun and pulls her bonnet nearer her brow to get some shade.

'Slow down, eh?' Will catches the crook of her arm.

'Do not touch me.'

His hand recoils as if she has smacked it away. 'What is wrong with you, Anne? I only want to be a friend to you.'

She blows her breath out between her teeth. She knows she is too hard on him, but really, he is so persistent! His company makes her awkward, his gaze makes her self-conscious. She has outgrown him completely. Even so, he is like a scolded puppy now, and guilt tugs at her conscience. 'Come on, then.' She walks on, slower this time, and allows him to join her.

'I love the summer,' he says, smiling once he's caught her up. 'It is the best time of the year. What's your favourite season?'

'Spring. The heat can be a burden in summer.' She wipes her head with her sleeve. She has put an old dress on to see her family, knowing they would not appreciate the red one from Miss Oliver.

'Mrs Oliver is starting to show now,' Will says.

'She is just fat.'

'You mustn't be so harsh with her, Anne.' He looks about him as if making sure there are no spies.

She rolls her eyes. 'Don't be so dramatic.'

'You mustn't let her hear you speak like that.'

'Do you think I'm stupid?' Anne swats at a fly that buzzes in front of her face.

'Of course not, I only ... It's only that I care for you.'

'You care for me?' She reels on him. They stand in the middle of a worn-out track amidst the heathland, the wind wrapping around their bodies and sending their hair into spirals.

'If you cared for me, you would be saying what a devil that woman is! You would be saying how she should not blacken my eye or pinch my arms. You would not be defending her, Will, if you cared for me like you say you do.'

Her chin wobbles, but the pity in his face makes her fists clench.

'Anne.' He comes closer, takes hold of her arms. 'Anne, I'm sorry.'

'I hate her. And I would prefer it if you did not walk with me, Will, I would like to have the time to myself.'

She leaves him standing scarecrow-like, cursing him and Mrs Oliver, and hoping that the powder around her right eye has not been ruined by her tears. She would not have her mother see the yellowing crescent where Mrs Oliver last took out her frustration.

IT IS A SWELTERINGLY HOT MORNING. The sun beats down upon him while heat emanates from his horse's body below. Tom pulls at his riding clothes, trying to create some air between his skin and his cotton shirt. His scalp is wet, and he removes his top hat for a moment to allow what little breeze there is to run through his hair.

'I am still not convinced you should be riding in your condition, darling.' Tom squints at his wife who sits with ease on her new white pony.

'Nonsense, I am perfectly well. The fresh air will do me good.'

Behind Tom, Liz hangs on to her own grey mare, forced to sit side saddle for the entire ride due to the company. He smiles at her terrified face, and she glowers back at him.

Behind her, by twenty yards or so, are Anne, Mr Chipman, and one of the maids. They carry the family's picnic between themselves like mules.

'Take your time,' Tom shouts at them. 'There's no rush.'

'Let's have a race, darling.' Mary turns to him. 'First one to the cliffs.'

'I don't think that is wise. It's not good for the baby.'

But Mary has already kicked her heels into her animal and is now galloping over the green fields and bounding up the hill.

There is no way Liz will be going anywhere near a trot, let alone a gallop, and Tom is not a confident horseman. He has been practising a few times a week ever since his arrival at Floreat, but still, the large snorting giants do not fill him with confidence.

Mary streaks ahead, her pale skirts flapping over her pony's rear. Reluctantly, Tom squeezes his stallion, and it belts away after her, scoring hoof marks into the soil as it goes. He clings on, hoping his fear does not show.

He nears Mary. The blue frills on her dress are visible once again, as are the strands of hair that have fallen loose from under her hat.

'Slow down, Mary.'

A cackle of laughter is her only response as they breach the hill. The grass slopes down and away from them, and close, getting closer, is the sapphire blue of the sea, stretching before them, as still as ice.

'Mary,' he calls. His horse snorts as it thrashes along just inches behind her. 'Slow down!'

The cliffs are approaching far too quickly. Tom drags on the reins, and for a second the stallion resists but then drops from a gallop to a trot.

Mary's pony is not as well trained. Tom can make out the strain in Mary's arms as she tugs at the reins, he can hear her frightened orders for the creature to slow down, but it takes no notice.

This is it! She will go over the cliff and fall to her death.

It would be quicker this way, he thinks, his eyes widening, his mouth drying with something like excitement.

Mary screams.

She and her pony are feet away from the cliff edge when the pony's hooves suddenly dig into the ground. It braces to the side, turning just in time to avoid the sheer drop. It is a tumble of white – the pony's body, Mary's dress, everything jumbled and unclear. Only when the creature rounds and heads back towards Tom can he see that Mary is no longer astride it.

The pony trots towards the stallion, its fear vanished. Tom dismounts, and for a moment, the pony obstructs his view, letting him imagine that Mary has been thrown down upon the shoreline.

But no, she is slumped on the grass, meringue-like in her crumpled dress. He runs to her and finds her shaking all over, tears slugging down her cheeks.

He brings her into his arms. 'It's all right, it's all right, darling.'

They sit together until the rest of the entourage emerge over the hillside.

'Ma'am!' Anne drops her bags and lets her hat fall from her head as she runs towards Mary, screeching at Clair to follow. Anne's breath is quick and heavy and her cheeks are scarlet by the time she drops to her knees in front of her mistress. 'Are you all right, ma'am? Are you hurt?'

Mary is recovering herself, her head cradled between Tom's arms.

'She had a fall. She just needs a moment, Anne.'

'Should I call for the doctor?'

'No,' Mary whispers, pulling her head upright and wiping away the tears. 'Help me up.'

The three of them take hold of Mary and bring her to her feet. As she tries to straighten, she flinches, crying at the pain, grabbing her stomach.

'Get the doctor,' Anne says to Clair, who is just about to run when Mary stops her.

'I am fine.' Mary stretches up again, wincing, but in more control than before.

'Ma'am, the baby. We must get the doctor.'

'I said no!' Mary's voice bellows in the quiet. 'Will you never listen?'

Anne's lips purse, the top of her dress tightens and loosens with each breath.

'I think we should go home.' Tom nods at Anne, indicating that she may leave them and gather their things. She does as he bids.

'I am well,' Mary says.

'You are not. We are going home. Take Mrs Oliver to my horse.' Tom transfers Mary to Clair. Together, the two of them stumble towards the stallion, who placidly chews the grass.

Liz joins Tom, and they stare over the cliff. The rock is a deep red where it has been gouged by centuries of wind, rain, and sea. The stony beach lies thirty feet beneath them, and white waves break over the boulders below, creating a noise like an agonising moan.

'She is a fool.' Liz's words disintegrate in the wind.

'She could have died,' Tom says, looking down at the waves, but he feels Liz's gaze slide his way.

'Sir?' Anne is behind them, shifting on her feet. 'Mrs Oliver is ready.'

'Thank you, Anne. Thank you for everything.' As he passes her, he touches her arm, then goes to his wife.

IT IS A STEADY RIDE HOME. Liz stays at the back, her mare plodding heavily, like everyone, for the heat is too much to bear. It is a relief, in all honesty; she could think of nothing she would rather do less than picnic under the midday sun, watching Mary eat for two.

They amble towards the stables. Liz's horse takes to a bucket of hay as Mary is helped from the stallion. The white pony is already in her block, shaking her head and stamping on the straw, rather pleased with the drama she has caused.

'She should be shot.' Mary lands with a thud. Her eyes are red, her nose running; she wipes it with the back of her hand as Chipman leads the stallion to safety.

'She's feisty, that's all.' Tom makes a show of brushing Mary's clothes straight, fussing over her, while Liz must get herself to the ground unaided.

'I want her gone, Tom. I mean it. The horrid thing would have killed me!'

'Anne,' Liz calls. The girl trots over immediately and curtseys. Poor girl, her skin is crimson, the sweat clear on her brow. She cares too much, it would seem.

'Does Chipman know where the guns are? A house as big as this must have some lying around.'

'I don't know, miss.'

'Well, ask him.' Liz shoos her away and watches Anne whisper to the man, and both of them flick their eyes worriedly at Liz. 'Go and fetch one, Chipman. Be quick.'

She takes the time to summon the pony to her with the lure of a carrot, provided by Will, and strokes its course mane as it chews. It is a wonder the creature held Mary's weight in the first place, for its head is only level with Liz's, and its legs look remarkably short this close. It's big, black eyes meet hers, as clear as mirrors, as Mary drones on and on in the background, her voice grating on them both.

'Miss.' Chipman waits behind Liz, holding the gun awkwardly before him. The sight of it has made Mary cease whining, and both her and Tom turn to Liz.

'Is it loaded?'

'Yes, miss.'

She takes it from him, liking its cold solidity in her prickling hands. She walks with it to Mary and holds it out. 'Shoot her.'

Mary gawps at Liz, then at the gun. The metal gleams in the sunlight.

'Liz,' Tom whispers, edging closer, 'what are you doing?'

'She wants the animal dead then she must shoot it. Come, Mary, take the gun and kill the beast.'

Mary's eyes fill again. Liz steps forward, and Mary jumps back. The air is ice between them, brittle and tight, as Tom and the servants watch silently.

'It is all you have been talking about for the last half hour. What is wrong? Have you not the nerve to do it yourself?' Liz waits for a second, but her anger is like a flare soaring into the sky, and it is like she is flying. In the quietness, her heels echo as she marches for the pony's stable, raises the gun, and aims between the animal's ears.

The gun trembles. The pony stares, unperturbed, and Liz sees her own smiling reflection in its eyes.

'Stop!'

There is a commotion behind. Mary has fallen into Tom's arms, her head lolling against his chest, tears streaking down her cheeks. He whispers into her ear, words that mean nothing, as he glares at Liz.

81

Liz returns the gun to Chipman, and the man runs inside with it. She wipes her wet palms on her skirts, squares her shoulders, and lifts her chin defiantly as Tom guides Mary towards the house. Only Anne remains, but she follows Tom with her eyes.

'You may go, Anne.'

'Can I get you anything?'

Liz shakes her head, returns to the pony. The creature greets her calmly, and she strokes its velvet muzzle.

'Miss.' Anne lingers nearby, her voice unsteady. 'You wouldn't really have shot her, would you?'

The pony blows through her nostrils, her warm breath like feathers over Liz's wrist, smelling sweet.

'Never.'

THE HOUSE HAS BEEN all astir since Mary's fall. Doctor Jameson has been and checked her. He said that the baby seems fine and that Mary suffered nothing more than bruising. She is to rest and not strain herself again. Horse riding is strictly forbidden.

They have not spoken about the incident with the gun. Liz is waiting for some admonishment from Mary, waiting in anticipation, but it never comes. Instead, they continue as if it didn't happen, and Mary has returned to her loathsome self.

Now, a week after the fall, Liz and Mary are on the lawn, arranging flowers just picked from the garden. Mary's vase is white porcelain, its neck moulded into the shape of two holding hands. Her flowers protrude in a proud display of colour.

'I think I should look in The Times. I do not want another girl from the village.'

'For what?'

'A wet nurse.' Mary rolls her eyes. 'Have you not been listening to me?'

'Sorry. I have been thinking about my flowers.' Liz picks up a delicate yellow rose, its tips blushing to a gentle amber. She puts it under her nose and inhales the sweet scent, imagining she might take a bite of it, it smells so beautiful. She places it into her vase, then stares again at the heap of flowers waiting to be chosen.

'Violet suits yellow.'

'But you already have those colours.'

'You can also. Here,' Mary leans across the flower-strewn table and plucks some violet petals. 'Freesias should sit nicely and be different from my roses.'

Liz takes the freesias, hoping that she looks like she knows what she is doing, but Mary is too busy with her own arrangement to notice Liz's hesitation.

'I was saying I should like a good, reliable wet nurse, with references, of course. I cannot take a chance when it comes to my son.'

'Shall you not nurse him yourself?'

Mary skewers a thick lily stem into the vase and snorts. 'No.'

'If it were mine, I should like to nurse it myself.'

'You wouldn't.' Mary stands back to assess her work and grins.

Liz imagines shoving Mary's vase to the floor, watching the ceramic hands smash into tiny pieces, the flowers splitting in the crossfire.

'Bravo, darling.' Tom saunters around the side of the house in grey striped trousers and a navy lounging jacket. 'That is a beautiful arrangement.' He kisses Mary on the cheek. 'Yours is … coming along nicely,' he says to Liz. 'I've told Chipman that we shall take tea in the garden now.'

On cue, Mr Chipman and Will emerge, carrying a table

between them. When it is all set neatly, Mary places her vase in the middle, and they take their seats. Liz leaves her arrangement where it is, noticing, now that she has stepped away, how small and meagre it looks compared to Mary's.

'I have been thinking ...' Mary slips a cucumber finger sandwich in her mouth and chews in the awaiting silence. 'I should like to hold a garden party soon.'

Tom has dispensed with the sandwiches already and helps himself to a large slice of Victoria sponge. 'Are you sure you are up to it?'

'I am with child, Tom. I am not an invalid.'

'But who would we invite?'

'Well, Aunt Emily.'

The thought of that woman returning makes Liz groan, but Mary is too distracted with her plans to notice.

'We need more than the four of us for a party, my dear.'

'There's the Reverend and his wife. Maybe the Lynches from Sidmouth?'

'Shall they not be in London for the season?'

'Why must everyone flock to that ghastly place?'

Liz bites into a jam tart. Tom gestures that she has some crumb on her cheek.

'Might we not invite the villagers?'

Mary turns to her husband as if he has suggested they might all walk into the sea and drown themselves. 'That is not the sort of company one invites to a garden party, Tom.'

'Why don't we hold it as a kind of fete? Have games, competitions?' Tom continues. 'Folk love that kind of thing. I should imagine it might boost spirits before the harvest begins.'

'I do not want the villagers here, milling about all over the place. Who knows what they might do.'

'It is a garden party.' Tom laughs with a hint of exasperation. He removes his hat and scratches the back of his head. 'No one need go inside.'

'I think it sounds lovely,' Liz says as she takes her second strawberry tart from the platter, wishing the tedious conversation would end so she could eat in peace.

'And if not them, there is no one else to invite. Go on, darling, it will be fun. I could captain a game of cricket. You and the women could enjoy croquet on the lawn.' Tom finishes his cake, places his fork down, and smiles at his frowning wife. 'I'm sure they would appreciate it. And they would think highly of us because of it.'

'They must think highly of us anyway.'

'Yes, but ... people like to know they are appreciated, dear. They are good tenants.'

Tom takes an eclair and cuts it with his knife. Liz sips her tea. They watch each other watching Mary.

'I suppose it would not hurt,' Mary says with a sigh. 'And I think it shall be a good harvest this year from what I have seen of the fields. Very well, I shall arrange it.'

'Marvellous idea, darling. Well done.'

THE DAY HAS BEEN full of excitement, yet Liz has done nothing but sit in front of her mirror or take dresses from her wardrobe to examine which would be most appropriate for the party. Anne has been buzzing in and out, commenting on the excellent spread of food that Mrs Beacham is preparing and talking of how the lawn has been cut so neatly that it looks like a swathe of green velvet.

'Can I bring you anything to eat, miss?' Anne says as the clock chimes one. 'You've not eaten all day; you must be starving.'

'I am saving myself for the picnic food.' She smiles at Anne, who is flushed from the business of the day and rolls back and forth on the balls of her feet, eager to attend some task or other. 'I am fine, Anne, honestly. Come back at two to help me dress, won't you?'

Anne curtseys then runs from the room. Liz sits by the window, hearing the seconds tick slowly onwards, watching the sky. It has been blue and brilliant all morning, but now it is greying in the distance. Clouds the colour of bruises sit on the horizon.

An hour later, Anne enters in the cotton summer dress her mother gave her on her last visit home. It is a pretty dress, but not flattering against Anne's complexion, and the years of use and wash have left the whites turning to yellow and the floral patterns fading to nothing.

'What have you decided on, miss?'

All of Liz's dresses are piled on her bed, as big and lifeless as dead bodies. On the top of the pile is a dress of pale green taffeta with delicate lace stitching along the bodice, sleeves, and skirt, and a large ornamental bow on the back.

'That one.'

Liz has already spritzed her clean skin with rose and lavender water, prepared only yesterday by Anne. Now, with her long hair protecting her back, she stands in her under-garments, waiting for Anne to tighten the corset. She had been enjoying the freedom, and now with each tug, she feels the familiar jab of pain in her stomach.

'Would you like some air, miss?' Anne turns to open the window but stops when she sees it is already as wide as it will go.

'There is no air today.'

'Are you all right, miss?'

Glancing at her reflection, Liz sees the paleness of her cheeks. 'It is just the weather.'

'Too hot for me as well, miss. I'm fair on sweating under here.'

Liz smiles at the girl's boldness. 'I think we are due a storm later.'

'I hope it don't spoil the party.'

With worry in her face, Anne begins fastening Liz's gown, her eyes flicking to the window as if she would halt the storm coming as long as she saw it in time.

'Are you wearing that dress for the party?'

'Yes, miss.'

'What about the white one I gave you? Have you not altered it yet?'

'I have, miss. Only ... I don't know whether I should. It's very grand.'

'Nonsense. This is a party. The perfect occasion for a grand dress.'

They share a smirk in the looking glass, and Liz senses the excitement building in the young girl.

'Now, go and see to Mary, then get yourself in that dress. Promise?'

'Yes, miss.' Anne curtseys and practically skips from the room.

Liz goes to the window again. The storm clouds are closer. A bee has found its way through the window and now buzzes in panic to be free. Liz brings over a chair, stands on it, and ushers the bee outside, feeling its wings vibrating against her fingers as she does so.

Below her, Tom strides across the lawn. After a moment, he slows, turns, and finds her, immediately. They hold each other's gaze. Then Tom turns again and paces away.

Tom sips his champagne and sees his carriage coming closer over the heathland with a group of villagers. His pocket watch tells him it is ten to three as he stands next to the marquee where the food is laid out and covered in starched cloths to keep off the flies. Chipman murmurs something behind him, and soon Liz appears by Tom's side with a foggy glass of champagne in her hand.

'Mary is getting dressed.' Liz drinks. She is pale, despite the heat. The pearls around her neck lie unevenly over her protruding collarbones.

'I think you should sit.' Tom guides her to a seat and orders Chipman to collect her parasol.

'Are you looking forward to the game?' she says. Her hand is cold through her glove as he holds it.

'Slightly.'

'Do you fear they shall beat you?' Her lips twist under her hat, her eyes sparkle. Tom shivers, swallows, forces his eyes from her pretty face.

'Your parasol, miss.'

'They are nearly here. I should go to Mary.' She rises, and Tom steadies her by the crook of her elbow when she stumbles.

'Are you sure you are all right?' He is close to her, whispering into her ear. He feels her hair touching his face as he speaks; he smells rose and lavender.

She hesitates for a moment as if she would say something, then pats her skirts. 'I am fine.'

He watches her go. She places each foot on the ground like she is creeping into a nursery in the dead of night. How he longs to follow her, but the villagers are approaching. He wonders if it is rude for Mary not to be present as the guests arrive, and smiles as he realises it is.

They parade up to him, each and every one of them beaming. They say hello, how nice it is of the Olivers to do such a thing, how they are so looking forward to the afternoon. The men joke between themselves, the women sneak up to the marquee to peek at the food. All of them, including the children, take a glass of champagne.

Anne's parents and a couple of older villagers dismount from the carriage that has parked on the drive and make their way towards the congregation. Mrs Witmore staggers as she holds onto her husband for support, her wooden leg difficult to manoeuvre.

'Good day, Mr Witmore, Mrs Witmore.' Tom ambles over to them, meeting them on the lawn and clicking his fingers at one of the maids who holds another tray of drinks.

'Thank you, Mr Oliver.' Mrs Witmore giggles as the bubbles catch her nose while she sips. She has the same colour hair as her daughter, but her features are daintier and lined with age. It appears that Anne follows her father in her looks.

'Very kind of you to send the carriage.' Mr Witmore doffs his hat.

It is the first time the two men have met, and the atmosphere is not quite as subdued as Tom would have liked. Mr Witmore's blue eyes move over Tom, surveying his suit, his hair, his face.

'No trouble. Shall you play today, Mr Witmore?'

Suddenly, two small red-haired boys collide into their father, grinning mischievously.

'Yes. And these two are certainly looking forward to it.'

'Boys!' Mrs Witmore pulls them from their father, chiding them for their unruly behaviour as Grace, Anne's sister, comes along. 'I told you to keep an eye on them. Sorry, Mr Oliver.'

'Not at all.' Tom winks at the boys who laugh wickedly. He smiles at Grace, a miniature version of her sister. 'I hope you enjoy the day. And here is my wife, looking as radiant as ever.'

Mary and Liz emerge from the house arm in arm. Liz smiles as she passes the crowd. Mary's face is flat.

'Darling.' Tom kisses Mary on the cheek as she unlinks from Liz. 'These are Anne's parents.'

'Hello.' Mary does not look them in the eye, and Mrs Witmore's smile fades as Mary shows no recognition of her.

'We best go and sort the children.' Mrs Witmore nods at the boys who have started to run around the garden amongst the women's skirts.

'Nice to see you again,' Liz says before Mrs Witmore leaves, and earns herself a smile in return.

'Is the Reverend here yet? Or Doctor Jameson?'

'Not yet, dear. It is only ten past.'

The three of them stand in the middle of the lawn, the ladies' parasols high, champagne flutes to their lips, smiling or unsmiling at those having a far nicer time around them.

To Tom's relief, it is only a minute before a carriage draws up to the house, and the Reverend Carey, a tall willowy man, and his wife, a short woman, similar in looks to the queen, dismount. Directly behind them, another carriage pulls up, and Doctor Jameson emerges on his own.

Tom readies himself, downs his drink, and strides towards his guests. He kisses Mrs Carey's cheek before she walks on to find Mary, then shakes the men's hands.

'You certainly look the part,' Doctor Jameson says, quickly removing himself from Tom's firm grasp.

'Yes, you shall make a fine cricketer, Mr Oliver. I hope I can only catch the ball if it comes my way. I was never one for sports at school.' Reverend Carey chuckles, shakes his head. 'My legs don't seem to do what my brain tells them to.'

'We shall have to have you as bowler then, Mr Carey.'

Mr Carey removes his handkerchief from his pocket and dabs his glistening forehead. 'This is a marvellous thing for you to do, Mr Oliver. Just marvellous. I have never seen the villagers so jolly. You have been in their prayers recently and shall continue to be so, I am sure.'

'Whose idea was it to invite them?' the doctor says.

'I thought it would be a nice way to introduce ourselves properly, get to know everybody, bolster them up for the harvest.'

'Ah, yes. The harvest. Now I see.'

'A marvellous idea,' Mr Carey says, oblivious to the politics in their circle. 'Mr Oliver, is there ... is there anywhere I might use one of your conveniences?'

Tom beckons Chipman over and instructs him to show Mr Carey to the water closet. Tom and Jameson turn towards the party, a reasonable distance between them, the silence expanding.

'How are they finding you?'

'Sorry?'

'The villagers. Your tenants.'

Tom clenches and unclenches his jaw, smiles through the stiffness.

'Pretty well, I should say.' He gestures to the crowd, who are all laughing and drinking and throwing happy glances his way. Jameson draws breath to speak again, but Tom is in no mood for him today. 'Darling,' he calls to Mary over the head of the doctor. 'I think it is time for some cricket. Are you playing, Doctor?'

'No. I prefer to observe, Mr Oliver.'

THE CRICKET MATCH is nearing its end when Anne descends the garden steps onto the lawn. The villagers have their backs to her, but she can see the blue and green shimmering dresses at the head of the crowd, lace parasols raised, the two ladies together looking like a peacock on display.

Her heart races as Mr Oliver bowls. The muscles in his arms have grown thick, and his cheeks have a rosy hue from the exercise. He bowls the perfect shot, and the ball glides effortlessly past Mr Marsh's defence, toppling the wickets. Mr Oliver's team cry in joy, and as he laughs, his gaze falls upon Anne for a second. The game continues as someone shouts about the looming clouds and how they'd better hurry up and win properly.

Anne finds her mother in the crowd, sat on the far side with Grace next to her. She sneaks up on Gwen and taps her on the shoulder, making her jump, so enthralled in the game she is.

'Anne! You scared me.' Gwen opens her arms, and Anne hugs her close for as long as is comfortable in the heat.

'You look well, Mother. And you, Grace.'

The glee in her mother's eyes wavers as she regards Anne. 'Where did you get that dress?'

'Miss Oliver gave it to me. It's fine, ain't it?' Anne twirls and some villagers stare at her.

'It is very fine. Too fine, Anne. Are you sure you should be wearing it?'

A heavy drop of rain falls on her bodice. Overhead, the sun is hidden behind grey curtains of clouds. She thinks she hears thunder, but it could just be the roar from the players as the final wicket is won and the game ends. In a second, Eddie and Paul run at her, crushing her in a long embrace.

'Anne, you look ... wonderful.' Will has come over. He is pink-faced, and Anne does not know if that is from playing or from something else.

'What are you wearing?' her father says on his approach, and Eddie and Paul disentangle themselves from her.

'Miss Oliver gave it to me.' Anne's voice is thin and child-ish. She thought she would walk out and be admired, not chided.

Her mother sighs. 'Anne, when your lady gives you clothes, it is better to sell them and buy something more ... suitable.'

Anne feels the cotton, how smooth and clean it is. The green stitched flowers are made of silk, something she has never worn before. She has been transformed into a beauty, like the butterfly she embroidered.

'You do not know Miss Oliver. She likes me to wear it.' She flounces away from them towards her mistresses, timing, nicely she thinks, with Mr Oliver who meets her there. He wipes the sweat from his brow, whistles through his teeth, and smiles as he holds her gaze. She knows she is blushing, but try as she might, she cannot make her skin cool.

'What on earth!' Mrs Oliver rises.

The happiness evaporates as Anne sees Mrs Oliver's face. She wishes she could run away, but there is nowhere to go. She is helpless.

'First of all,' Mrs Oliver hisses, prowling towards Anne and lowering her voice so the villagers cannot hear, 'you dress like a whore and, now, as if you were the lady of this house.'

'Ma'am. I ...' Anne does not know what to do. Everybody is watching. Her face stings and her fingers flutter involuntarily to her cheeks to hide her humiliation.

'Mary,' Mr Oliver whispers. 'Do not embarrass the girl.'

'Be quiet, Tom!'

The villagers gasp as Mr Oliver is silenced.

Miss Oliver stands. 'I am feeling a little faint.'

'Who do you think you are, Anne?'

Miss Oliver sways, and Mr Oliver rushes to his sister's side. Anne would go to her too, but she is pinned by Mrs Oliver's glare. Suddenly, there is a cry, and Miss Oliver falls.

'Doctor Jameson!' Mr Oliver cradles his sister in his arms as the village women form a circle around her and fan her with their hands. Doctor Jameson checks her pulse, feels her brow, retrieves his smelling salts. Gulping the air, Miss Oliver wakes, as if she has been brought back from the dead.

Rain splatters her forehead, and Mr Oliver takes his hand-kerchief to dry her.

'Get her inside.' Jameson clicks his fingers at Chipman and Will, who carefully, along with Mr Oliver, manage to get her to her feet.

'I think you should go with Liz now,' Mr Oliver says, and Anne is grateful for his command. Keeping her gaze averted from Mrs Oliver and her parents, Anne scurries after her mistress.

They carry Miss Oliver up the stairs and lay her on her bed. The doctor instructs Anne to get fresh water and to tell the cook to prepare some broth. After Miss Oliver has drunk a large glass of cold water, the doctor leaves, and tells Anne to keep an eye on her for the rest of the day.

'I think she has done you a favour.' Jameson leers at Anne down his nose as he goes.

Miss Oliver is as pale as her sheets. Anne frees her hair from its pins so that it cascades over her shoulders and back. Then, Anne carefully unfastens her clothes, peeling them away from her sticky skin, until she wears only her chemise and drawers.

'Some more water, miss.' Anne lifts her head and trickles the drink over her cracked lips.

'You do look beautiful,' Miss Oliver whispers.

Anne's heartbeat quickens. For all the shame, there is a fire in her stomach; the way that Mr Oliver regarded her was unmistakable. A smile spills onto her lips, but when she meets Miss Oliver's gaze again, the woman's eyes are hard.

'I'll go and fetch your food, miss.'

Anne slips from the room. She is just about to scurry to the back stairs when she hears raised voices from the hallway below.

'You will calm down this instant.'

'I shall not! Who does she think she is? She will be gone first thing tomorrow.'

'Don't be so rash, Mary.'

'Rash? No maid should look so … so …'

'Pretty?'

Silence. Anne's heart pounds. She holds her chest.

'What did you say?'

Anne should leave; she should run away like a good maid. She should not eavesdrop. But she is desperate to hear what Mr Oliver will say.

'Anne looked pretty.'

Anne's elation crumbles as she hears a slap and knows, with a terrible sickness, that Mrs Oliver has hit her husband. Then, there is the rumbling of a chuckle.

'I think you are not feeling well, my dear. Perhaps you should go to bed.'

Mrs Oliver's voice is low and rough, like a dog growling. 'I will not go to bed.'

'The party is over. You saw to that. Everyone has left.'

'I want her gone. Do you hear me, Tom?'

Mr Oliver says nothing.

'I want her gone!' The walls echo Mrs Oliver's scream.

Anne holds her breath.

'No.'

Silence.

How Anne wishes she could see the look on Mrs Oliver's face!

'I want her gone,' Mrs Oliver repeats, but the command is hollow.

'I said no.' He sighs. 'You look tired, wife. The party has taken its toll on you.'

'I am fine.'

'Are you really? You don't seem it.'

'I am well!'

'Go to bed.' His words send shivers through Anne; they are as sharp as a blade on glass.

Anne would stay longer, she would reach over the bannister to see those gorgeous green eyes, those full red lips as they speak to defend her, but then shoes tap on the stairs; Mrs Oliver is obeying!

Before Mrs Oliver has time to see her, Anne slips through the disguised partition door and runs to the kitchen, smiling all the way.

CHAPTER 7

 ctober 1869

THE RAIN HAS BEEN ALMOST constant for the past two months. Everywhere seems damp. The windows swirl with water, and the grounds are brown sludge. Even the walls cry in misery.

Liz has been inside for five days straight. The air is thick with dust, her clothes are heavy and cloying against her skin. She passes the time finding patterns in the streaks of rain on the glass panes, imagining forests or unfriendly faces.

She cannot stand it anymore. Another minute sitting here and those faces will come out of the windows and bite her.

She calls for Anne.

'Prepare my coat. I am going out.'

'Where, miss? You'll get drenched.'

'I need some air. Come with me if you like?'

Anne hesitates; she does not like the wet, but she likes Mary even less. 'I'll just be a minute.'

They meet by the front door, the two of them wrapped in dark coats, the hoods falling over their eyes.

'Should we take the carriage, miss?'

'No. I want to walk.'

Liz strides out. The wind is not as cold as she had imagined, and it breathes against her bare cheek in welcome relief. Underneath her vast cloak, she does not feel the rain, only the occasional drop on her nose where it falls from the rim of her hood. Her feet, however, grow wet and she wriggles her toes in her stockings, cringing at the moisture there.

'Where are we going, miss?' Anne says, struggling to keep up.

Liz slows. She has not thought where they would head, she had just needed to get out from the confinement of the walls, to stop the eyes in the paintings from looking at her, to stop the noise in her head. Most of all, she had wanted to escape before Mary joined her in the afternoon, as has been her custom these last few weeks, so she would not have to see the bump underneath Mary's dress, or hear talk of kicks, or knit gowns for the little boy that Mary is sure she will deliver.

The mist hangs so low that the clouds are indistinguishable from it. They could be miles from the sea for there is no evidence of it in view. The heathland is, now, a massive bog and unsafe to walk over. Only the shadowy trees are visible, like grey tombstones in the whiteness, and so she heads towards them.

Liz and Anne do not talk until they reach the woods where the leaves shelter them and quieten the noise of the downpour. Liz lets down her hood and breathes, inhaling freshness. It is like a long drink of clean, cold water.

'Do you know what sort of trees these are?' Liz meanders serenely between the trunks, pausing to pull on a branch. Fat splodges of rain drip onto her cloak.

'That is a beech, miss.'

'How can you tell?'

Anne draws closer. 'Its leaves have little wavy edges and fur. Can you see the hairs on them? The trunk also gives you a clue. It's almost grey in colour. And if you touch it, it's smooth.'

Liz strokes the bark. It is like a piece of new leather stretched too tight. She pulls her fingers away quickly.

This world of trees and leaves and fresh air is like being in a foreign land. She will never know the intricacies of nature, never understand why one tree bark is different from another. Looking at Anne, who could be a forest fairie with her wild hair, Liz is struck by her own strangeness here; the forest seems to be squeezing her out, pushing her away, turning their backs on her ignorance.

'What about that one?' Liz points at another, this one the biggest of all around. Knots and bulbous joints protrude from the trunk, and its branches stretch over their heads like hands clawing for something invisible. Any minute, one of those wooden fingers could fall and crush her.

'That is an oak, miss. The grand old oak. You can see all the acorns on it.' Anne does not fear the creature; she smiles up at it then stoops to pick an acorn from amidst the fallen leaves. She holds it out to Liz in her pink palm, but Liz keeps her distance, afraid the acorn might hatch and scurry like a beetle.

'This oak is the king of the woods, miss. And the beech is its queen. Da would bring me up here sometimes and sit me on that stump.' Anne points to an ugly growth near the base of the tree.

'He would tell me tales of how the oak were ever so lonely, up here, all on his own. He's very old, you see. Hundreds of years. And as the years passed by, he reached his hands up to God to pray for a wife. And the more lonely and the more desperate he got, the harder he would try and reach for God, and the strain of it made him ugly, and made him grow a veiny nose, on which I used to sit.'

Anne skips over to the stump and perches on it. For one dreadful minute, Liz sees the oak drag the girl into the earth and eat her whole, but when she blinks again, Anne is still there, still smiling.

'Finally, the old oak gave up. He looked down on himself and saw what an ugly creature he had become. And he began to cry. His tears were acorns that fell to the ground all around him. But the acorns brought squirrels and mice and rats and rabbits, which he let scurry over his feet and through his hair. And little oak trees sprouted up around him, giving him some company. The creatures brought seeds and nuts from other parts of the wood, and one day, he noticed a small shoot, just there.' Anne points to where the beech tree now stands.

'The old oak watched the shoot grow into a little branch. The little branch into a woody trunk. He scared away the animals who tried to eat it, shouted at the wind who tried to blow it down, and sheltered it from the storms that threatened to drown it. Eventually, the beech tree were full and strong and blossoming, and the oak tree thought she were the prettiest thing he had ever seen. Then, one day, he called over to her and talked to her for a while. He told her stories of how his cousin had once saved a king. He asked the animals to make a show for her that made her laugh. He told her how he had kept her safe all her life. And then, as her catkins began to fall and her flowers began to grow in the spring, he asked her if she would be his.'

Liz swallows. Her head is light, the ground uneven. She would lean on something to steady herself, but she cannot bring herself to touch anything in this place. She sniffs until the stars cease twinkling in her vision. 'What did the beech say?'

'She said yes. For she loved him and thought him fine instead of ugly. And now they stand with each other, their branches touching, their roots entwined, for eternity.'

Liz feels those roots now, stirring beneath her. She thinks of them growing and twisting. They will gobble her up if she stays too long, and shackle her forever.

She closes her eyes, breathes deeply, reminds herself she is safe. 'Let's keep moving. It's too cold to stay still.'

THEY SEEM to walk for miles through the woods. It is like a maze to Liz, and each time she thinks there is a break in the forest wall, it proves only to be a deception. All the while, Anne tells her the names of plants, and Liz must nod and try to smile as if she is interested, as if her heart is not pounding beneath her bodice, threatening to break her bones.

A cry scratches to come out of her throat. Tears brim against her lids. Her breathing is getting shallower as the trees darken. The more she tells herself to be calm, the more her feet itch to sprint out of this wooden tomb.

Then there is light. Liz runs for it, leaving Anne behind. She emerges from the trees into the whiteness, like stepping onto a cloud, and the relief makes her head spin. She grips her knees so she won't fall and sucks in the air as Anne catches up with her. The girl is mumbling to herself about the horrid weather before she stops abruptly several feet behind Liz.

'What is wrong?'

'It's filling up.'

Liz follows Anne's gaze. In front of them is a dip in the grassland, saucer-like and about the size, Liz would guess, of the walled kitchen garden. At the centre of the dip, a puddle of water has formed.

'What is it?'

'It is where the lake used to be. Where Mrs Buchanan drowned, miss.'

Liz remembers the story that Tom told her. She looks at the circular hollow in the surface of the earth and tries to imagine it brimming with deep water, adorned with lily pads and reeds, cradling the corpse of Mary's mother. She blinks the image out of her mind.

'Sorry miss.' Anne gathers herself. 'It gives me the creeps, seeing it like that, with water in it.'

'It's only a puddle, Anne.'

'Do you think it means –'

'I don't think it means anything!' Liz's voice echoes back at her; the sound of a madwoman.

She forces her eyes away from the dip. The woods have scared her, that is all; she has never been one for confined spaces. And who can blame Anne, a poor country girl, for believing in superstitions and in stories of trees in love? It is all just nonsense.

'The puddle is from all the rain we have had, Anne. It is nothing more sinister than that. Come. Let us continue. We were having such a nice time.'

Liz guides Anne away from the scene, holding onto her tightly for she is shaking. She lets Anne chatter for it soothes her nerves to hear talk of nothing but embroidery and Mrs Beacham's sponge puddings and Anne's excitement for Christmas, and finally, Liz's breathing returns to normal, and she forgets the corpse in the water.

They skirt the woodland as they walk home. The rain continues, but the drops are smaller now, and Liz can see the sea to their left and its black-grey waters breaking into white waves. The red faces of the cliffs frown at the water as it lashes against them.

'Your brother is a very nice man.'

Anne's voice had been nothing but a noise floating on the wind until now. At the mention of Tom, Liz pulls her gaze away from the waves and gives the girl her attention.

'I can't help but feel sorry for him ... with Mrs Oliver.'

'Why should you feel sorry for Tom?'

'Well, how Mrs Oliver treats him. It is not only me who she ...' Anne cannot say the words. It is too terrible to speak of a wife who hits her husband. Liz has seen his face, the scarlet mark of a small hand blazed across his cheek. It has happened twice now. When she has fussed over him, he has only laughed; he has taken worse.

'He has no need of your sympathies, Anne.'

'But I do, miss. I care for him.'

Liz stops. This is what she wanted, wasn't it? Anne's confidence, Anne's trust, to know the girl's secrets. And really, everyone sees the way Anne looks at Tom with round, wide eyes, hopeful and yearning. It should not come as a shock to hear Anne's passions said aloud, but for Anne to confirm them, only makes Liz's insides churn.

'I think he cares for me too,' Anne says.

Cold crushes Liz's lungs as she stares at the maid. 'What are you saying?'

'Nothing, miss. Nothing.' Anne is stumbling.

Liz knows her face must betray her rage, for the girl is blushing fiercely, regretting her moment of intimacy.

'Are you saying my brother has feelings for you? For a maid?'

'No, miss. I only meant –'

'I should hope not.' Liz bites her tongue hard enough to taste the sweetness of blood. 'And if I hear you spreading such lies I will throw you out of Floreat myself, do you understand?'

'Yes, miss.' Tears swell in the girl's eyes. Anne's chin wobbles.

Liz cannot look at Anne for another second; she will strike her if she does. She marches on, and Anne trots behind. She can hear the girl's feet squelching in the mud, and the girl panting and snivelling.

Liz walks faster, until Floreat comes into view, like a boil on the horizon. She does not wish to return to it, but where else will she go? She curses Tom for bringing her here. She curses Mary and the child for ruining their plans. She curses herself for agreeing to such a stupid idea, and it is as she is muttering under her breath that something catches her eye. Something unusual on the heathland.

It is coming closer, a small black dot growing larger. Liz stops. She is breathing fast, and the cold air stings her throat as she drags it in. She wishes this damn drizzle would end so that she could see clearly.

It is a figure. Its skirts are billowing in the wind.

'Who is that?' Anne breaks the silence, coming to her mistress's side.

'Don't you recognise her?'

'No, miss.'

They wait in silence, the wind rushing around them, rustling their dresses, pushing the rain horizontally across their vision.

The stranger nears them and is now on the fringe of the heathland just past the walled garden. Liz brings her hand to her forehead, blocking out the rain that pummels her face.

'Should we go, miss? Shall I call for Mr Chipman?' Anne shifts on her feet, but Liz stands firm.

There is something familiar about this figure. Liz cannot discern it, but the way the thin body is draped in black, the way the head sits rigidly on top of the spine, the way the legs jolt with each step. Finally, it reaches the walled garden and is shielded from the wind.

The figure pulls off its hat and net veil to reveal a face twisted and scarred crimson, the features distorted, melted out of recognition. The deformed mouth opens into a hollow smile. A gloved hand rises and points at the two of them.

Anne screams in horror. Liz is paralysed.

'It cannot be.'

'Miss!' Anne grabs Liz's hand and pulls her hard. Liz stumbles, but Anne catches her and heaves her upright. The girl never releases Liz's hand as they sprint over the lawn and crash through the front door, startling Chipman in the hallway.

'Miss Oliver!' He rushes to her side. 'Anne, what has happened?'

'Where is Tom?' Liz tears her sodden cloak away from her and throws it on the floor. Chipman barely finishes the word before Liz is running towards the study.

'THERE'S SOMEONE OUT THERE,' Anne says, pointing towards the walled garden. Her arm shakes as she holds it up and water splatters on the floor as it falls from her cloak.

Chipman runs outside.

'Who's there?' he bellows, over and over again as Anne follows him.

The rain is worse now – it slices into Anne's face like a hundred knives. She cannot see properly. She squints, and the whole world blurs into odd shapes.

'Will!' Mr Chipman shouts. Moments later, the young lad is racing towards them from the back door, coatless and fearful.

'Father?'

'Go to the other side of the garden. There's someone here.'

Will follows his father's order, and Chipman slows as he nears the wall. Anne is inches behind him, focusing on the water droplets running down his back, sure that as soon as they round the corner, they will come face to face with the hideous figure. She holds her breath, and her fingers grip Chipman's sleeve.

But there is nothing.

At the far end of the wall, Will is barely visible through the rain.

'Check inside the garden,' Chipman yells at his son. 'What did she look like, Anne?'

'She was dressed all in black. And her face ... it was awful, Mr Chipman!' She can feel tears threatening to silence her.

'All right, Anne. It's all right.' Chipman pats her on the shoulder. They do not like each other much, but she is grateful for his kindness now. 'And she came from the heath?'

'Yes.'

Chipman squints at the barren and wild landscape. There is nothing there but wet and wind.

'Nothing, Pa.' Will emerges beside them, panting, his face red and blotchy and soaking.

'Get yourself inside, Anne, and see to Miss Oliver.'

Anne does as she is told, staggering nervously to the front door now that she no longer has the protection of Mr Chipman.

In the hallway, the silence rings in her ears. She hangs up her cloak, then creeps towards the study, her own steps making her uneasy. She is about to tap on the door when she hears their voices. The sounds are a little muffled, but she can just about distinguish the words.

'How? Are you sure?'

'How many times, Tom? Yes, I am sure.' Miss Oliver is crying. 'I cannot ... I don't understand ...'

'It's all right.'

'You must find her, Tom!'

'I will. Do you trust me?'

The voices stop. Anne imagines Mr Oliver hugging his sister, comforting her like the good man he is. A little ball of fire stirs under her chest. She wishes Mr Oliver would comfort her like that. She imagines his arms around her. She imagines looking up at him as he brings his lips to hers, telling her everything will be all right.

She shakes off the thought.

Still, the study is silent. What are they doing?

Quivering, Anne kneels and presses her eye to the keyhole. Two figures stand close together. She is not sure where Mr Oliver begins and Miss Oliver ends, for they seem to merge together.

Her eye begins to twitch. If it would only focus better! But her eyesight has never been as good as Grace's, who could spot a hare a mile away. She blinks, and it is just as the figures are beginning to come clear that the front door crashes open and Mr Chipman and Will can be heard in the hallway.

Heart pounding, Anne grapples for the wall, pulling herself up as quickly as she can. Footsteps come from the other side of the study door and, suddenly, she panics. She remembers her mother telling her about a maid who had been dismissed for spying on the mistress in her bedroom. The mistress had blacked the keyhole, and the girl's crime was painted on her face for all to see.

Anne gasps at the thought, spits on her hand and rubs her eye. Her face is wet from the rain, and she is grateful for it. She does not have time to check herself in the looking glass before Mr Oliver careers out of the room and slams into her.

'Anne! Sorry –' He finishes his half-formed sentence with a nod, then moves her out of his way. His hands, firm and warm on her body, send a jolt of pleasure through her, and the little ball of fire in her stomach flips over.

Inside the study, Miss Oliver's gaunt face stares back at her with dark, wild eyes.

'WELL, WHERE CAN SHE BE?' Mr Oliver paces the hallway, raking his fingers through his hair. 'She has to be somewhere!'

'She is nowhere, sir. It is as if she has vanished.'

'People do not vanish, Chipman.'

'How did she make it across the heath, sir? It is one great bog out there.'

'Maybe that's it.' Anne whispers into the silence. 'Maybe she tried going back over the heath and got stuck? Maybe the bog's got her?'

Mr Oliver stands before one of the mirrors, leaning on the table before it.

'Yes. Perhaps Anne is right.'

Anne tries to catch his eye in the reflection of the glass, but he only looks at himself.

'Or she's a witch?'

Mr Chipman slaps his son across the head. 'Do not say such daft things, boy. You will only frighten people.'

Mr Oliver sighs. 'There is nothing we can do now. She is gone. In the morning, you shall go to the village, Chipman, and ask if anyone has seen such a woman.'

'What do you think she is doing here, sir?'

'I don't know.' Mr Oliver's voice is quiet. He looks at his sister. 'Liz needs some rest. She has had a fright. We will speak no more of this tonight.'

Chipman nods and leaves. Will follows his father,

glancing at Anne as he disappears through the concealed servant door.

'Prepare Miss Oliver a hot bath, Anne. She is like ice.'

THE TRAVELLING DRESS woman is here today. Elizabeth stands on a little round box while the woman flits around her with a tape measure. Mary sneaks a look at the woman's notes and discovers, to her horror, that Elizabeth's waist is over three times smaller than her own.

'I don't know,' Elizabeth says, as the woman asks her if she has any designs or colours or materials in mind for her four new gowns. Elizabeth has been distracted ever since the sighting of that strange woman on the heathland yesterday. Mary has no time for it.

'My favourite colour is green.'

'You have enough green gowns, Elizabeth, I think you should try something different.'

Mary sits in her chair, her stomach protruding before her. She thought the visit from the dress-maker might have cheered her, but her breasts still ache and her feet still itch. She feels as ugly as ever.

'Fetch me some tea, Anne,' Mary says once the dress woman has gone. 'I should like a little ginger in it too. And some for Elizabeth with sugar.'

'Yes, ma'am.'

'Can't shake this wretched sickness.' Mary holds her stomach as Elizabeth takes the seat next to her. They are both in their robes, their hair down, inside Mary's chamber.

Sighing at Elizabeth's lack of conversation, Mary fiddles with the sleeve of her robe. The baby kicks and makes her wince.

'Are you all right?' Elizabeth asks.

'It is just the child.'

Elizabeth's gaze returns to the window.

'I am worried,' Mary says.

Mary had thought she would not confide in Tom's beautiful sister, after all, they have not had the easiest of relationships. Yet, it seems she has no one else to turn to – certainly not her husband – and her mounting fears have been dancing through her mind for days now and torturing her dreams.

'About what?'

'About giving birth.'

Should she tell Elizabeth that she has been seeing her mother; that the ghost stands behind Elizabeth's chair right now, wet and dripping, black eyes staring at Mary accusingly? Mary looks to the floor instead of meeting that dark gaze.

'Will this child be the death of me?'

'No. You must not think like that.'

'Something is not right.' Mary's voice trembles. Her mother is getting closer. She can hear drips landing on the floorboards. She knows her mother is a figment of her imagination. She knows that if she were to reach out, her hand would slip straight through her mother's body and the apparition would vanish, but that knowledge does not ease her. 'Something with this child is not right.'

'You should not say such things. Every child is born innocent.'

Mary is not convinced. Everything can be cursed. 'Who was that woman on the heath?'

Elizabeth stills. Her fingers twitch as they rest in her lap. 'I do not know.'

'She is an omen. A ghost. Or a witch. Perhaps she has cursed me.'

'She is a human woman who likes to scare people!' Elizabeth shrieks. 'I gave her satisfaction yesterday. I should never have run. I should have faced her and told her to go away. I shall know for next time.'

'But why did she come here?'

'Why do beggars beg? Why do whores whore? Why do pickpockets take watches and purses? Why do we do anything? Because we feel we must. Because we are forced to. Because it gives us a thrill. I do not know why she is here. Stop asking me.'

Elizabeth's hands are shaking, and the shaking travels up her arms and into her body. She knows something.

Anne returns with the tea tray and sets it on the table.

'Why do you think that woman came here yesterday, Anne? Did she look familiar to you?'

'No, ma'am. I've never seen her before in my life.'

'Pour the tea, Anne,' Elizabeth commands.

'I think you should have some sugar with it, Elizabeth. You are quite clearly still in shock.' Mary drops two lumps of sugar into Elizabeth's china cup.

Elizabeth turns her silver spoon around in the liquid. Mary sips, tastes the bite of the fresh ginger as it slides over her tongue and down her throat. The baby kicks in response, but her second wince does not garner a response from her sister, who still stares out of the window intently.

'If you are so certain it was just an ordinary woman from the village playing tricks, why are you so scared?'

CHAPTER 8

 ecember 1869

HER CHAMBER IS thick with old, stale air as Mary passes another hour in confinement. Her night clothes sweat with the heat of the fire, and her stomach is like a mountain in the sea of the bed.

She has little company now. It is like she has been put here, out of the way, and no one cares to visit. Sometimes Mrs Jeffries, the newly hired wet nurse, comes to see her, but the woman is so dull that Mary would prefer it if she stayed away.

The only other person she can rely upon to visit her at night is her mother – her dripping, staring mother – who whispers insults at her through a tight-lipped mouth.

Doctor Jameson calls by every now and again to check her pulse, test the colour of her urine, ask how she is feeling in herself. He says he knows she is struggling with the confinement, but that she must rest, for the sake of herself and the baby.

It will not be an easy birth at your age.

She has never liked his honesty.

The only thing that occupies her mind is Tom and that night. That night before she was sent into the confines of her chamber. She replays it over and over again.

She had crept across the landing into his room. By the moonlight from the half-curtained window, she had found him asleep, the sheets halfway down his body. His face had been turned towards her, his mouth dangling open, his eyes closed and twitching. The fire had been low in the grate, and the room had a chill to it, so she had peeled back the covers and slithered in beside him. He had stirred a little when she had rested her head on his pillow.

Tom, she had whispered.

She had kissed his lips, as lightly as a feather quill. He had smiled, his eyes still closed and flickering with dreams, so she had kissed him again, gently at first, then a little harder until he was kissing her back, until his hands were sifting through her hair, until he was moaning, until she could feel him against her thigh.

Tom, she had said again, in pleasure at his touch, her voice louder this time. Her hair had fallen over his face, and at the sound of his name, he had lifted her from him, so that he could see her, clearly.

It was as if he had looked at a stranger who had come to strangle him. He had dived to the other side of the bed, told her to go, that she should not have come.

The struggle between them is a little blurred in her memory now. Was it she who first lunged at Tom, or him at her? Had she slapped his cheek, pushed at his chest before pulling him back on to her, knocking him off balance? Or was it he who had taken hold of her wrists and dragged her out of the sheets? She could not remember their exact movements, not until they were together in front of the bedroom door, her hands in his grasp.

Why did you marry me, Tom? You do not love me. You have used me.

Her words had made him stop. She had thought she may have hurt him. She had thought, for a moment, that tears would spring from his eyes, and he would apologise, and say that he did love her.

Yet, as the moonlight had shone on his face, she had seen the tinge of a smile stealing onto his lips.

No more than you have used me.

She had searched his face, trying to find his meaning.

Your father turns in his grave to know that I am in his place, and that is what you wanted, wasn't it?

The fight had left her then. She had been nothing more than a sack of trembling skin.

He had opened the door, taken a breath, and bid her goodnight, as coolly as if nothing had happened at all.

That was the last time she had seen him.

It was not a good way to begin her confinement.

ANNE LINGERS IN THE VILLAGE, gazing at the small, squat houses, wondering what her old neighbours are doing inside their homes. It is the first time she has not wanted to return to Floreat since moving there. The village is too cosy, too homely at this time of the year. If only she could sneak into her old bed, curl up beside Grace, and hear her family's soft snores. But that is a silly fancy.

She holds her oil lamp out before her and drags her feet into the darkness. Her father had offered to walk her back, but she had insisted that he stay inside in the warm. When her mother had worried about the strange woman who might be out there, Anne had reminded her that the woman had not been seen by anybody for over two months; she would be long gone.

Anne crosses the fields using the farm tracks, passing sheep and cattle who appear as solid lumps of black in the grey night. The moon is thin but bright, and the stars are plentiful. She gazes at the sky as she walks, trying to spot the constellations that her father once told her about, but forgetting their names and shapes.

The heath is already beginning to crisp up. Her footsteps crunch on the new frost. She wishes she had worn extra petticoats and stockings, for the cold seeps into her toes and ankles, into her calves and thighs, and makes her shiver.

She walks for a long time, until the magic of the starry night soon wears off. She is impatient to get into bed so that she may start to warm up. She longs to rest and sleep, for the day has been long, despite it being a Sunday. Already she is grimacing as she thinks of her work for tomorrow, wishing she did not have to deal with Mrs Oliver's giant, sweating body and ridiculous orders. Even dealing with Miss Oliver is now difficult; the woman has been distant ever since their walk in the woods, and Anne has not been able to fully meet her gaze without flushing.

'Anne Witmore.'

Anne screams and drops the lamp. It smashes, and the flame dies. In the darkness, something presses against her shoulder. She screams again and reels to find the strange woman looming above her, black skirts shimmering in the moonlight like oil on water, the netting on her hat covering her face.

Anne thinks she will die.

She tries to make a dash for it, but her toes jam into the uneven earth and she crashes onto the ground. She drags herself upright, tries to run again, but the woman clutches her arm. There is a brief tussle between them, but the woman is strong, remarkably so. Her grip burns Anne's skin as she pulls her close.

'What do you want?' Anne says, her breath catching in her throat as she speaks. She tries to swallow, but her mouth is dry. 'Are you going to kill me?'

The woman laughs, and it sounds like a man puffing rings of cigar smoke into the air. 'No.'

'What then?'

'I want you to do something for me.'

The woman's hand is still wrapped around Anne's fore-arm. Anne tries to shake her off, but she holds fast.

'I want you to spy for me. I want to know everything that happens in that house.'

It is the last thing Anne was expecting. The surprise makes her go limp, and finally, the woman releases her.

'Why?'

'That is no concern of yours.'

'It is if you want me to do it.'

The woman's eyes narrow. 'I have seen you with the man of the house. I have seen the way you look at him.'

Cold twists in Anne's stomach. 'So?'

The woman laughs again, that puffing sound, as if she has no voice box. 'I know you love him.'

'I don't.'

'I could give you something to help if you will do as I ask.'

It is too tempting to ignore. 'What?'

'Love potions. I could cast spells for you.'

'You are a witch?'

'All you need to do is tell me what you know.'

Anne recalls the last time she saw this witch, the terror in Miss Oliver's eyes as if she had seen a ghost, the worry in Mr Oliver's face as he looked in the mirror.

'No.'

The witch hesitates. Her hand dives into the lining of her skirt. Something clinks, tinkles, then she brings out a small bottle filled with clear liquid. 'This will make him love you.'

Anne swallows, forces herself to look away. 'I cannot help you.'

'Very well.' The witch hides the bottle again. 'Then you will have no spells from me, and you will live and die a spinster.'

Anne flinches but keeps her resolve. When the witch turns her back, Anne lifts her skirts and runs.

'You have a very pretty mother.'

Anne stops.

'It would be a shame if she were taken from you.'

The witch lifts her veil and reveals her face, showing the waxen quality of her flesh, like fat candles when they have spilled over and dried unevenly. Her mouth is nothing more than a dark hole. Her eyes are black marbles.

'Have you ever smelt burning flesh, Anne?'

Anne shakes her head.

'Fat bubbles and spits. Skin melts. Hair singes. The pain … the pain is the worst thing you can imagine.'

Anne tugs at her high collar, feels the heat against her neck as the witch approaches her, one step at a time.

'Many women die like this. Many die while sat in front of their fires. All it takes is one ember. It would be difficult for your mother to run away, in her condition.'

'Say another word,' Anne hisses, 'and I'll tell Mr Oliver about your threats. He'll get the police onto you.'

The witch tuts. 'Silly girl. You should not rile me so.'

'Don't speak of my ma again.'

'Would she like to know how her daughter whores herself for her master?'

Anne's jaw drops. 'That is a lie.'

'What would your father do, do you think? What would

Mrs Oliver do? Rumours spread worse than fire, Anne. You would be ruined. You would be out of that house in an instant, and you would never see Mr Oliver again.'

'It is not true!'

'It does not need to be.' The witch touches Anne's cheek and wipes away a tear. 'You will meet me here, every Sunday night, and tell me all that you know.'

THE AIR IS TOO STILL, the sky a fluffy grey-white as Anne trudges over the heathland. She carries a gift of lace that she ordered from the dress-maker all those months ago and a wooden toy soldier that she managed to procure from a travelling salesman at the back door one day. The two gifts have cost her nearly all her earnings.

Once home, she finds her family playing games in the parlour. Her brothers sit on the floor and roll their plain glass marbles at the one that has been placed as the marker. Eddie shrieks as he takes the winning shot.

'Merry Christmas,' Anne says.

Eddie and Paul spring from the floor and gather about her skirts. 'What have you got for us?' Eddie says.

'Have you brought us a present, Anne?' Paul says.

She takes the soldier from her basket. 'Will this do you?'

Eddie grabs it and holds fast when Paul tries to prise it from his grasp. They both marvel over its bright red and green paintwork and squabble over who will get to play with it first.

'Oh, Anne, it's wonderful.' Gwen opens her arms to her daughter. Anne hugs her mother then Grace, then takes her seat. 'How was Christmas at Floreat?'

It had been a day of forced merriment, helped along with extra allowances of beer and rich food. She had been grateful when bedtime came. 'Lovely. This is for you, Ma.'

'Oh! You shouldn't have.' Gwen unfurls the long piece of lace and gasps in delight. 'It's beautiful, Anne.'

'You should have kept the money,' her father says but smiles at her all the same.

Anne helps herself to a slice of cake as they talk, but from her seat, she can see the clock as it ticks away her time, and the cake grows stale in her mouth.

'Is everything all right, Anne?'

'Yes, Ma. I had a big dinner, that's all.'

'You seem a little ... I don't know. You're not quite yourself.'

'I'm just tired from yesterday.'

Her mother watches her as she sips her tea. 'You sure?'

'Let her be, Gwen. She don't need you nagging her. Let her rest while she can.'

'I'm just worried, I'm allowed to be, you know.'

How Anne wishes she could tell her parents about the witch. How she wants to unburden herself and cry in her mother's arms and have her father make everything all right like he always used to do. But she cannot.

So she stays quiet, and they laugh at Eddie and Paul as they thrash about on the floor, until the clock strikes. Anne tightens her shawl, and reluctantly eases herself out of her seat.

'I best be heading back.'

She kisses them goodbye, lingering a little too long in the comfort of her mother's embrace.

'You sure you're all right, darling?'

'Don't worry about me, Ma. You just look after yourself.'

She cannot look at her mother as she passes through the back door.

It is a black night, for the clouds have blotted out the moon and stars. She feels the first soft snowflakes as they fall upon her face, and her hand, which holds out the lamp, grows cold and wet beneath her glove.

She walks for a long time, slowing at the place where she thinks she last encountered the witch, but the witch is nowhere. She shines her lamp about herself, but the light is useless, and she sees no further than the length of her arm. She continues walking until Floreat comes into view. Perhaps the witch has forgotten, or better yet, died?

'What can you tell me?' the witch says, appearing out of nowhere.

Anne puts her hand to her mouth so her heart does not leap out of it. 'Nothing. Mrs Oliver has not yet had the child, though she's overdue. Doctor Jameson is worried.'

'What about Tom?'

'Mr Oliver is ... he is fine.'

'What does he do with his time?'

'He spends it in his study, mostly. I don't know what he does in there. Otherwise, he is in the library, reading. Sometimes he takes his horse, and he and his sister go riding when the weather is clear.'

'His sister?'

'Yes. Miss Oliver.'

The witch seems to consider this for a moment. 'And what does his sister do?' the witch slurs and some spittle reaches Anne's own lips. Anne shivers and brushes her mouth with her hand.

'She sews, looks at magazines. Sometimes she joins her brother in the library. She talks with Mrs Beacham about the food.'

The witch laughs.

'I have nothing more to tell you. There is no news.'

'What do you make of Miss Oliver?'

Anne has been thinking less and less of Miss Oliver as time has passed.

'Your silence speaks, girl.' The witch's eyes reflect the golden glow from the house. 'She is a very beautiful woman, do you agree?'

Anne nods.

'She is prettier than you.'

Anne's cheeks throb.

'They are close, Tom and his sister?'

Anne would speak, but humiliation has her tongue.

'How very infuriating for you.'

'They are siblings.'

The witch smiles then walks away. 'Next week,' she calls.

IN THE LIBRARY beside the fire, Liz cannot get warm. No matter how close she sits, she is perpetually cold.

Tom reads something. It seems to be all he does now.

'Anything interesting?' she says to fill the silence.

'It is a book about Venice.' He looks over the pages at her. His right cheek is flushed from the fire, and he has loosened his shirt. 'I am seeing where we might live.'

Liz cannot match his optimism. 'If we ever get there.' She stares at the logs which burn black and orange and cannot imagine the heat of the Venetian sun on her skin. 'If this baby ever comes.'

'We must be patient.' Tom brings his book up to his eyes again, ending the conversation. She would scream at him if she had the energy.

Clair bursts through the door. Her mousy hair falls from under her cap, her skin is white, and her eyes are wide. She dips into a curtsey and waits to be spoken to. Liz could slap her for it.

'What is it?' Tom says.

'It's Mrs Oliver, sir, she's having the baby.'

Tom pauses, as if unable to comprehend what the maid has told him, then says, 'Have you sent for Doctor Jameson?'

'No, sir.'

'Well, do it now, for God's sake!'

The maid flies from the room. Tom is on his feet, his hand scraping through his wax-less hair.

'So, it shall be tonight.' Liz remains in her seat, but her heart is battering beneath her ribs. 'Your son shall be born tonight.'

'You must go to her, Liz.'

She cannot believe what he is saying. She stares at him in horror. 'I can't. You know I can't.'

'She has no one else.'

'Do not make me!' Her breath comes hard and quick against her bodice. She can feel the butterfly fluttering in her gut, crawling its way up her throat. 'Tom, please do not make me.'

He kneels before her. He takes her hands, and his touch brings a spark of life to her cold body. He is crying.

'I am sorry. I am so sorry.' He kisses her wrists, and she sighs to feel his mouth upon her skin. 'I am sorry.'

She forces the butterfly down inside her. She has faced worse, she tells herself. Now is not the time for cowardice; one of them must be strong. 'Very well.'

He hangs his head near her skirts so that he may wipe his eyes. As gently as if he were a sleeping invalid, she moves him out of her way. She stands, steadies herself, and leaves the library.

ON THE STAIRWAY, she hears Mary groaning.

The doorknob is slippery as she twists it. Inside, the room is stale. Smoke swirls out from the fire and chokes the air. Mary writhes under her sheets.

'Elizabeth,' Mary says as she pants. 'They have all left me!'

Mary screams. Liz rushes to her side, takes her hand, not caring for Mary's vice-like grip. She peels back the covers to reveal the dark patch where Mary's waters have broken, and smells the acidity of sweaty genitals and unwashed nightgowns. Liz pulls the covers up to Mary's chest.

'It is all right, I'm here now, and Doctor Jameson is on his way.'

'Where is Tom?'

'Downstairs. He will come if we need him.'

'I need him now. I need him here.'

Liz could not stand to see Tom in this room, to see him witness the birth of his first child. His joy would be agony. 'You do not. He cannot come yet. This is no place for a man.'

'I want him.' Mary growls as another contraction passes.

'I said, no!'

'Mrs Oliver!' Anne runs into the room with her cloak still about herself. Her hair is wet; long, loose strands dangle beside her pink face, dripping water onto the floor. She scrambles to undo her brooch and cast her cloak aside, but her fingers are shaking, and her eyes are fixed on Mary. Liz unfastens the pin for her. 'Thank you, miss.'

'Where have you been?' Mary says, her teeth clenched, her hand outstretched for Liz's return.

'I've been home, ma'am. It's Sunday.'

'I don't care what day it is; you should have been here!'

'Sorry, ma'am.'

'That is enough squabbling. Anne is here. I am here. The doctor is on his way. You have nothing to fear. You must stay calm, Mary.'

Liz does not feel calm, but she hides her fear in her actions. She gets clean water, cloths, and towels. She wipes Mary's forehead and offers her hand for Mary to squeeze on each contraction. She makes Mary drink, makes Mary breathe steadily, tells her that everything will be all right.

It is almost an hour and a half before Doctor Jameson arrives with his assistant. He nods at the women around the bed and sets about sorting his instruments.

Liz sweats hard beneath her dress. She wishes that a window could be opened so that she may feel the cold breeze upon her damp neck, but it is pointless asking. She is only grateful that the doctor is here now and can take over.

She falls into one of the seats next to the heavy curtains, as far away from the fire and the bed as she can get, as Doctor Jameson makes his assessments. His assistant strips away the covers, allowing the doctor to look at Mary beneath her skirts. Liz is amazed that they do not flinch from the smell.

'Fetch me some sherry, would you?' Liz says to Mrs Jeffries, who waits in the corner of the room, her corset-less bosom heaving underneath her cotton frock. By the time the woman returns and Liz has the glass in her hand, there is excitement about the bed. It will not be long before the baby comes.

She gulps down the sherry.

Do not look, she says to herself.

She closes her eyes, fighting against the vision of rough-handed men and mean-eyed women, their hands shining red, peering down at her, frowning at the place between her legs, where she feels agony like she has never imagined.

Do not look.

She swallows the last drops of sherry. She fixes her eyes on the cut glass, on the way it throws shards of light off its engraved surfaces and blinds her, like the light that had swayed above her all those months ago. The brightness had broken through her delirium for moments at a time, and in those seconds of consciousness, she had heard pitiless words, seen something grey and shrivelled being taken away from her. She had reached out for her baby, only to be slapped down by one of the nurses.

It had been a bad birth.

Mary's screams merge into one long, head-splitting noise, shattering Liz's memories and bringing her back to the present. Mary's eyes are closed, her brows furrowed, and her lips white as she blows through them. Another hard push and Liz hears the slip of a wet body breaking free in a torrent of blood, and a baby cries.

LIZ IS rigid in her seat. She watches, like a spectator in a theatre, as the assistant lifts the naked, writhing, blood-covered child in the air so that the doctor may examine it.

'Tom,' Mary grunts.

Tom enters as the baby is made clean. He looks at Liz before he glances at the baby or his wife.

'Mr Oliver, you have a healthy son.' Doctor Jameson steps aside so that Tom may have sight of his child.

'Tom?' Mary's white hand protrudes from the covers, and she holds it out to Tom. He takes it, gingerly, and seems pained to return Mary's smile. The assistant brings the newborn, still screeching, to its parents and lays it on Mary's chest.

Liz swallows down the butterfly.

Then Mary's smile begins to falter, and her gaze draws upwards. 'Get it away! Get it away from me!'

She twists deeper into the bed, recoiling from her child, her gaze flicking madly between her baby and the empty air above her.

Doctor Jameson pins her arms still and orders Tom to do the same as his assistant takes the child and gives it to Mrs Jeffries, who leaves the room.

With the child gone, Mary begins to regain some control, but still, she looks into the air and cries. Tom strokes her forehead, shushes her, tells her everything is fine.

'Stay with her,' Tom says to Anne, who is pale and shaken from the traumatic night. 'Call for me if anything else happens.'

Quietly, as if it is Mary who is the child, Tom, Liz, Doctor Jameson, and his assistant, leave the room. As they make their way down the stairs, the grandfather clock strikes three.

'Why was she like that?' Tom says.

The doctor shakes his head. 'Sometimes, some women find it hard to ... love their children at first. It will pass.'

'I hope it does.' Tom stands firm before the doctor and makes the man meet his gaze.

The doctor nods and accepts his coat from Chipman. His hand trembles as he does so. 'Everything will be well, Mr Oliver. Give it time.'

Tom's lips peel back over his teeth, but Liz grazes his hand with her fingers, and he says nothing.

'Thank you for your help, Doctor.' Liz ushers Jameson and the assistant to the door. 'Goodnight.'

Tom and Liz watch them mount their carriage and stand rigid as the horse trots away into the falling snow.

'She is mad,' Tom whispers into the airless night. 'What other proof does the damned man need?'

'You have a son.'

'Yes.' He sighs, then, as if a thought has suddenly struck him, he turns to her. 'How are you?'

She waits until the carriage has disappeared. 'I am tired.'

'Would you like –'

'Goodnight, Tom.'

CHAPTER 9

 anuary 1870

THE CRYING IS CEASELESS. It echoes throughout Floreat, breaking through the walls and clawing at everyone's minds. Liz's reflection, whenever she looks these days, is ghostly; her eyes have sunk in their sockets, and the skin around them is like a sooty shadow. How she wishes the child would be quiet! How she wishes she had a room further away from the nursery.

She lifts her covers from her, not caring about the cold that hits her through the thin material of her nightgown, makes for the window, and draws back the curtains. Beyond the glass, the moon is high and clear, and the heathland is spotted black and silver for as far as her eye can see.

She leans against the cold stone wall and stares, unseeing, until her feet begin to prickle and goose pimples stand rigid over her body. She wonders if Mary wakes like she does. She wonders if Mary's breasts ache and ooze with milk turning sour as her baby calls for her. She wonders if Mary would care if the baby died.

The child screams louder. It is as if he is tearing the flesh from his throat in his efforts to reach his mother.

What is Mrs Jeffries doing? But it is no use blaming Jeffries; the child cries no matter how many times he is fed, no matter how many times he is held close to her warm chest, no matter how many times he is swaddled in clean gowns.

Liz hits her head against the wall, hoping to drown him out. As she lifts her heavy eyelids, something moves on the heathland.

The witch.

The child falls silent.

Liz screws her eyes shut. Her mind is playing tricks on her. It is not who she thinks it is. It cannot be. The witch has not been seen for over three months now. No, it is only the moonlight, the lack of sleep, and the piercing agony in her stomach that are making her delusional.

She looks again. The witch is gone.

LITTLE THOMAS'S cries can still be heard, for the nursery is above them, but Mary and Elizabeth sew as if all is calm in the drawing room. It is how Mary likes to spend the afternoons nowadays; she finds the repetitive action soothing, a welcome distraction.

'Mrs Jeffries is fitting in well.' Elizabeth loses the end of her thread, finds it again, licks the tip of it, and slides it through the eye of the needle. 'But I think Little Thomas does not like the taste of her milk.'

'Please stop talking about him.' Mary jabs the needle through her material and pulls back too hard; her cloth tears.

'I think Tom is doing well. Don't you?'

'How do you mean?'

'He is doing well as a father.'

There is a spike of jealousy in the base of her stomach. Since the birth, Mary has not seen her husband at all except at meal times. Even then, he barely looks at her, and when he does, she can sense his disgust.

'He spends much of his time with the child.'

'Please, Elizabeth! No more.'

Mary does not want to think of the child, for whenever she does, her mother returns, and she has been enjoying her time in the presence of the living. But it is too late.

Mary's neck suddenly grows chilled. She is sure that if she were to crane it, she would see the white face, the dark eyes, the purple lips of her mother, just inches away from her.

'Go away,' she begs.

'Mary?' Elizabeth leans forward in her seat. 'What is it?'

Mary clenches her jaw. She does not want to admit to it, but she cannot keep it a secret anymore. 'My mother is here.'

Elizabeth looks about herself. 'What do you mean?'

'She is behind me.'

Elizabeth stares past Mary's shoulder. Is that fear in her pretty green eyes?

'How often do you see her?'

Mary fixes her gaze on her material. She sews, concentrating on the motion of pushing and pulling the needle. She will not admit that Mother visits her daily.

'Mary?'

Mary's thread is running out. She has perhaps five more stitches before she must tie off.

'How often?'

The thread is gone; Mary ties it and searches for more.

'Where is the blue reel?'

'That was the last of it. I told you when you started.'

With a shriek that bounces around the pictured walls, Mary throws her sewing at the window. It falls to the ground slowly, gracefully, like a bird shot from the sky. For a moment, the whole house is still. Mother vanishes.

Then Little Thomas's cries begin again.

'I can't stand it,' Mary whispers. She rummages for her silk handkerchief in the pocket of her dress and cries into it. 'When will he stop?'

'He needs his mother.'

The hatred in Elizabeth's voice makes Mary glance up, but Elizabeth begins to sew again. Every so often, her gaze flicks up to beyond Mary's chair, anxiously.

'I can't Elizabeth. Don't you see? I just ... I can't bring myself to look at him.'

She recalls the last time she saw her son, after the trauma of giving birth. She had smiled at the curl of his hand, and his grumpiness at being plucked from somewhere warm and safe. Tom had held her gently, and the three of them had formed a perfect triangle together. She weeps for the memory.

If it weren't for her mother. If it weren't for the way she had slipped into the room and stood menacingly in the corner, her wet lips open, uttering words of warning that this child brings death.

Mary had looked at Little Thomas and had seen his eyes open; they had been black like her dead mother's. His cries had turned into her mother's voice, and his curled hand had stretched up to Mary, reaching for her throat.

'It is not the child's fault,' Elizabeth says.

'She has brought him. She has brought him to avenge herself.'

'Do not talk such nonsense.'

'He will be the death of me.' Mary senses the creeping

hands of her mother return and take hold of the back of her chair. 'Please go away.'

'Fine. I shall leave you.' Elizabeth rises.

'No! I didn't mean you.' Mary grabs her sister's hand as she makes for the door. 'Don't leave me with her.'

Elizabeth retracts her hand as if it is a corpse who has hold of it. Her glance shifts around the room – does she see Mother too? But no, that queer look in Elizabeth's eye is only for Mary.

'I should just like to sit for a while.' Mary forces a smile. She must learn to control herself. She should not have mentioned Mother at all. 'Please, stay. We were having a pleasant afternoon, weren't we?'

Somewhat reluctantly, Elizabeth concedes, and the two of them study the view as the child cries on.

ANNE HAS HAD A RESTLESS NIGHT; her dreams are never peaceful anymore. The cries from the baby do not help. She is sure Mrs Jeffries is no good as a wet-nurse. How can one child be so unhappy? When Anne offered to help, she received a swift and curt rejection. She had explained her years of experience, helping with her siblings, of taking them from her weary mother, of how she was better than anyone at getting a child to sleep, but Mrs Jeffries didn't care. Anne was a lady's maid, not a nurse.

She finds her clothes in the dark and puts them on in a trance. She creeps along the attic landing, avoiding the creaks for she has learned where they lie – Mary had often scolded her in her first few months for making so much noise – and begins her descent to the kitchen.

The wailing is louder as she reaches the second floor. She has never been able to resist the cry of a child. Indeed, her mother had chided her for fawning over her siblings if they so much as grimaced. She hesitates by the hidden servant's doorway.

No one seems to care for the poor babe, apart from Mr Oliver, who she sometimes hears in the nursery shaking a rattle and cooing silly words at his son. Mrs Oliver keeps as far away as she can. Even Miss Oliver has not been near the child, although Anne has heard her asking Mrs Jeffries about him and has caught her lingering outside the nursery on more than one occasion, her fingers inches from the door handle.

Anne can take it no more. She opens the door and steps out onto the dark landing. The maids have not yet lit the lamps; they will be downstairs, one dusting the drawing room, the other blacking the range. All is quiet, but for the baby. She will just take a peek, just to reassure herself that the child is wrapped warmly in Mrs Jeffries' embrace and that there is nothing she can do.

She tiptoes towards the nursery, turns the handle as quietly as she can. The room has one single candle burning far away from the cradle, and it does little to illuminate the space, but there is no doubt that Mrs Jeffries is not there. Anne curses the heartless woman and promises that Mr Oliver will hear of this, but for now, she must see to the babe.

He is wriggling in his cradle like a little worm, bound tight in his muslin cloth. Anne frees his arms, and they spring upwards, his tiny hands grappling at the air, reaching for her. She shouldn't, but she cannot help herself. She lifts him up and cuddles him close. He has that smell she loves, and she smiles as she places her cheek upon his soft, downy head and remembers how she used to do this with Eddie and Paul.

She rocks on her feet, swaying him backwards and forwards, telling him there is no need to cry, telling him what a wonderful father he has, telling him what a handsome little boy he will be. And finally, he stops crying. How she wishes Mrs Jeffries would find her with the child now, silent and content in her arms, and she could gloat and say I told you so.

She strolls around the room. He enjoys the movement, as most babies do, but the space is too small. She is going round and round in circles. Now that he is quiet, she will walk him on the landing.

She meanders along the carpeted floor and points at the paintings of the child's ancestors, whispering speculations about who they were, what their names might have been, what significant contributions they might have made to the world. Little Thomas follows her finger, his mouth opening and closing, chewing on his gums, his blue-grey eyes ogling his surroundings. He frowns at the sight of one particularly ugly man who sits proudly upon his horse against a Devonian background.

She is near the top of the stairs when she feels him beginning to wriggle. Perhaps she should return to the nursery, lay him down, and see where Jeffries is with his milk. Just as she has made up her mind to do so, a door across the landing opens, and Mrs Oliver's wan face stares at her.

'What are you doing with him?'

'Nothing, ma'am. He was crying, I was just seeing that he was all right.' Anne backs towards the nursery, eager to put the child down for he is stronger than he looks and her anxiety is causing him to struggle. Mrs Oliver follows her, gaining on her.

'You would steal him! You would steal my son!'

Anne runs into the nursery and bundles Little Thomas into his bed. Mrs Oliver is upon her in an instant. Her hair is wild, stuck up with grime that has not been brushed away. Her face is white, and her hands are clenched at her sides.

'Please, ma'am, I was only trying to help.' Anne reaches in to comfort the child as he cries.

'Do not touch him! You would steal him! You would raise him to kill me!'

Mrs Oliver dives on Anne and tackles her to the floor. Anne is blinded by the woman's hair, and she feels hands strike her face, the sting of fingernails as they score her cheeks, her neck, her mouth. Anne would push Mrs Oliver off, but her arms are pinned to the ground as Mrs Oliver sits on her chest. Anne struggles and cries out for her mistress to stop, to no avail.

Suddenly, Anne is freed. Her lungs fill with air. She rolls onto her side, holding her face.

At the end of the room, Mrs Oliver writhes against her husband. She is spitting and cursing and stamping at the floor like a bull before it charges. Mr Oliver hauls her out of the room, shouts for Chipman, urges his wife to be still, to calm herself, to compose herself.

Mrs Jeffries, who must have been watching for some time, helps Anne to her feet. 'What happened?'

Anne cannot answer, she is too stunned to speak. She lifts her face and Jeffries gasps.

Anne staggers out onto the landing as Mr Oliver and Chipman drag Mrs Oliver into her room. Standing before the looking glass, it takes Anne some moments to realise that the face staring back at her is her own.

Blood seeps down her skin like red ribbons. Her right eye is already swollen; she winces as she touches it. Her dress is ripped at the throat, revealing more gouges where Mrs Oliver's nails have wounded her. Her hair has fallen from its pins, and her curls are askew about her face. She raises a trembling hand to her head and brings away a clump of loose hair.

The sight of herself is too much to bear. She has never been so ugly, never been so battered and sore. She cannot stand the thought of anyone seeing her like this, least of all Mr Oliver, and so she darts to the servant's passage and retreats to her room, where she weeps in the darkness.

TOM LEAVES Mary in her chamber. Liz doesn't know what he has done to placate his wife; perhaps stroked her forehead, probably kissed her, maybe hit her. He is in his room now, for there is a shadow in the gap between his door and the floor, and she goes to him.

Inside, Chipman helps Tom dress.

'You may leave, Chipman.' The man exits on his master's command, dropping into a bow for Liz as he passes her.

Tom is in his trousers and shirt. The buttons down his chest are loose, and his white, firm flesh shows between the material.

'You look tired. The commotion woke you?'

'I don't sleep anyway.' Liz touches one of the dark circles under her eyes.

'Neither does Mary. She is insane.' He has reached the final button at his neck, and he pinches it together. His breath is short and quick. His blood is up from all the excitement.

'What will you do?'

'I have told Chipman to summon Doctor Jameson. He cannot ignore this any longer.'

'You said that last time.' Liz leans against his bed and looks about the room. It is grander than her own, with more fine murals, larger oil paintings, and thicker rugs.

'Poor Anne,' Tom says under his breath as he trails his hand through his hair. He slumps into his chair beside the low burning grate and fixes his sleeves.

'What was she doing with the baby?'

'I don't know. Trying to help, I suppose.'

'It is not her place to help with Thomas.'

Tom laughs. 'You cannot think this is Anne's fault?'

'I think you place too much upon the girl.' Liz's body is rigid. 'I think we should find another maid.'

Tom is on his feet, pacing towards the window. He is annoyed; she can tell by the way his shoulders sit beneath his shirt. 'I don't understand you sometimes, Liz. You know why we have Anne.'

'I can't say that I do, really.'

'For God's sake!' He slams his hand against the wall. 'You know that Anne has her part to play in all this. We need her. Why are you being like this now?'

'I don't like her, Tom.'

'She is how I have made her. It is all for a purpose.'

'And how exactly have you moulded her to your purpose?'

He sighs. 'Don't look at me like that. It is not what you are thinking.'

'Really?'

'I would never –' He shakes his head, but there is a faint tinge on his cheeks that Liz spots immediately.

'I want her gone, Tom.'

Tom looks at his feet. The distance between them has never seemed so vast as she waits for his agreement.

'I am sorry, Liz, but she is too valuable to lose now. She is the proof of Mary's madness; she's covered in it. Please, just … for Venice. We are close, can't you see? Doctor Jameson is coming today.'

'Doctor Jameson?' Her palms smack into the mattress, her voice bounces off the walls. Never has Tom sided with another against Liz, and fear and rage erupt from within. 'What will Jameson do? He hates you. He will not help us. He will not be persuaded by your charm like her.'

'He is stubborn, yes –'

'Stubborn?' She laughs, too hard. 'Is that what you call it?

And what will you do if he remains stubborn, Tom? What will you do if this wonderful plan of yours fails?'

'You must be patient, Liz.'

'We have been here a year already!' She spits the words at him, grabbing hold of one of the bedposts to steady herself, for sparks are flying across her vision.

He shies away from her. 'I will sort it.'

'Make sure that you do. I will not be here another twelve months, I promise you that.' She gasps for breath. She has not been so forceful in weeks, months, and it has robbed her of her strength. The room blackens, the ground moves beneath her feet.

'Sit down.' Tom helps her up on the bed. She would shrug his touch away, but she feels it so seldom these days that, despite her anger, she longs for it. He lies her down and props himself up beside her. 'Everything I do, I do for us. Please believe that.'

She forces a nod.

'It will be all right.'

Those words have been said too much; they have lost their meaning. 'It was never meant to last this long.'

'I know.' He runs his fingers over her hair like he used to do when they were little. 'But this is only temporary, I promise. I will sort it. Do you trust me?'

It is like looking into a mirror as she stares into his green eyes. Of course, she does. He is the only person she has ever trusted.

AFTER BREAKFAST, Doctor Jameson arrives. His usual bluster has returned, and the doubt he showed when last here delivering Mary's child has vanished.

'Mr Oliver. How may I help you this time?'

Tom does not invite him to his study. Instead, he meets

the wiry old man in the hallway with Anne behind him. 'Chipman, take the doctor's coat.'

Chipman does as he is told and disappears out of sight.

'Have you not noticed our maid, Doctor?'

Jameson doesn't even glance at Anne. Tom steps dramatically to one side so that Anne stands alone in the bright space.

'Ah.'

'That is the work of my wife. And you tell me she is perfectly well? She has been seeing the ghost of her dead mother and attacking the servants until they are bloodied and blackened. Do you think that is how a sane woman behaves?'

'I think you should calm down, Mr Oliver.'

'Do not speak to me as if I am a child!' Tom prowls towards the doctor. 'Now, you will help my wife this time. Do you understand me?'

Jameson flinches. 'Are you threatening me, sir?'

Tom pauses. He can hear Anne shifting on her feet. He stifles his response, stretches his fingers out of their tight grip.

'Anne, take the doctor to Mary. He will need to see the state of her.' He backs away, though his stare remains fixed on Jameson. 'I will be waiting for you in my study.'

It is only ten minutes before the doctor returns from his patient. Tom has promised himself to be calm from now on; he must show that he is more civilised than the pauper Jameson believes him to be.

'How did you find her?' Tom says as he nods at the chair.

'She is unwell, I grant you.'

Tom motions at the whiskey, but Jameson declines.

'Don't mind if I do? It's been a long day already.' Tom

pours himself a half measure, although it is not yet midday. 'I didn't want it to come to this.' He sighs and sips his drink. 'Where is best for her? Money is not a problem.'

'What do you mean?'

'Which institution do you recommend? Is there one nearby?'

The doctor laughs, showing his crooked, yellow teeth. 'I am not putting your wife into an asylum, Mr Oliver. I am prescribing her laudanum.'

Tom's glass is warm in his sweaty hand. He downs the last of the whiskey and bites his lip. He must remain calm. 'You think laudanum will work?'

'Your wife is sleep deprived, that is all. The baby has taken its toll. Other than that, she is perfectly healthy. Once she starts to have a decent night's rest, she will soon be back to her old self.'

Tom smiles as he meets the doctor's eyes. 'I hope you are right. Although you will understand if I am not as confident as you. It was you who told her father that she would be well once she was married. It was you who told me that she would be calmed from pregnancy. So far, Doctor,' he says, his lips curling into a snarl, 'you have been wrong in every case.'

'I am not in the habit of sending my patients to the madhouse, Mr Oliver. No matter how much they might inconvenience you.'

'How dare you!' Tom is just about to haul the doctor out of his chair when Jameson gets to his feet.

The doctor sniffs through his hooked nose and then calmly opens his medicine case, pulling out a bottle of brown liquid. 'She must take a teaspoonful of this each night before bed. She must take no more. I trust you will contact me again if you have any other concerns.'

'Oh, I will!' Tom shouts after Jameson as the man stalks out of the room, then he throws his glass against the fireplace, watching it smash into diamond-like shards and fall into the flames.

IN HER BEDROOM, Liz sits before the looking glass in her nightgown while Anne brushes her hair. They do not speak to each other as they used to. Though Liz knows she must try, the effort to maintain the pretence of friendship is too hard when she is so exhausted. So, she says nothing as she watches Anne's wounded face in the mirror and realises she feels nothing for the girl.

'Has Mary had her medicine?'

'I gave it to her just after dinner.'

'Did she take it?'

Anne pauses. The brush rests at the top of Liz's neck.

'Anne, did she take it?'

'I'm not sure, miss. I didn't stay to watch.'

Liz sighs. 'I will check on her before I go to bed.'

'Thank you, miss.'

Anne finishes with Liz and leaves her alone, staring at herself.

She does not know how much more she can take. Tom failed in his promise, and now Mary remains, still haunting their days and ruining their nights. Little Thomas cries on. Nothing has changed.

She slips from her room and crosses the landing to Mary's chamber. She does not knock for if Mary is asleep, she does not want to wake her.

Inside, Mary's room is dark, the only light is from the low burning fire. She can hear heavy breathing coming from the bed, and she tiptoes towards it. Mary is curled into a ball on her side, like a baby, and sleeps soundly. The glass on the bedside table is empty apart from the trace of the laudanum resin clinging to the sides of it.

Liz runs her finger around the glass, puts her finger in her mouth and sucks. It tastes of nothing much, perhaps a little bitter, and she waits for a few moments to test if the drug will have any effect, but, disappointingly, it does not.

She is about to return to her room when the child's cries draw her towards the nursery.

Her hand has wavered over this handle so often. She has been too much of a coward to enter before, but now, what does she have to lose?

Inside, Mrs Jeffries rocks in the chair, the child held close to her exposed breast in case he might wish to feed. As Liz closes the door behind her with a click, the woman's eyes pop open.

'Miss! Excuse me.'

'It is perfectly fine. Stay as you are.'

Mrs Jeffries smiles but covers herself as best she can. She seems to have aged ten years since the baby's birth; she must be feeling the strain of sleeplessness worse than anyone.

Liz creeps towards the two of them. Little Tom's face is puce and wrinkled, his body is wrapped tight. He feels trapped, Liz guesses. Who would not howl if they felt so imprisoned?

'Let me take him from you.'

'Are you sure, miss?'

'I should like to get to know my nephew. I have taken too long already.'

Liz holds out her thin arms, and Jeffries transfers the baby into them. He is already a weight, but he is warm and soft and wriggling with life. She rocks on her feet and kisses his head.

'Are you all right, miss?'

Liz is crying, and she has not realised it.

'Very well, Mrs Jeffries.' With the child held close to her

body, the pain in her stomach has disappeared. 'I am very well now.'

She walks about the room, keeping her gaze locked on this beautiful, miraculous child, and finally, Little Tom quietens. His frown smooths, and his skin calms, though his cheeks remain rosy. His little eyes squint open and look at her.

'How have I left you for so long?' she whispers.

She holds him until her arms tremble. Even then, she does not wish to part with him, but her strength is failing; both she and the child are almost asleep. When she turns, she finds that Jeffries' mouth has dropped and her eyes have closed. Liz taps her on the shoulder, and she jumps awake.

Liz hands Little Tom over as if he were a doll made of crystal. 'Take him out of the swaddling. He does not like it.'

Back in Mrs Jeffries' grasp, the child begins to grow anxious again.

'Miss, I think it's best to keep him in –'

'I said, take him out.'

Mrs Jeffries does as she is ordered and covers the child in his warm gown instead. Immediately, the boy eases. In his cot, his eyelids droop, and his rosebud mouth puckers. Liz strokes the back of his chubby cheek.

'Sleep now, my darling,' she leans in and kisses his forehead, 'and everything will be better in the morning.'

CHAPTER 10

 ebruary 1870

THE WEEKLY MEETINGS with the witch are becoming more tiresome than terrifying. Anne has no news to give her other than how wretched Mary is being, but the witch does not seem to care for that, nor for the wounds to Anne's flesh.

'What does Tom do?' the witch says again in the dim glow of Anne's lamp.

'What he always does.'

'What of Lizzie?'

'Why do you call her that?' But the witch does not take kindly to questions. Anne sighs. There is little use arguing. 'What she always does.'

'You shall be no use to me, girl, if you do not talk. I do not like your attitude.'

Anne clenches her jaw, pushes her frustration away – it is not wise to rile the witch. 'Miss Oliver is now fond of the baby – that's the only difference. She plays with him most days, takes him for little walks about the house, that sort of thing.'

'Better,' the witch says. 'And you do not like this?'

'Never said that.'

'It is in your face.'

The rain is coming heavier, the slime is building beneath her bodice. Anne would have this meeting over with.

'I just don't see why she's so keen on him now, when before the only people who cared for the child were Mr Oliver and me.'

The hole of the witch's mouth tilts, and her rough hand cups Anne's cheek. Anne remains as still as if she is in the jaws of a fly-catcher, and any movement might mean death. 'You really are in love with him. Silly girl.'

Anne dives away from the hand. 'Is that all you want from me?'

'Do you think Tom loves you back?'

Mr Oliver has looked at Anne like no other person has, as if he sees not a lady's maid, or a daughter or a sister or a stand-in mother, but the real Anne; who she wishes to be. He has talked to her and has valued what she has had to say. He has protected her from his own wife.

'I am sure he has feelings for me. He has kept me here long enough, despite Mary. He must think something of me.'

'I'm sure he thinks something of you, girl.' The witch laughs. 'And what do you think he thinks of his wife? What do you think he thinks of his sister?'

Anne swallows and straightens her spine. 'If you have nothing more to say, then I shall go.'

'Wait.'

Anne stops.

'You will do something for me. You will call her Lizzie.'

Anne folds her arms. 'Not until you tell me why.'

144

The lamplight catches the witch's eye, makes it glimmer. She smiles. 'You will find out.'

'SHOULD you like to stop in France?' Tom says. 'Or perhaps Spain? I understand the Alhambra Palace is very impressive.'

Tom pours over the globe on the table by the fire in the library. Little Tom sits upon Liz's lap, and she makes silly faces at him.

'I should like to see it.'

'Would the boat stop there?' Liz blows kisses at the child.

'It should stop there if we told it to.'

'Isn't Daddy pompous?' she whispers to the baby and laughs when he burps in response.

'Excuse me.' Anne is at the door. 'Mrs Oliver is in bed.'

'Have you given her the medicine?'

'Yes, miss.'

'Good.' Liz returns her gaze to the child and tickles his tummy. 'You may go.'

Anne dips and turns to leave until Tom stops her. 'Have you ever studied the globe, Anne?'

'No, sir.'

Tom beckons the maid over, and Liz detects smugness in the girl's grin.

'I was just saying how I should like to visit the Alhambra.' He points at the spot on the globe. 'It was built by Moors, did you know? Then the Christians slaughtered them and took it for themselves.'

'They stole it, sir?'

Tom shrugs. 'Evolution, I believe we must call it now.'

'Do you believe in all that, sir?'

The two of them stand very close together as they study the world.

'Yes, I do. Do you, Anne?'

'I can't say I know enough about it.'

'I can teach you if you would like? I have the book over here.' Tom saunters to a shelf in the wall and plucks out Charles Darwin's *On the Origin of Species*.

'Anne does not have time for evolution, Tom.' Liz interrupts their little discussion, reminding Tom that she is still in the room. 'She is already stretched with two mistresses to serve. She probably has duties to be attending to right now.'

'I don't, miss.' Anne's grin is too bold, triumphant. The girl inches nearer Tom, her fingers close to brushing his sleeve. 'I have done everything for tonight until you retire for bed.'

The two women hold each other's gaze. Anne is testing her, Liz knows it. When did the girl start thinking she was better than Liz?

Tom breaks the silence. 'Well, it is too late now, anyway. Another time, perhaps, Anne.'

Anne drops her eyes to the floor. 'I shall prepare your bed, miss. Would you like me to take Little Thomas to Mrs Jeffries?'

Before Liz can say no, Tom answers for her. 'That would be most kind of you, Anne. Liz was only just saying how tired she was feeling, weren't you, Liz?'

Liz nods stiffly as Anne comes before her. The child wriggles as Liz tries to set him straight so that Anne might get a hold of him, but Anne pushes Liz's hands out of the way.

'Let me see to him, Lizzie.'

Liz reels, the breath forced from her. It is as if she has taken a blow to the stomach. When was the last time she was called that? She dares not think about it.

'What did you just say?'

Anne bobs the child up and down on her hip. Her eyes are wide. 'Sorry, miss?'

'Is everything all right?' Tom says.

'Yes, sir.' Anne turns her back on Liz. 'Goodnight, sir.' Anne dips low for her master and then leaves the room, all the while whispering and giggling with the child, as Liz struggles to find some air.

ANNE HAS DONE EVERYTHING PERFECTLY; the fire is burning well, not too high or too low; the bed sheets are toasty but not uncomfortable; she has lit candles beside the bed and on the dressing table to bathe the room in a golden glow. She has even spritzed some perfume in the air to make it more pleasant. Now, she waits for Miss Oliver's arrival with a sickness in her stomach. It is a mixture of nerves and excitement.

'I can undress myself tonight, Anne.' Miss Oliver does not meet Anne's gaze as she comes into the room. 'You may go.' She picks the pins from her hair so that it falls loose.

'That is a fiddly dress, miss. I should help you.'

Miss Oliver twists her arms about herself trying to find the buttons and discreet ties, all to no avail. Anne brushes away her hands and takes over, leaving Miss Oliver standing like a doll in the centre of the room as something to be toyed with.

'Have you enjoyed your day, miss?'

'Yes.'

Miss Oliver is awfully pale, and it is an ugly pale, with a sheen of perspiration that makes her skin ashen-grey.

'You feeling all right, miss?'

'Perfectly well, if you would only work quicker so I could lie down.'

Anne finds the next button and pretends it is stuck. She takes her time to undo it. 'I've been meaning to ask you, miss. This dress,' Anne gestures at the red one she is wearing, 'when I came to alter it all those months back, it had a mark on the bottom of it. Like it had been singed?'

'Oh?'

Anne pulls away Miss Oliver's coloured skirts. 'How did that come about?'

Miss Oliver swallows hard. A bead of sweat trickles from her temple down her cheek.

'I'm not sure. It is an old dress, and the material is not of high quality. Perhaps it caught on a grate once, and I never noticed.'

'It's a bit odd not to have noticed your dress catching fire, miss. I hear many a woman has died from such a thing. You should be more careful, miss.'

'Yes, thank you, Anne. I shall be from now on.'

Anne rips the corset away so that Miss Oliver is left in just her chemise.

'My robe.'

'I think you are too warm, miss.' Anne dabs a handkerchief over her mistress's brow, then pushes her down onto the stool. 'I can brush your hair like this.'

'I would like my robe,' Miss Oliver's voice is strained. The glass reflects a face with tight lips and darting eyes, but Anne has already begun to scoop her mistress's hair into her hands to brush it. The chemise is low at the back for it is too loose on Miss Oliver's skeletal frame, and as Anne looks down, she sees the network of scars across the woman's back, like a thick spider's web.

'Oh, my! What –'

'My robe, now!'

Miss Oliver pushes her stool back so that it slams against Anne's foot. A bolt of pain shoots from Anne's big toe, and she grabs hold of it as Miss Oliver rushes for the robe that is lying on the bed.

'You will leave, Anne.'

But Anne is too shocked to move.

'Get out!' Miss Oliver charges at her. Anne sprints for the door, ignoring the agony in her toe, and slams it shut just in time to feel Miss Oliver's punches crash into the wood.

ANNE HAS no lamp to see by as she runs to the attic, but she knows her room by the familiar stench of it. She falls onto her bed, beside which a great patch of mottled damp is spreading by the hour, and weeps angry, frustrated tears.

She could spit at how she has to spend her nights in this hovel in the rafters, where the wind whistles ceaselessly and blows through her hair as she lies asleep, while underneath her, Mrs and Miss Oliver rest in warm, dry luxury. What makes either of them any better than her anyway? What kind of lady has scars upon her back like Miss Oliver? A lady's skin should be pure, clean, unblemished. And what sort of lady attacks her maid and her husband? No, she must serve two women who are no better than herself; who are worse than herself!

Snatching the tears off her face, she rips off the red dress and throws it in the corner of the room. She will not wear anything that vile woman has worn. She thinks of those scars again, imagines them seeping some kind of terrible fluid which sticks on the dress, the dress she has worn for so long already! She cringes and shudders, then buries herself under the thin covers and winces as her toenail catches on the sheet.

There is something disturbing about Miss Oliver. And the witch was right; Miss Oliver does not like Anne one bit, and Anne does not like her either.

LIZ SHAKES as she sits on the edge of her bed, her knees

clamped together, her arms wrapped suffocatingly tight around her body. Her fingers reach to the scars on her back. Under this thin chemise, she can feel them. The once torn skin has long healed, but it still seems thinner, weaker, as if it could rupture at any moment.

The cries from that night echo inside her skull. The screams, the sobs. How she begged for the man to stop, her wrists bound to the top of the bedpost, her naked body pressed against the wood, as each skin-splitting slap was followed by a moan of pleasure.

She had wailed for Mother, the person who had ordered it in the first place, as punishment. She had promised that she would never see him again, that she would stop loving him if only the torture would end. How she had pleaded, how she had wished for Mother to enter the room and make a deal with her!

But Mother never came.

Hours later, the whip left with its master to lie in some secret cupboard in a hidden room in a house in Marylebone.

Sophie, her only friend, treated the wounds. How they had bled! How her skin had wept for days after, scabbing over and tearing open again and again. She remembers the sting of the remedy even now, how she had to bite on a wooden spoon so she would not scream as Sophie dabbed at her back.

After a few months, the pain had ended, and she had thanked the Lord that Mother had not bargained with her that night.

SOMETHING BRUSHES against Anne's face. It is like a feather against her cheek, or perhaps a strand of her hair moving in the breeze. She lies there half-conscious, wracked with dreams thick with fire and smoke and tortured skin until a squeak startles her. She lurches out of bed. Wide awake, she can hear them scurrying and talking to each other. She has been sleeping with a family of mice.

She runs to Mrs Beacham's room. The woman is fast asleep, and Anne's bangs upon the door are not well received.

'What do you expect me to do about it?' Mrs Beacham grumbles as she sits up. 'You shall have to poison them or lay traps.' Mrs Beacham rubs her eyes and settles herself back into her bed, which is almost the same width as her body.

'What should I do now? I can't go back to bed in there.'

Mrs Beacham's mouth opens into a yawn. 'What time is it?'

'I don't know. The maids aren't up yet.'

'Well, I'm going back to sleep. I suggest you get up and make yourself useful now you're awake.' Mrs Beacham rolls over; the conversation is finished.

Anne slinks back to her room and finds her clothes for the day. She dresses in the hallway, then walks down the stairs and out onto the landing. Behind the door, the child is quiet in his nursery. She grips the handle, but her nerves are still too frayed from last night to be so bold, so she backs away.

She tiptoes down the main staircase and finds that the grandfather clock has not yet struck four. She goes to the library and opens all the curtains to let in the moonlight, then takes the globe to the window. She finds Britain and marvels at how small their little island is compared to the lands it has conquered. What a lowly position it should have in the world, and yet it rules most of it.

Her gaze lands on the book by Darwin, which has been left on the opposite table.

Evolution.

The idea is a Godless one. Anne thinks He may strike her dead where she stands for entertaining the notion. Yet, she does not die. And she has been praying for weeks and months, and God has not stopped Mary from beating her. God has not made Mr Oliver kiss her when nobody is looking. Years ago, God did not save her mother's leg. It is as if God has never even heard her.

She slumps into one of the chairs. It is not as comfortable as she thought it would be. She can feel lumps under her bottom where the stuffing does not lie properly.

She plucks at her skirt. She has almost three hours before the maids rise, and another hour on top of that before she must breakfast and wake Mrs and Miss Oliver. She cannot go back to bed. She cannot light a lamp to read or sew by. She has nothing to do.

So, she gathers her cloak and boots from downstairs, takes the key for the back door and lets herself out of the house to begin the long walk home. She will collect some rat poison from her father who will be awakening by the time she arrives, then have a ride on his horse back to Floreat in time to start her working day. Tonight, she will be free from scurrying bodies.

'Please leave me. Please ... please ...'

Mary sits in the centre of her bed with her chin tucked into her knees.

Mother stands at the foot of the bed, staring. She raises her hand and points one long, skinny finger at the daughter who killed her, all those years ago.

'Please ...'

Mary has heard the clock strike eleven, then twelve, then one, then two, then three, then four, then five. The fire in her grate has extinguished, and her bare feet are now numb. The full glass of water and laudanum sits on her bedside table; her mother pushed her hand away when she went to drink it.

152

'Please leave me.'

It was once a comfort to hear the child cry, for then Mary knew he was far away from her. Now he is silent, she does not know his whereabouts. She imagines him crawling like a beetle across the landing, scratching under her door, waiting for the lock to be forgotten one night so that he can break through and strangle her while she sleeps. So, she locks her door, but locks do not mean a thing to ghosts.

'What do you want from me?'

A change somewhere in the atmosphere. Mary lifts her head. Her mother has moved; the ghost now hangs limply by the bedroom door, a pointed finger on the handle.

Mother is answering Mary's question.

In her nightdress, for she has no time to change, Mary slides out of her bed and follows the phantom down the stairs where it slips through the front door of the house, yet when Mary tries to turn the handle, she finds it is locked. Chipman will have the keys.

She curses him. She is being kept a prisoner in her own house. Her mother is on the other side of the door, her presence sliding further away, the answer to Mary's question receding from her grasp.

She runs through the servant's passage, her feet slapping against the bare stone. The narrow corridors do not affect her as they once might have done, and she scurries through them like an ant in the dirt. She is keen and focused. She will find Chipman's keys, and she will take them from him. If he wakes, she will silence him. Yet, as she emerges into the servant's quarters, she can feel a draught upon her ankles. She searches for the source until she sees the back door is ajar. She has no need for keys. She is free.

Outside, the gravelled path around the perimeter of the house induces no feelings on her naked soles. She dashes to the front where her mother waits for her at the bottom of the steps, then follows, as her mother sets out into the gardens.

Her mother glides as if she is blown on the breeze, like a sailing boat across the sea. Mary has to run to keep up, falling every now and again, her feet tripping over themselves or catching on a stump in the earth.

They are out of the lawned area now and heading into the parkland. The grass is higher here, but Mary's shins feel nothing as the blades slice against her flesh.

'Where are we going, Mother?'

In the distance, the sea swells. The wind is getting stronger, and it blows Mary's loose hair around her head so that she has to push it from her eyes every minute or so. Moon shadows dance across the landscape, distorting the world.

Amidst the confusion, the woods appear, and the faint ghost of Mary's mother slides amongst the trees. The broken branches cut into Mary's feet and calves as she follows. Dead leaves and undergrowth squish between her toes, making her slip.

'Mother? Mother!' Cold sweat clings to her skin and soaks through her nightgown. She cannot see the white figure anywhere. 'Mother!'

She runs on. She cannot turn back.

'Mother?'

Her legs are heavy. The trees crowd around her, muttering to themselves.

'Mother, please. Where are you?'

A cloud covers the moon, and there is total darkness. A breath blows against her ear, and she shivers, turns, twists, casts her arms out to feel who is there.

Then the cloud slips away, and in a beam of silver light, she sees her mother before her, beckoning her to follow. Mary drags her body on. Hours of relentless traipsing pass, until the weak dawn light bleeds into the sky and the two of them emerge from the forest.

Slowly, she joins her mother and realises where they are. It has been almost twenty years since Mary was last here.

SUNLIGHT FLASHES into Mary's mind. A hot day, too hot for the dress her governess had made her wear. A brilliant day with the sky as blue as sapphires and dragonflies lazily buzzing around the reeds.

There had been a picnic, and the unwanted food had laid upon the blanket attracting wasps and blue-bottle flies. Her mother had lounged on the grass, her large skirts forming a mountain of pale pink against the greenery.

Mary had left a birthday present at home. She cannot remember what the toy was now, but it had been so important that her mother had insisted that the governess go and fetch it.

She had waited for the governess's return so she could play with her toy, but the woman had taken so long! Her mother had been dozing. Mary had passed the time by watching the birds flitting between the trees, listening for the frogs in the water, making a daisy chain for her hair, but she had grown bored.

And it had been so hot! The heat had prickled her skin and had made it itch. She had pouted and sighed, but Mother had not removed the hat from her face or asked what was wrong.

So Mary had tugged away her dress, ripping it in her fury, until she had been in nothing but her undergarments. The heat had been instantly relieved, but her arms and back had still felt as if someone were sticking hundreds of needles into her flesh.

The water had looked so inviting; still, apart from the ripples from the skater flies upon its surface.

She had swum in the sea many times before. Her mother had told her what a wonderful swimmer she was. So she had walked to the edge of the pond, feeling the heat from the long grass gather about her legs, and smelling the scent of muddy water as her toes had soaked into the spongy ground.

It had been blissful to feel the cold water against her stinging back, and for a while she had floated in the middle of the pool, staring into the cloudless sky, imagining that she might have been anywhere in the world, as her mother had slept.

Then, a dragonfly had dived too close and startled her. She had kicked her legs to swim away when slimy hands had swirled around her ankles. She had panicked.

Mother had woken up as Mary had screamed, and in an instant she had rushed to the water and waded in. In her haste to get to her child, Mother had not had time to remove her clothing. She had walked into the water until it was up to her waist, her chest, her chin, and had told Mary to swim as she pushed Mary towards safety.

That was the last time Mary had felt her mother's skin upon hers.

Mary had kicked with all her strength, until the ground had returned beneath her feet, wet but firm, and she had pulled herself from the water.

She had turned just in time to see last dry curls of her mother's hair disappearing under the water.

She had screamed. Mother's drenched face had resurfaced, her mouth had opened and sucked in some air, her eyes, wide and wild, had found Mary for a second. Then she had slipped under again. Bubbles had popped on the water. Mother's thin fingers had clawed the air until they too, vanished.

Mary had screamed until she thought her throat had burst open, until the water finally grew calm.

She is screaming now. She is reaching for her mother, who, they said, after the body was dragged from the lake in sediment smeared skirts, had not been able to swim in such heavy clothing. She is crying and apologising and looking at the dead woman beside her, who is nothing like the elegant mother of her memories.

'I'm sorry! I never meant it ... I never meant to kill you.'

Her mother's ghost points at the dip in the earth where the pond used to be. There is water there. The lake is filling up.

'What do you want from me?' But the answer is obvious.

Her screaming subsides to shaking sobs. She nods.

Her feet refuse to move for a moment, then they stumble forward towards the water.

The pool is big enough for Mary to wade in until her hips are submerged, her arms breaking the thin layer of ice all around her. She looks over her shoulder to see her mother watching. She leans back, lifts her feet and floats for a while, seeing the faint stars in the dawn sky. Her eyelids close as the water laps over her ears and onto her cheeks. With one last sigh, she welcomes oblivion.

CHAPTER 11

The four of them stand around the bed. Mary lies between the sheets, her hair brushed neat by Anne, a new nightgown placed on her, the cuts on her feet and legs bathed clean. The fire is high, and the curtains have been drawn. It is stiflingly hot.

Doctor Jameson performs his medical checks. Her pulse is quick, he says, but her breathing is shallow.

'Will she survive?' Tom chews the dry skin on his lip.

'She must be kept warm and dry. I believe she might develop a fever. You must keep her inside.'

Tom nods and scratches at his eyes.

'How did she get out?'

'This is not a prison, doctor,' Liz says, halting Tom's furious response – which she can feel buzzing through his skin – by placing her hand on his shoulder. 'We do not keep her under lock and key.'

'The front door was locked, though? I am asking in case she has fallen, perhaps from a window. We do not yet know the extent of her injuries.'

'Chipman tells me the back door was open,' she explains. She does not trust Tom to speak – he is too desperate, too excited at the possibility of Mary's demise, sure that she will now either die, or be carted to the nearest asylum. 'That's how the maids became suspicious. Chipman sent Will out to check the perimeter, in case it was ... someone else, and Will heard screaming.'

'And she was unconscious by the time he found her?'

Liz nods. The doctor sighs, the air forcing its way through his nostrils. 'Has she been taking her medication?'

Liz turns to Anne, who stands in the corner of the room, quiet and with eyes cast to the floor.

'I think so, sir.'

'What do you mean, girl? Has she taken the laudanum or not?'

Anne's cheeks are pink. She ignores the doctor, and her blue eyes flick at Tom though he does not meet her gaze, much to Liz's relief. 'I don't know, sir.'

Where were you this morning, Anne?' Liz shoots the question.

'Here, miss.'

Liz knows she is lying. Mrs Beacham told Liz that Anne had been in to see her in the middle of the night because she was scared of some mice. Anne had not been seen again until Mary had been carried home, at which point, she suddenly appeared.

Surely, Anne cannot have anything to do with Mary's accident, can she? She is too simple. But the girl is different now than how she was at the beginning. She is too bold, and remarkably cunning when it comes to Tom and those who are close to him.

'What will you do, Doctor?' Liz says, dragging her suspicious gaze off Anne's blushing face.

'We must wait and see. Mary is getting stronger already,

the life is coming back into her. But we do not know how her mind will have been affected.'

'I should say it was rather affected before this happened,' Tom says. 'And you told me then that she would get better. Tell me, how did you become a doctor, because you don't seem to be a very good one.'

'Tom.' Liz's squeezes his shoulder to remind him of his promise. With a look, she apologises to Jameson, though he ignores her.

'If she had been taking her medicine, this would never have happened.'

Jameson rises and makes his way to the door. Liz escorts him down the stairs after glaring at Tom so he will remain with Mary – Tom has had his chance with the doctor. Now it is her turn.

When Jameson has his coat, Liz takes him by the arm. 'I hope you do not take offence at my brother, sir. We are not of this ...' she gestures at the wealth around them, 'this world, as you know. He fears that he is not good enough, not able to look after his wife like a husband should. This is all a great strain on him.'

Jameson, who is an inch shorter than Liz, removes his arm from hers and straightens his hat – he is a challenge to soften, she will give him that. 'Perhaps he is right, madam.'

'Perhaps. What I mean to say to you is that Tom only wishes to protect Mary, and he thinks a professional solution is best. I understand your own views, however. I applaud you for them, in fact. So we shall look after her here. I will make sure that Anne attends solely to Mary without any other distractions.'

The doctor inclines his head ever so slightly, and his words, when he next speaks, are not quite so clipped. 'Can you trust the maid?'

Liz hesitates. 'What do you mean?'

'Mrs Oliver has been hard on the girl. I believe you and your brother thought her too harsh at times. I have checked the laudanum bottle and the measurement is correct, I grant you, but the girl could be pouring it away.'

'You think Anne would do such a thing?'

'Jealousy is a serpent, madam. It sneaks inside a house and poisons it from within.' His eyes are dark and small as he squints at her. 'You may be surprised what young girls are capable of.'

She leans in so she can whisper, 'Thank you for the warning, Doctor. I shall keep an eye on her.'

A small smile puts dimples in his cheeks. She holds his gaze as he backs away, and as he turns to descend the steps, he glances back at Liz. She nods at him, and waves from the threshold as his carriage rolls away.

MOTHER HAS GONE. It is a miracle. No longer does Mary feel the room grow damp, hear the dripping, nor smell the boggy water clinging to her nostrils. She has peace, at last.

The nursery is brighter than her own darkened room. She blinks, and it takes a moment for her eyes to adapt before she sees Mrs Jeffries rising from her chair, smiling in alarm. Between them both is the cot where the child sleeps.

Mary treads carefully upon the floor. It has been years since she has been in this room, but she still remembers where the creaks lie, as she often snuck out while her governess dozed in the afternoons.

She reaches Little Tom's cot in silence and looks down upon him. With her mother gone, she no longer fears him quite so much, and discovers, to her amazement, that he is really rather beautiful. Tears fall down her face as she gazes at the boy she has chosen not to love, until now.

'Ma'am?' Jeffries whispers, and joins Mary's side, stepping

on a squeaking floorboard as she comes and waking the child. His forehead creases into little lines, he squints hard, his pink lips pucker, his hands twist into fists and punch the air, and then he begins to wail.

'Sorry, ma'am.' Jeffries bends over the cradle and lifts him free.

'I will take him.'

There is a moment of hesitation before Mrs Jeffries hands him over.

Mary has never held a baby before. He is much more substantial than she thought he would be. His limbs stretch and bend as he protests against being held so awkwardly. Mary giggles at his stubbornness, then gets a firm grasp of him so that his movements slow and his eyes open.

She sees him properly then. She sees the fullness of his lips and the darkness of his soft hair; she sees his father in him, and she forgets what her husband said to her before her confinement, she forgets the terror her son provoked in her, she forgets the horrors of pregnancy. She feels only love.

She stays with the child for an hour before she leaves to ready herself for dinner. She tells Jeffries that she will take her son down to dine tonight.

At seven o'clock, the dinner gong sounds and Jeffries waits outside Mary's bedroom with Thomas in his fine cotton and lace gown. Mary takes him in her arms and dismisses the nurse.

The drawing room door is open, and inside, Liz and Tom wait for Mary before they go to dinner. With her bonny son on her hip, she joins them. Her smile falters when she sees their expressions.

'Darling.' Tom jumps to his feet and rushes to her side, his hands out towards Little Tom. 'Are you all right?'

'I'm perfectly well.' She keeps hold of the baby as Tom tries to prise him away. Eventually, her husband lets go and meets her gaze. 'I wanted to do something to celebrate the occasion.'

'What occasion?'

'My recovery.'

'I see.' Tom nods, sniffs. 'Yes, well done, darling. You are much improved.' He moves back to his seat.

'Yes, I am.' Mary laughs into Little Thomas's face as he stares up at her, his mouth open and drooling. 'I don't know how I could have thought such dreadful things about Little Thomas, our gorgeous baby boy.' She kisses him on his button nose. 'Shall we go through to dinner?' Mary rallies the two of them, who seem stuck to their seats.

Little Thomas wriggles. Who knew something so small could be so strong?

'What do you want, little man?'

He is rocking back and forth, as if impatient. Turning, Mary finds Elizabeth has come behind them, and it is she who the child's eyes are fixed upon.

Elizabeth smiles, and the baby smiles back. He has not smiled for Mary yet.

'Hello, Little Tom.' Elizabeth touches his fist. He grabs her finger and pulls her closer.

Mary yanks his hand away from Elizabeth and ignores his cry. 'Come along now.'

THE PACKAGE WEIGHS heavily in Anne's arms as she rushes to her room. Flinging the door open, she curses at the mice who still pester her, and who now dash to their hiding places. She throws the package onto the bed. She shivers as she looks at it; it is impossibly imposing.

What can it be?

It is of great importance to the witch, that is certain. The hag had pushed it upon Anne, telling her what she must do with it and ignoring her questions. When Anne had refused, the witch had said it would cost her her family if she did not do as she was instructed. So, Anne took it, and now she stares at it, fearing that she has brought a piece of pure evil into Floreat.

She straightens herself out and washes her hands and face. She is a mess from the heathland, and her boots have let the wet in so that her toes are soggy. She brushes off the sprigs of dry gorse that cling to her skirts and wipes the mud from her heels. Her hair has come loose, and she attempts to fix it, but it is no use, her fingers are too stiff. She lets it tumble free, and it falls in thick red curls to her waist.

She slinks downstairs and leans over the bannister on the landing, listening. The Olivers are nearly finished with their dinner.

She returns to the package, unties the string, and unwraps the scrappy, brown paper. She smells the witch – that peculiar smell of earth and damp and dirt and smoke as if the fire that burned her has never left her. Then, a small hand appears, which is attached to an arm and a body and a head. A doll. It is dressed in rough grey clothes, and over its permanently opened eyes, the witch has pressed grass, to hide the blue that the artist had painted them originally. Its head is slightly cracked, and the skin has browned in areas. In its hand, is a tightly folded piece of paper.

The witch told her not to read the note, but Anne is desperate to know what it says. Hearing the witch in her ear – *I'll know if you read it* – Anne slips the paper free.

Trembling, she unfolds the note, but just as she is about to smooth out the final crease, a baby cries. In her fright, she believes it is the doll come alive with the witch's spirit, come to slit Anne's throat for disobedience, and she springs from the bed, letting the note fall from her fingers.

The doll is lifeless; it is Little Tom's cries that she hears permeating through the walls. But she does not open the note again. She folds it back into shape and, hoping she is not too late, creeps downstairs and peeps through the servant's door.

Jeffries scuttles from the stairs to the nursery with the child in her arms. The nursery door clicks shut. Now Anne must set the doll where the witch told her to before the rest of the Olivers make for bed.

With bare feet, she flits to Miss Oliver's chamber. The fire has been lit, but it is too high, and she thinks that Miss Oliver will be too warm in bed tonight. Then again, the doll may chill her to the bone.

With that thought, Anne places the doll in the centre of the bed just as the witch instructed, straightening its legs so that it sits upright and angling it so that it faces the door as if it is waiting for its mother to return.

We'll turn her mad, the witch had cackled, and Anne had smiled as well.

LATER, Anne goes straight to Mrs Oliver's room and prepares the laudanum. In a minute, her mistress enters.

It is hard to be in Mrs Oliver's company, brushing her hair as she simpers on and on about how much she loves her little boy and her little family, and how everything shall be right from now on. But for the first time ever, Mrs Oliver thanks Anne for her help, and so, it is with some sense of guilt that Anne hands over the cup of tea with the laudanum mixed into it, and watches as Mrs Oliver drinks it all.

'Sleep well, ma'am.'

On the landing, Anne listens for any disturbance coming from Miss Oliver's chamber. Just as she thinks there is nothing but silence, she detects the faint gulps and gasps of sobs.

She should relish the sound, but she cannot. It is all too much – what has she become? Despite how much she dislikes Miss Oliver and how much she thinks herself above the woman, Anne has brought evil into Floreat. She has conspired with a witch! What would her mother think of her if she knew the truth? Shame makes her eyes sting with tears.

'Anne?' Mr Oliver stands beside his bedroom door. His jacket has been removed, and his shirt sleeves are loose, the buttons about his neck and chest are undone. 'Are you all right?'

Anne snorts and wipes her wet face. She looks to the floor, the ceiling, her twisting hands, Mr Oliver's frown, Mr Oliver's naked collarbones. She can feel her cheeks burning.

'Come here.' He beckons her across the landing and stands aside so that she can enter his room. She follows his command without a word. The door remains ajar.

Inside, the air is still. Anne has never been in here before. She is keenly aware of the space between them; of the way his shoes have been kicked carelessly from his feet to lie crookedly at the foot of his chair; of his red silk robe hanging off the corner of the wardrobe; of the giant bed in the middle of the room and his pillow which she is sure holds the imprint of his head. It smells different than the mistress' bedrooms as well; there is less perfume here. Instead, there is the faint scent of beeswax, and an earthiness which she believes can only ever belong to a man.

'Why are you crying? Has Mary upset you?'

She turns towards him and finds he has come closer while she has been observing his chamber. Now, she can smell the brandy on his breath, see the dots of whiskers breaking over his chin which he will shave off come morning. She cannot lift her eyes to meet his, so she fixes her stare on the pulse that throbs in his neck.

'No, sir.'

'You can tell me anything, you know.'

The room feels as if it is drawing in, as if she is trapped between the vibrant tapestried walls and the hard body of her master. How can she tell him what troubles her? How can she tell him of the wicked deeds she has done? How can she tell him about the doll that has left his sister, his dear, dear sister, heartbroken?

'I ... I can't ...' She shakes her head and feels mucus drip from her nose. She wipes it away, embarrassed.

'Tell me.' He takes hold of her arms. His hands are hot through her dress. He steps closer again so that her forehead is parallel with his neck, her lips parallel to his chest. Her breathing quickens.

Mrs Oliver has had this, she thinks. Mrs Oliver has had Tom's bare flesh beside her, on top of her, between her. She has kissed his lips and felt his beautiful hair between her naked fingers.

Miss Oliver, too, has held him close and felt his brotherly love and protection.

And as quickly as it came, her guilt slips away.

'I was just upset, sir,' she says, attempting a smile. 'I am worried about Mrs Oliver. I think she is ill.'

'She seemed much better tonight.' Mr Oliver's voice is soft and low. No one can hear them.

'I think it might be another delusion. She is too happy. Sorry, sir, I hope you don't think me too ...'

'Not at all. You have no need to apologise. Mary's behaviour is certainly manic. We never know where we are with her, do we?' He sighs, and his breath blows the hair about her face. 'You are so good with Mary. I don't know what I would have done without you.'

Her face burns. He raises his fingers to stroke her fiery cheek.

He wants me, she suddenly thinks, and the air is snatched

from her lungs. All this time, and she was right! He has given her special treatment. He has trusted her above all others.

She can do nothing but feel his fingertips on her skin, as his eyes shine down upon her.

'You know,' he whispers, his lips just inches away from hers, 'I think you are right about Mary. And, when the time comes, you must state all of your fears, all of your concerns, to the doctor. It is the only way she will get the help she needs.'

There it is! The glint in his eye, the emphasis in his words – he wants his wife gone too! And still, his fingers linger on Anne's jawline.

'You must tell the doctor of the madness you have heard from Mary's lips. You must tell him how you fear for the safety of Little Tom. You wouldn't want any harm to come to him, would you?'

'No! I love him.' And she loves Mr Oliver too, but the words do not need to be spoken; they both understand her infatuation.

He smiles, and his thumb rolls down her neck. She dares not breathe. What would happen, she wonders, if Mrs Oliver were already gone? Would Mr Oliver's hands journey on? Would his lips meet hers?

'Then I need you to help me.'

She watches his lips form the words, and she nods. She has known all along that he has needed her, that the witch was wrong to say he did not love her.

'I know I can rely on you.' He kisses her forehead, and it is like his lips have branded her. 'No more tears, eh? I do not like to see you upset.'

'Yes, sir,' she whispers.

'That's better.'

He pats her arms, then the heat of him disappears as he steps back. The loss of him is overwhelming. Her fingers flutter, trying to reach for him, but she forces them to her side. He is only biding his time, she tells herself.

And so must she.

'Goodnight, sir.'

He opens the door for her, but does not step back to let her through easily. She must squeeze between him and the doorframe, and as she pushes past him, he breathes, 'Sleep well, Anne.'

CHAPTER 12

*M*arch 1870

SHE CAN SEE her bones now. She looks in the mirror and runs her fingers over her ribs. She never thought she would see her skin so taught, so transparent, as if the blood has been drained from her.

The thought of blood makes the saliva dribble from her mouth. Mary does not bother to reach for the bowl. Instead, she leaves a trail of vomit on her rug. Anne will have to clean it later.

She returns to her bed, which is damp and sour. Her skin screams as she crawls between the sheets. She lays her head on the pillow, and winces as her skull hits rock. Her stomach simmers, she clenches, then wrenches her legs out of bed once more and lunges for the pot, making it just in time.

It is the child making her like this. Her mother was right. He has come to kill her. His gummy grins and silly giggles sent poison out on the air, reeled her in, brought her closer to her doom. It was mere days after falling for him that she noticed a dizziness in her head, a creeping nausea in her stomach, the taste of blood in her mouth, though no wound could be found.

He will kill her if she lets him.

Her door creaks open. She curls into a ball and shrinks away from the light from the hallway. Anne comes to her and groans in disgust as she steps into Mary's vomit.

'I left the bowl here for you.'

The chill porcelain is pressed against Mary's arm. Mary slaps it away, making Anne drop the thing so that it shatters on the floor.

'Stupid bitch,' Mary says, though the words are lost in the chattering of her teeth.

'You haven't eaten your soup.'

'Don't want it.'

'You need to eat. You are nothing more than a skeleton.'

Mary grabs the girl's arm and pulls it before her. She scrapes her brittle fingernails across the top of the girl's hand until the skin peels back and blood seeps through. But Mary's strength is short lived. She has no stamina anymore.

'You are poisoning me.'

Anne pulls her hand free and sucks the wound, then disappears from the side of the bed. For a while, she is lost to Mary, but then she returns, and Mary can just make out the white cup she holds.

'Drink your tea, Mary.'

Mary burrows further down into her bed, but Anne drags the covers away.

'You must take your medicine.'

'Get away!' Mary pulls herself off the bed and falls onto the floor.

Anne is upon her in a moment, crushing her. The pain of skin against skin! The agony as Anne's weight bears down on her! She screams, and with her mouth open, Anne pours the cold tea inside her. She chokes, and the drink splutters out of her nose, stinging her raw flesh as it does so. She must swallow or drown. So she swallows, cringes at the bitterness, and crunches on some grains which litter her tongue, as hard as egg shells.

'Good.' Anne gets to her feet, sighs, and walks away.

'You ... you are evil.' Mary cowers on the floor beside her bed, feels death swimming down her throat.

Anne rolls her eyes before she leaves the room.

Mary stumbles to the door and locks it. She is safe. Now, no one can enter and drip poison into her mouth as she sleeps. No one can cut her feet so that the blood drains out of her.

She is so tired, so very, very tired. Her eyes are like boules rolling in dry earth. She rubs them, but then stops, imagining they may fall from their sockets if disturbed too much.

She curls onto her bed. She hopes that sleep will take her quickly, so the pain may be relieved. She hopes that she will have dreams instead of nightmares. She hopes that when she wakes, she will rise with ease and eat something.

The thought of food makes her stomach growl. A memory flashes in her mind, the memory of the night her virginity was taken from her, the night when Tom's body thrust against her and the seed of evil was spent inside her. The night when all of this began.

But the memory does not last long. The laudanum has found its way to her bloodstream. Her limbs float away from her body and dance in the air. She watches her feet tap, her legs and arms sway on the breeze, her torso twist to an unheard tune. The rhythms ease her mind until the fog descends, and she sleeps.

ANNE HAS WATCHED the sun set through the little cottage window until there is nothing but a black expanse dotted with diamonds of white stars.

Her mother is talking too much about nothing in particular while Anne nibbles at a leftover slice of cake from Paul's birthday. Paul has been wittering on about how he can scare crows with a single stare – he is convinced he has some godly power over the creatures. Mother tells him to be quiet about such superstitious nonsense.

She is eager to leave, for the conversation is dull, and Eddie and Paul's constant bickering is grinding on her nerves. She waits until the clock strikes seven, then makes her excuses.

Outside, she slips into her father's shed and, with her lamp, finds the arsenic. She refills her bottle with the fine powder and slips out into the night, over the heathland, towards Floreat.

The witch is in her usual place between a high clump of gorse and a glassy pool of stagnant water.

'Mary is mad.' Anne says before the witch has time to ask her usual questions. 'Elizabeth is ill. Tom is anxious.'

'How ill?'

'Elizabeth? Sickness, same as Mary. She's stayed in her bed these last few days.'

'Is it serious?'

Anne recalls Elizabeth's damp, grey skin, the way her teeth chattered, the foulness in the pot. 'I'm not sure.'

The witch sighs and shakes her head. 'Do you know anything? The baby is not ill, too?'

'Oh, no. He's very well. He gets stronger by the day.'

'And Tom?'

Anne cannot help the smile that steals over her face. 'He is in love with me.'

The witch waves her gloved hand across the air, tuts. 'Is he well? He has not fallen sick also?'

'No, he's fine.'

'And what does he plan to do about Mary?'

'He has found another doctor. A better one from Exeter. He says I must tell him how wicked she is to me.'

'And you are not wicked back?' The witch grins. 'You hope she will be taken away?'

'She is mad.'

'So you say.'

Anne kicks at the gorse bush and ruffles some animal that has taken shelter there. She hears the scurry of tiny feet as it runs away from her. 'I still have those damned mice. Just can't get rid of them. And I need more of the potion.'

'I have none left.'

'You must.' Anne's pulse is fast. 'I need it.' She has been slipping it into Tom's whiskey for weeks, and he has been growing closer to her by the day. She is sure he will not be able to control himself for much longer.

'I don't have any.' The witch walks away.

Anne has only drops of the potion left. She cannot lose Tom now, when she is so close to having all of him!

'I'll tell them if you don't give it to me.'

The witch stops.

'I'll tell them that you're spying on them. I'll tell them it was you who planted the doll. Miss Oliver hasn't been right since then. What did it mean to her?'

The witch does not respond.

'I'll tell them that you're living in the woods. You didn't know I knew that, did you?'

The witch turns on her. Anne's bluster blows away.

'You tell them, my dear.' The witch approaches Anne and caresses her face. 'You tell them all about me. What do you think they will do? They may hunt me down. I can go somewhere else – I move with the wind and the moon. But what do you think they will do to you? You have been meeting with me for months. It is you who planted the doll, not me. It is you who will have nowhere to go, no money to your name ... a fallen woman.'

'Tom wouldn't let that happen.'

'So he knows that you meet with me? He knows what you have done to Liz? He knows about the potion you have been giving him?'

Of course, he does not. Anne's fear must show in her face, and she tries to move away, but the witch grabs her loose hair and jerks her close enough so that Anne can smell the hag's rancid breath as she speaks.

'Do not threaten me, girl.'

Anne quakes, but dares not struggle.

'We can help each other, you and me. We want the same thing.' The witch drops Anne and retrieves a small bottle from somewhere inside her skirts. 'This is all I have left.'

Like a puppy, Anne waits for the potion to be transferred into her own bottle. 'Thank you.'

'You say Lizzie has been ... out of sorts. Where is the doll now?'

'I don't know. I never saw it again after that night.'

The witch smirks then vanishes into the blackness.

ANNE STRIDES through the back door of Floreat. She is keen to get to her room and smarten herself up in time to see to Mary and, then, after her goodnight kiss from Tom, she will go to the study and slip a few more drops of the potion into the full bottles of whiskey there. She is on the stairs when Will stops her.

'Had a nice night?'

'Yes.' Anne continues up the stairs, but Will clutches at her through the banister. She tugs her hand away.

'Sorry, just ... come down here for a minute, will you?'

Groaning and hiding her potion, she follows Will as he leads her into the kitchen. The place is unusually empty.

'Sit down.' Will gestures at the bench. 'How's your ma and da?'

'They're fine. What do you want, Will?'

Despite the coolness, Will's forehead has a sheen to it. Anne imagines it would be slippery if she put her fingers to it.

'I ... I was thinking.' He licks his thin lips. 'I am very fond of you, Anne, as I think you know. And I was thinking that we may start walking out together and that you might ... consider me ... that you might accept me ... that you might be my wife?'

He is met with silence. Anne does not know if she has heard him correctly, but his fiddling and his sweating indicate that he might, indeed, be asking her to marry him.

'No.'

His big brown eyes stare at her.

'No, Will. I will not be your wife. As I have said before, I am a lady's maid, and you are a hall boy.'

'I'm not. I'm not a hall boy anymore. Mr Oliver has promoted me. I'm a footman now.'

Why did Tom have to do that? Now she has no excuse. The truth must suffice. 'I said no, Will. I do not love you.'

'You could. Remember when we were little? We'd pretend to be husband and wife –'

'We were children.'

'You felt something for me then. You could feel something for me now ... in time, at least. Lots of marriages start like that. They grow into love. You could love me in time.'

'I could not love you, Will.' Anne stands to get away from

his clutching hands, but he follows her; it is like they are playing a game of cat and mouse around the kitchen table. 'I said no.'

'Please, Anne, just walk with me.'

'No.'

'I love you, Anne.'

'And I love someone else!'

Will stops. Anne catches her breath. They are standing at opposite ends of the table in the dim light of the moon.

'Who?'

'I can't tell you that.'

'Who is he?'

'Will.' Her warning tone quietens him.

He looks to his feet. His lips are even thinner now and have begun to wobble. She would not have the embarrassment of seeing him cry.

'Goodnight, Will.'

DOCTOR KERSHAW IS a rotund man who wears spectacles. His belly precedes him, and Tom likes the way the middle-aged man smiles, oblivious of Tom's history.

Doctor Jameson, on the other hand, is not enamoured with his peer, or rather, rival. How Tom had to stifle his sniggers as the waspy old crone dismounted from his horse beside an elegant Exeter carriage, his face puzzled, his frown deep. The introduction has been nothing less than glacial.

'On matters so delicate and so important, I feel it only right that I should seek a second medical opinion. I believe it is the scientific way?' Tom says.

'Quite right, Mr Oliver. We understand, don't we, Doctor Jameson? We are men of science, after all.'

Tom indicates that they should make their way upstairs.

177

He lets Doctor Kershaw into Mary's room while he remains on the landing with Anne and Jameson.

'I know what you are doing, Mr Oliver,' Jameson says while fiddling with his pocket watch.

Tom is acutely aware of Anne's gaze; he feels like a prize bull at an auction. Every now and again he looks back at her, sometimes grave and solemn, sometimes exasperated, sometimes he even gives her a little wink when he is sure Jameson is not looking. She likes that.

Finally, Doctor Kershaw returns, and Tom allows Jameson to see to Mary. Once Jameson has gone, Doctor Kershaw begins.

'Your wife is terribly ill, sir.' He dabs the sweat from his face with a clean handkerchief. 'I have to say,' he continues in hushed tones, 'I think it is appalling that you have had to endure this. She should have been hospitalised weeks ago, looking at the state of her.'

'Jameson has known her since childhood. I thought he would know what was best for her, but ...'

Kershaw touches Tom's arm in a small gesture of condolence.

'I should also like you to see Anne here. She is Mary's lady's maid. I'm afraid she's not had a very good time of it of late, have you, Anne?'

Anne's head is dipped low. Her hands are held neatly together, though they shake. She is on the brink of tears when she looks up. She plays her part well.

'Show the doctor what Mary has done to you.'

Anne removes her gloves so that Kershaw may inspect the deep gouges on the thin, pale flesh of her hand that are forming thick crusts of scabs. She undoes the first two buttons on her blouse to reveal a floret of dark purple bruising on her neck and jawline where Mary struck her with a cold fire-iron over a week ago.

'She's taken whole clumps of my hair out, sir. She's thrown things at me. I've had glass stuck in my skin from where it's shattered against me.'

Kershaw takes her hand to examine the wound, then gently tilts her head so he may see her bruises. 'You shall heal, but what a dreadful ordeal for you.'

Anne's tears trail down her cheeks. 'She talks so badly of the baby, sir. She talks about killing him! I am scared of her, sir.'

Doctor Kershaw clears his throat, nods, but purses his lips before he speaks.

'You may go now, Anne.' Tom squeezes her shoulder, and she runs away. 'You see what we have been living with, Doctor? What is wrong with my wife?'

With Anne gone, Kershaw begins.

'Firstly, I think she may be suffering from gastric fever. You must keep away from her to stop the spread. Then I suggest we get her moved as soon as possible. Her mind ...' Kershaw shakes his head. 'She is not only a risk to herself but to you, your sister, the staff, and, most importantly, your son. As the girl just said, she wants him dead. She was just talking about how I should go and kill him now!' The doctor's eyes bulge. 'She thought me an angel sent from God. She believes your son is the devil.'

Tom slides against the wall. 'How could I have let it get so bad?'

'Here, now, man, there's no need for that. You must not blame yourself.'

'Why do you think ...?'

'I understand there is a history?'

'Her grandfather. I don't know the whole story,' Tom says, 'but, it was thought that he took his own life by jumping from the cliffs. He had been the melancholy sort.'

'Yes. It can run in the blood, you see, and the tragedy of

179

Mary's mother can't have helped. Your wife has a weak disposition, Mr Oliver. The birth of your son has brought back unpleasant memories, feelings of guilt and shame that can take hold of a child when a parent dies.'

'I just can't understand Jameson. Her aunt told me he had once suggested she take rest in a suitable establishment, back when her father was alive. It was George who forbade it. Now, when she is most in need of that kind of help, Jameson has refused.'

'I shall call him out on it, Mr Oliver, don't you worry. Any doctor can see she should not be at home.'

Tom wipes his hand over his face, sighs. 'Thank you, Doctor Kershaw. Sometimes I felt like I was the one going mad.'

'Don't think such things. I will sort everything with Mary, and if Jameson denies what is clear to everyone with a brain, I shall send for a colleague of mine. We will have her taken care of in no time, and once the fever passes, we can address her habit as well.'

'Her habit?'

'The laudanum.' Kershaw rests his belly on the banister. He removes his glasses and cleans them with the same hand-kerchief that he used to wipe his face. 'That is a cruelty in itself. Many women must take the stuff, but then, you see, they cannot do without it. That can cause troubles like nothing else.'

'Should we stop her taking it?'

'Not yet. It would be too traumatic for her, and for you, sir. Many meek creatures turn into beasts if deprived of their habit, and Mrs Oliver is already ... strong-willed. Continue with it until we find her a place where she can recover properly.'

'And when do you think that will be?'

'I shall produce the certificate today. I should think she

could be out in a day or so. It is an extreme case.'

Tom smiles his thanks, weariness painted across his features.

'My sister is not well, either. Her stomach.'

Kershaw nods and makes his way towards Liz's room. He emerges only minutes later. 'Rest. She must rest. Keep her warm and give her plenty to drink. Again, you must keep your distance for your own sake.'

'Will she be all right?'

Doctor Kershaw sighs. 'She has the fever, Mr Oliver. We must pray for her and for your wife's recovery.'

Tom tries to swallow, but his mouth is dry. 'Thank you,' he whispers and manages to instruct Kershaw to go to the library where Chipman shall pour him a drink. The doctor accepts and hobbles down the stairs.

'I'll be with you shortly.'

Jameson has still not left Mary's room, and Tom is growing suspicious of him. The door is ajar, and Tom creeps towards it, his ear to the crack.

'Who? Who was it?' Jameson whispers.

'Red. Red ... Red.' Mary's throat is thick with tears and anger and confusion. 'They will kill me ... He will kill me.'

'Who was it you saw, Mary? Tell me. I am an angel, remember?'

Tom throws the door open to find the doctor leaning over Mary like a gargoyle on a church roof. 'Doctor. I think that is enough.'

Mary's face is contorted. There are dark circles under her eyes, and her skin is grey and wet. The room produces a stench something like sweat and blood and dried herbs.

'You shall come away now!'

Jameson marches from the room, then reels on Tom. 'How did she get that bad?'

'She has been worsening for days.'

'You should have called for me sooner.'

'And what? Have you insult me again? Have you tell me she will improve? Each time I have called you, you have done nothing!' Tom edges closer, his voice low. 'You should have taken her away months ago.'

'You would have liked that, wouldn't you?'

'That's it, isn't it?' Tom shakes his head. 'You have put my whole family in jeopardy because you cannot stand the fact that someone like me pays your wages.'

'It is you alone I cannot stand. You may have fooled everyone else, but I have seen what you have been doing from the start. You have never loved her. Why would you? You love only yourself. You brought me here, thinking I'd sign the papers and make your life easy. You knew I had advised on her incarceration before, and you thought you could make me do it again so that you could spend her money. Her father will be turning in his grave.'

Tom releases the tension in his jaw. There is no point in denying it anymore. Jameson is no longer needed. 'Will you provide your report or not?'

'I will not see her lose her fortune to scum like you.'

'Fine. Kershaw will help me instead.'

Jameson swallows. His breath rasps sharply. 'I will provide my report,' he growls, 'for I see I have no choice now. But I will visit her every week. I will ensure she has the best care possible, and I will do my damnedest to see that she comes home as soon as possible.'

Tom smiles. 'We both know, once she's in there, it is me who must sign her out.'

Jameson exhales, his face falls. He steps back. 'You are a clever man, Mr Oliver.'

Tom nods. 'Those years in Rugby looked like they paid off, eh?' He steps aside, gestures at the stairs. 'Don't let me keep you.'

CHAPTER 13

*H*er eyes open, take in the darkness, blink again. Eyelids as sharp as crushed glass over her eyeballs. Her tears swamp but do not soothe her. She feels the clumps of her own hair laced across the pillow as she rolls her head to one side, unable to lift it, unable to sit up, unable to stand, no matter how hard she might try.

Her body clenches involuntarily. Her muscles bunch, spasm. Her stomach heaves again, her arse pushes, but she is dried out.

The convulsion ends. She gasps, but the air does not come to her. And still, the sickness remains. Liquid swims in her mouth. Stale. Foul. The stench of her. God! She would shudder at the sight of herself if her mind were clear, but it is not. It is as if someone has taken hold of her brain and is squeezing it, crushing it into confusion, blinding her with agony.

Slow. She is slowing down. Every movement is hard.

She tries to breathe, but she has not the energy. Breathe ... breathe ... but what is the use? It will be better this way.

At the foot of the bed, a woman shines in pale pink skirts. She smiles, her chestnut eyes glow, she holds out her hand. Her flesh is warm and soft in Mary's palm and tightens in a reassuring grip.

'Mama.'

She closes her eyes. She is slipping away ... the pain and the fear are all slipping away.

CHAPTER 14

A red poker sears her insides. Vomit rushes up her raw throat, and as she spits it into the bowl, she sees spots of blood lying amidst the cloudy contents. Her head pounds with each pulse, but she must rise, she must make her feet move, for it is too quiet in the house and she must find out why.

She drags her naked toes across the rug. She stumbles but manages to steady herself by grabbing hold of her dressing table. The glass perfume bottles and pomade jars jingle, as she tries to straighten her spine.

It seems to take hours before she reaches the door handle. It is shockingly cold in her sweating palm. Squeezing with all her strength, she manages to turn it.

The air from the landing slams against her skin. The lamps dazzle and triple in her vision. In the distance, if she squints, she can make out a figure. She focuses on that as she walks, but the landing is so long! The forms are receding. Darkness is coming. Another heave wracks her body, and her legs collapse.

The figure swirls around her head, creating wafts of air.

Soft fabric catches against her cheek, and she imagines she is being stroked by birds, black, shiny birds, who have come to carry her away.

'Liz?'

The sound is sweet in her ear. She smiles. It is so long since she has heard that voice – what has kept him away?

A plump little face with cherub red lips and long dark lashes appears in her mind.

I'll always look after you, he whispers to her, his eyes startlingly green in the shadows, his podgy hand soft and outstretched for her. *Do you trust me?*

'Yes.'

Cries of anguish. She understands the tone but not the meaning.

Her tongue flicks across her lips, but they are as dry as stone. Then her head is lifted, cold is pressed against her, and water seeps into her mouth, catching on her tonsils and making her choke, making her eyes pop open in panic.

Tom kneels beside her. His hand is on the back of her thighs, the other underneath her armpit, strong and steady, as he has always been.

'We must get her back to bed.'

The pressure grows harder as he lifts her. Her feet dangle in mid-air, and her head flops back. She notices Anne then, the unusual blackness of her dress, too harsh against her white skin.

'What has happened?'

'Nothing, Liz. Don't worry about anything.' His words are gentle. It would be easy to follow his commands.

'Tell me.' But they carry her across the landing and into her bedroom without another word. 'Tom, tell me what has happened.'

He lays her on the bed. She tries to rise but his hand presses on her shoulder, too heavy to fight against.

'Stoke the fire, Anne, and help me wrap her up.'

'No!' Liz drags her body upright. 'You will tell me what has happened.'

Tom and Anne are silent. Liz does not like their joint conspiracy. Her stare never wavers; it breaks him.

He sits beside her and takes her hand. His eyes are dry, but there is something there that she has not seen often before. Fear.

'Mary is dead.'

She looks at his mouth, at his red lips, seeing a peel of dry skin that strikes her as odd and wondering if she has heard him correctly. Shaking her head, the room swirls. Sickness crawls up her throat. With effort, she forces it down.

'What?'

'Mary died. Sometime in the early hours, we think. It must have been. Anne put her to bed last night before she saw to you.'

Somewhere in the background, Anne sniffs, affecting tears.

'How?'

The Adam's apple in Tom's throat bobs up and down. His fingers wrap tightly around her own. 'She was sick. I think you should lie down, Liz. The doctor is on his way.'

'Mary is dead.' The words form stiffly on her tongue.

'Yes, Liz. She is gone. Are you all right?'

Does he mean about Mary? Does he mean about her illness?

'I should like to lie down.'

He lifts her ankles and places them under the sheets. She thought she was hot, but now she realises, as his heat touches her, that her skin is cold. On the other side of the bed, Anne raises the quilt to Liz's chin.

'Leave us.' Liz thinks she is not heard, for Anne continues to pester.

'Leave, Anne.' Tom says.

Liz catches Anne's wounded look before the girl exits. Tom tucks the quilt around Liz. She watches him fussing, feels his weight beside her, smells his freshness as it wafts from his clothes. It is a delight to have him all to herself again.

'When did you last visit me? I can't remember.'

'Last night, love.' He strokes her forehead. 'I thought you were better, but …'

'What did we do?'

'I read to you.' He gestures at the volume of Browning's poetry on her bedside table.

'My favourite.'

'I know.' He leans closer, his forehead creased. 'Oh, Liz! You look so … I thought you were recovering yesterday. I thought you were getting better. If I hadn't brought you here … Oh God! If anything happens to you –'

'I will be well, Tom.'

He gasps as he teeters on the brink of tears.

'Do you remember that day?' she whispers. 'I have been dreaming about it. The sky was so big! The gallery, the ices we ate, that secret little spot beside the Serpentine we found.'

'I remember.'

'Just you and me. It was so perfect.'

He nods. 'But then –'

'It doesn't matter what happened afterwards. It was a perfect day.'

'It was.'

She feels the sun on her now, warming her back, her pure, beautiful back. She smells the water, clean and mineral. She tastes sugar on her tongue, parts her sticky lips, remembers his kisses.

'Do you trust me?' she whispers.

He laughs softly. 'Always.'

His palm soothes her forehead, brushes her hair away.

'You should sleep now, love. You must get better. Then we can go to Venice.'

His warm, dry lips press against her cheek, next to her mouth. She closes her eyes. She can rest now that Tom is beside her.

CHAPTER 15

$\mathcal{T}$he house is in a state of panic. Liz is still bed-bound, still saying queer things, still sweating as if she is melting, fast. Chipman is useless. Mrs Beacham acts like nothing at all is wrong. Will has not spoken to her since she turned him down, and the twins do nothing but cry.

Only an hour ago, Anne was taken into Mr Chipman's parlour and sat amongst the silverware in the dim half-light. She was soon joined by Police Inspector Edwards. He is a large man, with an upturned, pointed nose and a thick, broad chin. It was clear he had not shaved that morning, and the stubble made him look grubby. Anne imagined wiping his face with a damp cloth, like her mother does with Eddie and Paul after they have eaten, as he sat opposite her, clasped his hands in front of himself, and began his questioning.

She answered him as thoroughly as she could. *Yes, Mr Oliver is – was – a doting husband. Yes, Mr Oliver was always kind to his wife. No, I never heard Mr Oliver speak harshly towards his wife. No, I was never suspicious of Mr Oliver with regards to his wife.*

Now, the ground squelches underneath her feet, and each

step makes the mud splat over her clothes, but she must hurry, for she does not know what else to do, or who else to turn to.

'Witch!' Anne shouts as she reaches the fringes of the woodland. 'Witch, where are you?'

She stumbles through the trees, passing the beech and the old oak and dipping them a curtsey as she goes. It is a habit formed in childhood – to forget would bring bad luck.

'Witch!' Her words ring about her, bouncing off bark. She continues her quest. She will cover every inch of this woodland if she must.

Suddenly, something has a hold of her ankle and yanks her hard. She falls, crashing roughly onto her hands and knees. Something in her wrist snaps and she cries with the pain.

'Be quiet!' The witch crawls on top of her and pins her to the ground.

The witch's palm crushes Anne's mouth. Anne cannot breathe. She wriggles and writhes, but the witch holds firm, taking no notice as she glances around the woodland.

'What is wrong with you?' The witch slaps Anne's face. 'Anyone could have heard you! Have you been followed?'

Anne sucks the air into her starved lungs and shakes her head as tears stream down her cheeks. 'Tom's been arrested.'

'What? Why?'

'Mary died.'

The witch heaves the girl up into a seated position and rests her against the tree trunk. Anne tries to compose herself.

It is the first time Anne has seen the witch in daylight. Her scars are not quite as gruesome without the silver sheen of the moonlight, and her eyes, which before had appeared black, are actually a rich dark brown, the whites of them clear and bright.

'How did she die?'

'Gastric fever. Although, Doctor Kershaw was on about her mind and the laudanum. She'd been ill for weeks. She wasn't eating. There was nothing left of her.'

'But they must think that Tom has something to do with it. Why else take him away?'

'I don't know.'

'It is common for men to kill their wives.'

'Tom would never kill her!'

'I know that.' She looks to the heavens. 'Perhaps they suspect poison. The effects of poisoning have been mistaken for gastric fever before.'

'He would not poison Mary!' Anne's chin begins to wobble. 'Oh God, what will they do to him?'

'Shut up, girl. You are making a fool of yourself.'

Anne snorts back her tears. Then, she thinks she has it. 'It is the doctor.'

'What do you mean?'

'I heard them only a few days ago. They'd fallen out. Doctor Jameson's never liked Tom. Who else would blame Tom for Mary's death?'

'You're sure?'

'It must be. No one else could ever think such a thing. There's no way Tom would ever hurt a hair on that ungrateful woman's head. He only wanted to help her.' If she tells herself that often enough, she will believe it.

The witch nods. 'He is too soft.' The witch looks into the distance.

Anne wipes her face with her handkerchief. The brown cotton comes away mottled black with tears. 'How do you know Tom, anyway? You've never told me.'

The witch's brown eyes slide sideways and fix on Anne. 'You are right. Tom is innocent.'

'But they have him locked up! They have the doctor's word.'

'They have the doctor's suspicions. It has not been proven. The body will be examined, tested for poison. There will be no proof. He will be released.'

Perhaps. Anne does not know how such things work – proof and evidence and post-mortems – but she must believe the witch. The alternative is too dreadful.

She rests her head against the tree trunk, sighs. How has everything gone so horribly wrong? She wishes she could stay like this, breathing in the cold air, letting it clear away the worry and fear, until all of this is over and Tom is back at Floreat.

'How is Lizzie?'

'Worse than we thought.'

'She shows the same symptoms as Mary?'

Anne nods. 'She's worse than ever today. I think it might be the shock of Mary that has done it.'

'It would be best if Lizzie had a swift death, don't you agree? It would be best to bring her suffering to an end sooner rather than later. Kinder.'

Anne doesn't know if death is ever kinder. 'Perhaps.'

'And with Tom out of the way ...'

Anne regards the witch. The woman is staring at her, eagerly, but Anne can't make sense of anything at the moment. 'I don't understand.'

'If she dies while Tom is locked up, surely that will prove his innocence?'

'How?'

The witch's jaw tenses. 'Mary and Lizzie have both suffered similarly. The bobbies think Tom poisoned Mary, but if Lizzie dies too, they will know he did not poison his sister, because he would not have had the opportunity. And what would be the point? Brothers do not murder sisters. If

Lizzie dies of gastric fever while Tom is away, they will know that Mary died of the fever also.'

Anne lets the concept float in her mind. 'I suppose.'

'For goodness sake, girl! Of course, I am right.'

'So?'

'You want to help Tom?'

'Yes, I love him.'

The witch leaps before her, grabs her shoulders, and shakes her. 'Do not say that. Don't you see that saying such stupid things will only make things worse?'

'How?'

'Christ! Never mind. Listen to me. If you want to help Tom, you must make sure that Lizzie does not wake in the morning.'

'You want me to kill her?'

'No.' She takes Anne's hands gently. 'She is already dead, my dear. You are just ending her suffering. And saving Tom.'

An amber leaf flutters from the sky and lands into a pile of other dead leaves at Anne's feet. She watches it for a moment, thinking. 'How?'

'Take the covers from her. Extinguish the fire. Open the windows. Give her no water. Tell everyone she is resting. If she is as ill as you say, she will not last long.'

Anne imagines it, and her flesh crawls. 'It is too cruel.'

'You have been cruel to her before.'

Anne flushes. 'This is too much. I can't.'

'Then, Tom will hang.'

Anne sobs into her handkerchief. She will not let them kill him.

'What if the police find me?'

'Why would they? No one wants to go into a sick room. Just do as I say, be quick about it, and if they do go into her room, deny you were ever there. Do you understand?'

Anne nods.

'Remember, Anne, no one can know that you and I have been meeting. It will be bad for you if they find out. Now go, before you are missed.'

Anne staggers to her feet and stumbles through the woodland. She will do as she is told, for what would be the point of life without Tom?

TOM IS in what constitutes a cell, out here in the country, and through the bars next to him is a drunk man, his face bloodied, his hands cut. Tom has not seen a drunkard for a long time. The old, familiar sight is comforting.

The weather outside rages. The station door keeps blowing open with each gust of wind, making Tom think that the Inspector has finally returned. Yet, it is not until many hours later, with Tom's backside stinging from the hard chair that Mr Edwards saunters into the station. His plain clothes are worn at the hems and elbows. It is as if he has a layer of dust upon him that he cannot shake off, yet he removes his bowler to reveal shiny brown hair slicked back carefully. He must be married, after all.

'Mr Oliver. Comfortable?'

'Not really, but I can't say I care much for myself while my sister lies ill at home and my wife has just died.'

'Yes, your wife's death.' Edwards unlocks the bars, brings a spare chair with him and sits opposite Tom. 'That is why you are here.'

'I thought as much.'

Inspector Edwards leans back, his hands linked before his soft belly. 'I will get to the point, Mr Oliver. It has come to our attention that you may have had some kind of involvement with your wife's death.'

'Come to your attention? How?' Tom is not shackled; they knew they would have no trouble from him. He folds his arms across his chest. 'Are you saying that Mary was murdered? She died of gastric fever.'

'We'll know once the coroner has done his job.'

An image of Mary, peculiarly thin, her naked body laid flat on a cold table, her bones protruding out from her skin as men ogle her, invades his mind. He wonders if she has been cleaned before the examination, or if she still smells? He wonders when they take their knives and cut through her chest if her tits will perk up at their touch.

'How was your marriage?'

'Good.'

'We have heard that Mary could be difficult at times.'

'Isn't every woman?'

Inspector Edwards laughs.

'Mary was high spirited. She could have moods. It must have also come to your attention that she was going to be put into an asylum? She required some rest.'

Mr Edwards nods.

'Mary was very ill. She could be hard to live with before Thomas was born, but afterwards, she worsened. She had notions that the child was going to kill her.'

'And did that concern you?'

'Of course, it concerned me, he is my son. We thought, at one point that she was recovering. She grew fond of the child and spent more time with him. She said how much she loved him.'

'What changed?'

Tom shrugs. The drunk next door snorts, turns over so he lies flat on his back, and returns to sleep.

'I don't know,' Tom says, and it is no lie. The workings of Mary's mind were always a mystery. Really, he didn't have to do much at all to turn her mad.

'One day she was fine with him, the next she didn't want

to see him again. She said he was trying to kill her, that he was making her ill.'

Edwards nods, waits a moment. Tom cannot read him – perhaps Tom is losing his touch? The thought unsettles him.

'I believe you counselled Doctor Jameson many times throughout your marriage?'

'I sought his professional advice. He had been Mary's doctor all her life. I thought he might provide a solution.'

'Solution?'

'She needed more help than I could give. Her tempers were violent. She often hit the staff, her lady's maid in particular.'

'I believe she attacked you also?'

'She tried. She could be strong when she wanted to be, but I managed to keep her at a distance when she became like that. I was never frightened of her if that is what you were wondering.'

Inspector Edwards rubs his hand over his shadowed chin. 'Doctor Jameson believes you were trying to get rid of your wife, sir.'

'We did not agree, the doctor and I. I was not trying to get rid of her, I was trying to help her. I didn't feel that I was ... capable of taking care of her.'

'Were you having an affair with Anne Witmore?'

Silence. The change in direction comes as a shock. The two men stare at each other.

So, Tom thinks, this is what this is all about.

'No.'

'Doctor Jameson informs me that when he recently examined your wife, she said that she saw ...' he rummages in his pocket and retrieves a small, scruffy notepad. The accusation is left hanging as he tries to find where he has written it down. '*Him and her. At night. Together. Red. Red. Red.* The doctor says that you heard her saying this when you came to collect him.'

Tom takes a moment. 'And this is supposed to mean I was sleeping with Anne?'

'Jameson says Mrs Oliver was very distressed. It was clear to him that *red* meant the colour of Anne's hair.'

'Yes, the doctor is fond of thinking he always knows everything. That is why I brought in Doctor Kershaw, for a second opinion on Mary. It seems I had left it too late, I should have called for Kershaw sooner.'

'Are you doubting Doctor Jameson's abilities as a doctor?'

'I believe he took a dislike to me, and now he is trying to accuse me of being unfaithful to my wife. I hasten to remind you, Inspector, that my wife was suffering from terrible delusions. I am sure you know that she thought Kershaw and Jameson were angels sent by God to kill my son.'

Mr Edwards is quiet.

'Or did Doctor Jameson fail to mention this to you?'

The silence is confirmation enough.

'I admit, I think perhaps that Anne – Miss Witmore – may have certain ... feelings for me.'

'What makes you say that?'

'I'm sure you know when a woman is admiring of you, Inspector. You can just tell, can't you?'

Edwards does not falter at Tom's charm. Tom checks himself – the inspector is used to dealing with liars, after all. He must be cleverer than that. He continues earnestly:

'I believe it is common for young maids to develop feelings for their masters. No one takes them seriously. Only last week, I promoted my hall boy to footman. He has a liking for the girl, you see, and I wished to improve his chances of wooing her.

'I employed Anne because she was recommended to me by my manservant and her mother had worked for the

Buchanan's when Victoria was alive. In truth, I felt rather sorry for the girl. And once Mary began beating her, I thought it would be damned shameful to fire her for no fault of her own.'

Mr Edwards nods but it is unclear whether he is satisfied with Tom's explanation. With some difficulty, for his jacket appears a little too tight, he pushes his notepad back into his pocket.

'Look, Inspector, if I might set your mind at ease so that I may be free to bury my wife in peace, Mary was due to be hospitalised by today at the latest. If, as Jameson believes, my sole aim was to get rid of my wife, she was already leaving. To be crass, I had no need to kill her.'

Mr Edwards swallows, nods, then rises.

'May I go now? I must get back to Liz. She has a fever also.'

'Not just yet, sir. We must ask for your patience until the cause of death is ascertained.'

CHAPTER 16

*A*nne scampers into the house. She does not stop to remove her cloak or change her boots. She makes sure her steps are light in the servant's passage and on the staircase.

She can hear them all about her. They are like her mice, those policemen, scurrying and scratching. She does not like them one bit.

She slides through the secret doorway onto the main landing. Little Tom's room is quiet. Her heart throbs for the child, whose world is in peril right now. She is doing this for him, as well.

She creeps over the carpet. Both Mary and Tom's chamber doors are ajar, and she can hear the opening and closing of drawers, the shifting of bedsheets, heavy footsteps over the floorboards.

She is getting closer to Liz's door now, and she prays that it is closed.

It is. The witch was right; the police would never risk a fever, even to find a killer.

SHE MUFFLES the handle with her cloak and slips inside. The room is sweaty, and urine and faeces lie in the slop bowl under the bed. The fire burns high, the curtains are drawn. Under the tight covers, Liz sleeps deeply. Her lips are rosy. Her pale lashes are thick and long against her porcelain cheeks. Her white-blonde hair is like spun silver upon the pillow. Even in sickness, she is beautiful.

Anne thinks of what lies beneath the sheets. She wishes she could wake Liz and ask about those scars, about why Liz has such moments of panic, about why Liz holds her stomach at times as if it has a knife stuck into it. She wishes she could ask Liz, but she cannot. If Liz were to open her eyes, Anne could never do what she is about to do. So, she lets Liz sleep.

The witch's words chant in Anne's mind. She whispers them under her breath as she quietly pulls the curtains back, pushes the windows wide, and douses the fire with the jug of water from the bedside table. She peels back Liz's bed covers. The gale from the open window catches on Liz's thin cotton nightgown and makes it quiver. Liz shivers, her teeth gently rattle. A soft moan escapes from her lips, but it is too quiet for anyone outside the chamber to hear.

Anne takes Liz's frigid hand. It is as light as a sparrow and just as bony. She remembers how things were when she first arrived. She recalls Liz saying she wished for them to be friends. She remembers how she used to relish the thought of spending idle afternoons with her favourite mistress.

In that moment, she wishes everything could go back to how it used to be. But that is impossible.

'I'm doing this for Tom and the baby. You'll understand.' A teardrop hits Liz's knuckle, and Anne quickly wipes it away. 'I'm sorry. For everything.' She places the hand back onto the bed. 'Goodbye, Miss Oliver.'

ANNE IS SNEAKING across the landing when she hears a door open.

'Excuse me!'

Anne turns, catching a glimpse of her red face in one of the mirrors as she does so. 'Yes, sir?'

The policeman is young, perhaps mid-twenties, and walks towards her with his nose in the air. 'I've been looking for the key to the desk in the study. I thought it might be in Mr Oliver's room, but I cannot find it. Do you have any idea where it might be?'

'No, sir. Sorry, sir.' Anne exhales the breath she has been holding as she turns to walk away.

'Just a moment. It's Miss Witmore, isn't it? Is everything all right?' He stands in front of her, blocking her exit through the concealed doorway.

'Yes, sir.'

'You seem upset.'

'Just about Mrs Oliver, sir.'

The boy looks down at her over his pig nose. 'What are you doing up here?'

'I ...' Anne clears her throat. 'I was going to clean Mrs Oliver's room, but I see that someone is in there.'

'You were going to clean the room in your cloak?'

Anne stares at herself. There is mud on her skirts and boots, and small twigs and leaves cling to her outdoor clothes.

She tries to smile. 'My head is all a muddle, today, sir. Forgive me. I will go and change.'

'You are filthy, Miss Witmore. Where have you been?'

'Nowhere.'

'You have been in the house all morning?'

'Yes.'

He sighs, and his sour breath blows against her face. 'You were perfectly well put together when Inspector

202

Edwards spoke to you. I will ask you again. Where have you been?'

Will the words come out of her mouth? They seem lodged in her throat, suffocating her. 'I just went for a walk.'

'In this weather?'

'I needed some air.'

'Where did you go?'

'I don't know. Just around the estate.'

He quietens for a moment, which only makes his stare more intense. She feels like a bug under a magnifying glass. 'May I go now?'

'Where did you walk, Miss Witmore?'

Anne sighs, almost sobbing. 'Around the estate.'

'Why?'

'Fresh air!' The answer feels feeble even to her own ears.

'Pickman?' he calls, and an even younger uniformed policeman pokes his head out from Mary's room. 'Get your coat.' He turns back to Anne. 'There is something you are not telling me, Miss Witmore. Don't go anywhere.'

THE MINUTES DRAG INTO HOURS. Every so often, the drunkard rallies, gets to his feet, drops down again, utters some form of abuse at no one in particular, and then falls asleep.

Tom stands. His muscles in his backside and legs are cramping. He paces his cell, rolling his head left to right, listening to his bones crack. He pulls on the bars to see if they might bend for him, when the station door opens and he drops his hands.

Inspector Edwards enters.

'May I go now?'

'Not just yet, sir.'

'Do you know what killed my wife?'

'We shall soon.'

203

Tom grabs at the bars, and his knuckles whiten. 'My sister is ill. I do not think you realise how ill she is.'

'Would you like me to call a doctor for you?'

'I would like,' he says between his teeth before steadying himself, 'to go home.'

The door to the station blows open. There is a moment of confusion as the door hits the wall, and the wind blows in a small tornado of leaves. Then, she appears.

It is all he can do to keep standing. He anchors himself to the iron bars for support.

She is between the arms of two uniformed boys, who do not seem strong enough to hold her writhing body for much longer.

'Sir,' one of them begins. 'We found her in the woods.'

'Could this be the woman your staff were telling us about?' The inspector says. 'The woman who scared your sister?'

Tom does not know if he can speak while she stands there, looking at him. 'Perhaps.' His voice is nothing more than a breath. 'I don't know. I never saw her.'

Mr Edwards sniffs. 'Take her next door. I shall be with you shortly.'

'Sir,' one of the constables holds out his hand, and the Inspector takes what dangles from it. 'Found this near her.'

Mr Edwards inspects a square piece of brown cotton. The young lad points at something in the corner of it, before Mr Edwards nods and slips it into his pocket, then follows the three of them out.

It is an agonisingly long time before anyone returns. The day has drifted into night. Tom's stomach growls, and his throat cracks with thirst.

Finally, Inspector Edwards storms back into the station

with a loop of keys in his hands. He opens the drunkard's cell, picks him up by the collar and drags him outside where he hurls him on the floor and shouts at him to think on his actions. He shuts the door on the startled man and comes to Tom, locking the cell behind him.

'Do you know that woman?'

'No. There is talk she is a witch. She came to the house once and scared my sister.'

'Does your sister know her?'

'She didn't say.'

Mr Edwards leans on his knees and rubs his eyes.

'Why did she come here?' Tom says.

'She says she is here to help you. Why would she say that, do you think?'

'I don't know.'

'She says she is your mother.'

It takes a moment before Tom can bark out his laughter. 'The woman is insane.'

'She's been living in the woods, we think, inside a dead tree. We think she might have a connection to the house. She knows a lot about you and about what happens at Floreat. She knows about your child.'

'Is she threatening us?'

'Is that woman your mother, Mr Oliver? Tell me the truth now.'

Tom wipes the back of his neck and rubs the moisture from it onto his trousers. 'My mother died before I ever knew her. We – Liz and I – were raised by our grandparents, Reverend and Mrs Oliver. I have my birth certificate at home somewhere, if you would like to see it?'

Inspector Edwards shakes his head.

'Bring her in,' Tom says.

'Excuse me?'

'I should like to see her.'

'Why?'

'I think I have the right, do I not, after all the trouble she has caused us?'

Reluctantly, Mr Edwards goes next door. When he returns, the witch is on his arm, handcuffed but calmer than before. He puts her into the cell where the drunkard had been.

'Tom.' The black hole of her mouth widens into a terrible smile. There are tears in her dark eyes.

'I do not know you.' He hopes his voice is cold, but the feeling of strangulation is so strong that his words are nothing more than a whisper.

'She says her name is Charlotte Carter. She says your name is Thomas Jacob Carter.'

'She is lying. My name is Thomas Oliver. I have the papers.'

'Tom.' She comes to the bars, and Tom edges as far away from her as he can.

'My mother is dead. She has been dead for many years.'

'Tom, please!'

'Why would a mother try to hurt the ones she is supposed to love, Mr Edwards? Why would a mother want to see her child unhappy? Why would a mother spy on her own flesh and blood? It makes no sense.'

'Tom, I love you.'

Tom flinches. 'I'm sorry, Inspector. This woman is clearly insane.'

'You fool!' She screams.

Inspector Edwards bangs the bars, scaring her away. 'That's enough of that.'

'She has mistaken me for someone else, it would seem.'

The door opens, and the young constable enters. 'Telegram for you, sir.'

Inspector Edwards takes the note. Tom waits for him to

say something as his eyes scan the paper, but he remains silent.

'What is it?'

'Arsenic.'

Tom is confused. 'What is arsenic?'

'Your wife. She died from arsenic poisoning.'

Tom's mouth drops.

'Mary was murdered, Mr Oliver.'

The cold from the open door bites at Tom's bare neck. Their eyes bore into him.

'I did not poison her, Inspector, I swear to you. I told you I had no need.'

'Anne.' The words echoes in the silence.

They turn to the lunatic in the next cell.

'It is Anne Witmore,' she says, stealing closer to the bars. 'I have been meeting with her in the woods. She is my spy. She has told me how much she hated Mary. She has often wished her dead in my presence. It is Anne, sir, not Tom.'

More silence. Tom cannot comprehend. How could Mary have been poisoned? How could Anne do such a thing? It is all lies, it must be lies! It was a fever, so Kershaw said, nothing but a fever … Then, his stomach plunges.

'Liz.'

When nobody responds, he leaps to his feet and shakes the bars. 'Let me out! Don't you see?' Tom grabs Inspector Edwards' jacket. 'Liz has been poisoned, can't you see, you fool? She is in danger! She is at Floreat with Anne. Anne is trying to kill her. I must get to her – I must save her. Let me out! She will die if I do not save her. Let me out now!'

Mr Edwards rushes the key into the lock. 'Put him in cuffs.'

Tom yanks his hands free. 'I am coming with you.'

'You will come with us, but you will be in cuffs until we can prove your innocence.'

Tom cannot risk any delay. He must get to Liz. The cuffs tighten around his wrists, and the men march for the door.

'Leave her, Tom!'

He does not look back at the woman in the cell.

'Tom, please! I love you.'

The station door slams shut as they climb into the cart and begin the grinding journey over the black heathland towards Floreat.

FLOREAT IS RUDELY AWAKENED as they storm into the house.

Tom hears nothing, sees nothing, feels nothing, as he takes the stairs three at a time, his cuffed hands swinging from side to side, his breath coming hard into his tight lungs. He is through Liz's bedroom door before the others have reached the landing.

The room is icy and dark. Liz's bed stinks from the vomit on the pillow and the diarrhoea on the sheet. She looks as if she has been caught in a downpour; her skin is as blanched as chalk and covered in sweat. Her face is contorted in agony as she shudders in nothing but her nightgown.

'Help me!'

He tries to talk to her, to get her to recognise him, as the others come into the room, gasping at the sight of her. The inspector pulls on the lever to summon help. All is panic and confusion as Liz is lifted between two constables and carried through the house. Inspector Edwards orders Cate to go with Liz to the hospital. Tom tries to follow as Liz is wrapped in heavy blankets and loaded onto the cart.

'You will stay here.' Mr Edwards rips him off the cart and shoves him to the floor.

'Liz!' The horse is whipped into a gallop. 'Liz, I love you! I'll be with you soon.'

They will not make it in time, Tom thinks. She shall die in

that filthy cart beside strangers. He lumbers to his feet and charges after the wagon. He will make it. He will be by her side; no one will stop him anymore. But then something smacks his legs from under him, his head smashes on the ground, and the cart vanishes.

When he regains consciousness, he is lying upon one of the sofas in the library. All is calm, and for a moment he forgets that any of this has happened. He thinks that Mary and Liz are reading in the drawing room, that Little Thomas is asleep in his nursery, that he himself has only the worry of choosing whether to drink whiskey or brandy tonight.

But he cannot fool himself for long.

Out in the hallway, the staff stand before the inspector, heads bowed, hands folded before themselves. All of them are present; all except one.

Tom watches from the doorway as Mr Edwards interrogates them.

'Where is she?'

The staff look sideways at each other.

'Where is she?'

'She said that Miss Oliver did not need her tonight, so she went,' Clair whispers, too scared to meet the inspector's glare.

'When was that?'

'I don't know. About four, maybe?'

'She was told to stay here. Where did she go?'

'She didn't say.'

'Where might she go? Think!' Mr Edwards' voice clatters in the quiet.

'She has nowhere else to go but home,' Chipman says.

The inspector nods as another constable, who Tom

vaguely recalls from earlier today, dashes down the stairs with something in his hands.

'Sir.' He breaks through the semi-circle of people and comes before his superior. 'I found these underneath her bed.'

The officer holds out two bottles. One is only a quarter filled with fine, white powder while the other is almost full of clear liquid.

'She's been laying it down for the mice. There's a few dead under the floorboards. Accounts for the smell.'

'Well done, Roberts. You shall stay here, continue searching. Look after Mr Oliver – he must stay inside. Ackley, come with me. And bring a lamp.'

'WHAT'S WRONG WITH YOU? You can't sit still,' Gwen says as she spreads a thin layer of dripping onto a slice of bread.

Anne nibbles at the grainy meal. The cottage is quiet for a change; the boys are worn out from their long day's work and have gone to their bed. Grace leans on the table, yawning. Da is smoking his pipe outside.

'You're white as a sheet.'

The dripping clings to the insides of her mouth. Her tongue runs over her gums, which feel coarse and tacky. She places the slice of bread back on the plate.

'You need to eat something.'

'I'm fine, Ma.'

Gwen leans across the knobbly table and strokes Anne's head. The action brings back a memory of the time when Gwen was recovering from her surgery. She had been sitting in the exact same place in front of the fire, propped up against the bare wall, a blanket wrapped around her leg, looking so small and frail and not at all like the mother Anne knew.

Anne had begun to cry, out of fear, out of worry, out of anger, out of uncertainty, and Gwen had leaned over, wincing from the pain of the movement, and had run her soft, warm hand over Anne's hair. It had been all that Anne had needed to stop her tears. This time, it brings tears to the fore.

'Oh, Ma!' She wishes she had better resolve, but she can't stop herself now.

Gwen sends Grace to bed and calls Anne to her. Anne falls into her mother's arms, her body wracked with sobs, her face buried deep into the nook of Gwen's collar bone.

'What's wrong, love? Please just tell me.'

She can't admit her sins to her mother. She can't accept her feelings of passion, of jealousy, of envy. She can't say what part she has played in the tragedies at Floreat.

Her father swings in through the back door. 'Someone's out there. I can hear them coming.'

Anne freezes. The warmth from her mother drains. She straightens.

They wait, all three of them, fixed in their places, barely breathing as they hear the cries of men coming closer. One voice is familiar. And then, just as she places it, Inspector Edwards barges through the front door and strides into the kitchen, the young constable with the pig-nose panting beside him.

'Anne Witmore. We need to talk to you.'

The severity of his stare causes her to bolt. It is her father who stops her, and makes Anne return to her chair. Inspector Edwards takes the only other available seat, leaving the constable and Anne's father to stand in the cramped space.

'The maid said you left Miss Oliver at four o'clock today because she had no need of you. Is that right?'

Anne nods.

'When we found her, she had no fire, no quilt, and the windows were open. Do you know anything about that?'

'She was fine when I left her.'

Mr Edwards rubs his chin. 'You were told to stay where you were.'

'I ... I just thought ...' What did she think? Nothing. Sheer panic had made her run to her mother, naively believing that no one would find her here.

'You have arsenic in your room.'

The change of subject confuses her for a moment. 'Yes. For the mice. I got it from Da.'

'Where were you this morning?'

'At Floreat.'

Her answer is met with a sigh. 'Do you know a woman who goes by the name of Charlotte Carter?'

'No, sir.'

'She might not have told you her name. Mr Oliver called her the witch.'

Anne's tongue almost slides down her throat.

'She has very distinct features. She was burned. You would know her if you saw her.'

'That was the woman you said you'd seen that time, way back. She'd scared Miss Oliver,' Gwen says, squeezing Anne's hand to encourage her to talk. 'But, she hasn't been seen for months. I thought she'd gone?'

'She's been living in the woods. We found her this afternoon. She's in the station now.'

Anne's saliva runs thinly round her mouth. She will be sick.

'She's been spying on the house. At least, she has had a spy in the house, perhaps acting on her behalf. We don't know yet. When Ackley, here, spoke to you before, Anne, your dress was muddy. You told him that you'd been walking around the estate, but you couldn't tell him where exactly. Did you go to the woods?'

Silence.

'It would be much easier if you would talk to me, Anne.' Inspector Edwards waits, but still, Anne says nothing. He takes something from his pocket.

'That's yours, Anne,' Gwen says. 'That's your hanky. Where ...?'

'In the woods, Mrs Witmore. Close to Charlotte Carter.'

'Anne?'

Anne cannot look at her mother. Her skirt is growing damp from her tears that drip upon it.

'We discovered these in your room as well.' The Inspector displays the two bottles. 'What are they?'

Anne swallows, curses herself for not finding a better hiding place. 'Arsenic. For the mice.'

'And this?' He holds up the clear liquid.

She tries to swallow again, but there's nothing there but her fat, greasy tongue.

'Is this from your father as well?'

'No,' her father says when she does not respond.

'I will ask you again, Miss Witmore. What is in this bottle?'

'It's just a potion!' she screams for she cannot bear the questions any longer. 'It's just a silly potion.'

'What kind of potion?'

Anne is sure her skin must be scarlet. 'A love potion.'

'For who?'

She can look nowhere but the floor as she answers. 'Mr Oliver.' She recoils as she hears the sharp intake of her mother's breath.

'Where did you get it from?'

She can't answer that. She glances at her father, who is as

rigid as the fire pokers which he stands beside. 'Da?' Her father does not look at her.

'Where did you get it from, Anne?' Mr Edwards says.

What is the point in pretending anymore? Everything has gone wrong. She has nothing left to lose. 'The witch.'

'So, you do know her. How?'

'She found me one night when I was walking back to Floreat.'

'What did she want from you?'

'Information. About what happened in the house.'

'Why?'

Anne shrugs.

'You did not ask?'

'Of course, I asked! But she … She scared me. She said she would do things if I did not do what she wanted. She is dangerous!'

Mr Edwards sighs, hands the bottle to Ackley, who sniffs the contents then puts the bottle to his lips and takes a sip. 'Gin.'

The shock dries her tears. 'What?' She thinks about all the effort she has gone to in order to get it, to slip it into Tom's drinks. And it was working! Tom was falling in love with her.

'Mrs Oliver has died from arsenic poisoning. Miss Oliver is also suffering. She has been taken to Exeter hospital.'

'It was gastric fever.'

'No, Anne. It was murder.'

It can't be. That was just a rumour, a lie made by the doctor so Tom would hang. Tom! She thinks of him locked away, terrified. He cannot die. The thought is unbearable.

'Miss Carter – the witch – says you poisoned them.'

The breath is knocked from her lungs as his words echo in her mind.

'We understand you had a difficult relationship with Mrs Oliver. And you are in love with her husband. Will Chipman told us you rejected him because you hoped to marry Mr Oliver one day. How did you think you could marry Mr Oliver when he already had a wife?'

The question lingers in the air.

Suddenly, her father slams his fist into the fire-irons, and they crash on the stone floor. 'This is all his fault! It is him you should be questioning, not Anne. She is only young and foolish. It is him who is in the wrong here. I have seen how he is with women. He is a snake!'

Mr Edwards holds up his hands to stop the tirade.

'Exactly what I thought, Mr Witmore, which is why I have had him in the cells all day. But I have a problem now. Miss Oliver has also been poisoned. By all accounts, Mr Oliver loves her dearly. So, tell me why he would poison his own sister?'

'I didn't kill Mary,' Anne whispers. It is all she can manage to choke out.

'You liked Miss Oliver at first, didn't you, Anne? I believe she gave you gifts, nice dresses, that sort of thing. What happened? Will tells me you grew distant from her. You were not as kind about her as you once were. Did she snub you? Was it jealousy? Did she discover your feelings for her brother? Did she anger you?'

'I did not poison Miss Oliver!'

'And then there's the baby. You are very fond of the baby, aren't you? Did you think you might be a mother to it once Mary had gone?'

'No! Please, Ma, Da, I did not! I did not kill Mrs Oliver! You must believe me!'

Mr Edwards sighs. 'The problem is, Anne, you have done nothing but lie to us all day.'

CHAPTER 17

pril 1870

THE COFFIN'S polished lid shimmers in the last few rays of sunlight before it descends into the shadows. As it goes, a breath escapes from the congregation, and it is like the ocean sighing.

Reverend Carey begins the committal, but Tom doesn't listen to the words. His concentration is upon the bare earth, the ground that has been cut through with a shovel, dissected, left naked, open and exposed. He notices some worms and imagines that, soon, those little pink strings of flesh shall be feasting on Mary's body.

Aunt Emily is the first to take a handful of earth and toss it upon the coffin. She says nothing as she does so, keeping her features controlled and neutral. She seems smaller than she was all those months ago, her shoulders crowded in against her chest, her face bent to the floor. It will not be long before she too is food for the worms.

It is Tom's turn next. He takes some earth and is surprised at just how cold and damp it is as he stares at it in his hands. Everyone lets him take his time. No one coughs or sighs or tuts or asks him if he is well. He can do as he pleases.

He throws the dirt, watches it cascade down, and smiles. He retrieves the book from his coat pocket. 'Liz wanted you to have this.' He drops *Ruth* upon the coffin lid. 'It was her favourite,' he tells the congregation, who cringe at the hollow thud.

As they stroll back to Floreat, Tom hears Doctor Kershaw whisper to the Reverend that Jameson is no longer practicing.

'To think this could all have been avoided. He is a disgrace to the medical profession, Mr Carey. A disgrace.'

Tom wishes he'd insisted on taking the carriage with Aunt Emily, so he would not have to hear these snippets of conversations, but Emily was too stubborn. She'd wished to experience the estate how she used to when she was a little girl, on foot, with the ground crunching beneath her feet and the sun warming her face. At least the fresh, open air serves as a reminder of his freedom, he reasons with himself, which was so recently threatened.

'I never liked her.' Aunt Emily has hold of Tom's arm, and her movements are jerky, as if the floor is uneven, although it is perfectly flat. 'I'm not sure I even loved her.'

Tom could say something, but he doesn't. Aunt Emily does not need sympathy; she just needs to be heard.

'I could never take to her, even as a babe. I think she reminded me too much of my father.' She inhales deeply, shaking with the effort.

'Should you like a rest?'

217

'Pah!' She swats her free arm at him. 'I am perfectly fine. How is Elizabeth?'

Tom welcomes the change of topic. 'She is recovering well. We got to her just in time. Any longer and I ...' He regains himself. 'It seems she did not have as much in her system as Mary. She should be home soon.'

'And the murderess?'

Tom clears his throat. He hopes the staff cannot hear their conversation. 'Awaiting trial. I imagine she will be hanged.'

Emily nods. 'I may never have liked my niece but to be murdered by one's own maid.' Tom feels her shudder. 'It is the devil's work.'

'It was in the laudanum,' Tom says when the silence becomes uncomfortable. 'That's how she was poisoning Mary. She mixed it in and poured it into her tea at night. She thought no one would suspect.'

'And Elizabeth? She wasn't also taking ...?'

'Oh, no.' Tom pulls his top hat lower to shield his eyes from the sun. 'We don't really know. Perhaps sprinkling it on her food. Liz never ate that much, though.'

They reach Floreat. Emily stops before the open front door and peers at the inscribed letters. For the first time, there is a faint mist in her eyes. 'What a ridiculous name for it.'

CHAPTER 18

*M*ay 1870

LITTLE TOM WRIGGLES as he lies in the middle of Liz's bed. He spurts dribbly laughter as she tickles his nose with the fur shawl that Tom bought her for the journey home from the hospital, although now the weather has changed and it is a hot spring day.

The doorknob twists. Tom enters, peering through first to check if Liz is sleeping or awake. When he sees her and the child playing, he strides over to them, kisses them both, and lies beside them.

'He has a tooth coming through.' Liz moves the silk handkerchief which Little Tom is sucking on so that his father might see the white edge peeking out amidst scarlet gums.

'And no tears? You are a brave boy.' Tom tickles his son's neck, then turns to Liz, suddenly serious. 'I have news.'

She stills. It has been such a long wait. She has tried to keep her mind occupied, but her thoughts keep slipping back to Anne. Her nightmares are filled with the girl crawling out of gaol and over the heathland, back to Floreat, to wreak her revenge.

'She has been found guilty.'

The breath rushes out of Liz's lungs. She collapses onto the bed. Her limbs are numb. She thinks she might cry or laugh, but she does neither.

'She will be hanged, as we thought.' Tom rolls over, props himself onto his elbow, and strokes her hair.

Liz closes her eyes. The image of Anne dangling from the rope fills her mind. Will Anne's fiery red curls break free of her white cap when she is dropped? Will they tumble over the rope and down her back, blowing in the wind, making it look as if she is still alive? Will Gwen weep? Will Mr Witmore despair? Will Anne look to her mother in her last seconds, or will she look to God?

'You know, I never ...' he begins, then coughs. 'I never encouraged her.'

Liz smiles. She knows exactly what he did and did not do.

'I never liked her ... in that way. She was just here to serve a purpose.'

'I know.'

'I never slept with her.'

'You don't have to tell me.' She smooths the frown off his forehead.

'You know me better than I know myself.'

'I always have.'

'I'm so sorry, Liz. It's all my fault. It was all my idea – Mary, this place, Anne. If I'd have lost you ... if she'd ...'

'Hush.' She presses her finger against his lips. 'You will never lose me.'

She looks deeply into his eyes, and he nods as his son begins to cry. She sits up and scoops the child into her arms.

'What is wrong little man? What are you crying for? You have nothing to cry about now.'

Little Tom's face is red and lined as he pushes his fist into his mouth.

'Shall I call for Jeffries?'

'No.' Liz stands and rocks the child on her hip. She goes to her dressing table, picks up the hairbrush, and puts the ivory handle to his mouth. He bites on it hard, and the tears subside. She turns to Tom with a smile as he saunters towards her.

'You are extraordinary,' he says against her neck, but then wipes away the bead of sweat that she has felt trickling from her hairline.

'You need rest, love.' He takes the child from her, and she lets him go without a fuss, for she will have plenty of time with him soon enough.

Tom guides her back to bed. 'Sleep now. And dream of Venice.'

Her eyes close as he kisses her forehead. 'When?'

'Soon, my love.'

A BITTER WIND trickles through every crack, every layer of brickwork, every window ledge, engulfing everything in a miserable chill. Anne cannot feel her extremities.

She had taken to pacing her cell to try to ignite some warmth in her body but found the exercise fruitless. It served only to remind her of how she will soon be forever cold, for the blood in her veins will have ceased to flow and her heart, which she has always imagined as a kind of pulsating fire within her body, will have been extinguished.

She had grown hysterical when she had found out what was to become of her. She had not been able to stop scream-ing. Somewhere, in the back of her mind, she had remembered rumours about people getting away with murder on the grounds of insanity. They had been locked up, yes, but they had not been executed. Perhaps it was this thought that had made her so wild, that had made her bite the guards, that had made her piss herself. Maybe it had been a calculated effort of self-preservation. Perhaps it had been just sheer terror.

Either way, it had not worked.

When she had discovered that the witch had walked free, her fear had turned to rage. The witch had given evidence against Anne. She had told the police that Anne had ideas above her station, that she resented the ladies of the house and was determined to marry Mr Oliver at whatever cost. She had said Anne was willing to use potions and poisons to get her way.

Her mother had told Anne, on her one and only visit, that the witch had been released. She had been a nuisance but nothing more; just some old hag with fanciful notions about having a son in a grand home. Wrong in the mind, but seemingly harmless. After all, her potions had been nothing more than alcohol. It was Anne who had administered the arsenic.

Now, something white is pushed through the bottom of her cell door. It scratches over the grit and muck, and she tiptoes towards it as if it might come alive and lunge at her, but on closer inspection, she sees it is only a letter with her name upon it.

The paper is deliciously smooth between her fingers. Nothing is soft in here; the floors, the walls, the bed, the clothes, are all as coarse as sand. She rubs the paper over her face, breathing in the scent, and smiles. It is from Tom – she would know that smell anywhere. It is his study. It is his papers, his books, his whiskey – it is him.

She could cry for the pretty way in which his hand has made out the letters of her name, as if he could caress her through the medium of the quill. She lifts the paper free from its red wax seal and unfolds it, her stomach flipping with excitement.

There is just one line of writing and an ink drawing of a butterfly in the top right-hand corner. The words are faint. She goes to the small, barred window to catch the last of the daylight.

She wishes she had not. If she could only un-see the words on the page.

The letter is not from the man she loves. The words do not warm her heart. Indeed, she thinks the message may have rendered the hangman's job futile.

Five little words. No one would suspect a thing. But Anne knows what they mean.

She screams. She shakes. She trembles as tears splat onto the stone floor. No one comes. No one cares about those five little words on the paper.

MAY GOD SAVE YOU.

LIZZIE

CHAPTER 19

une 1870

TOM WALKS between the feathery heathers, the orchids he has never bothered to learn the names of, the birds that dart away from his stride. He takes it all in, smiling at nothing in particular, enjoying the simple pleasures of unfamiliar bird-song, hot summer sunshine, and the adventures ahead.

Indeed, he is not in the best frame of mind for what he is about to do. It would have been better if the day had been damp and grey, cloying and oppressing, rather than azure-skied and tranquil. He should look tired, drained, sorry, rather than healthy and carefree.

Never mind, he tells himself. After all, it is not him who should be sorry.

The village is lively on this glorious day. Less than a week ago, the villagers had held a summer fair, with beer, and dancing, and singing, and games where young boys wrestled on a makeshift stage. Tom had contributed one of his own favourite bottles of brandy to a prize draw, and his gesture had been well received. He had done it as a kind of tester, to see whose side the villagers were on. He'd had nothing to worry about.

The cottage at the edge of the village is quiet and still. He knocks on the door. It takes a while until he hears footsteps. Perhaps the person is deciding whether to open the door or not. Maybe they have been suffering abuse.

His breath is caught when Anne opens the door, staring at him with those pale blue eyes of hers amidst a freckled face.

But no, it is not Anne. It is Grace. Anne is dead.

'Is your mother in?'

Grace nods, seeming not to notice his shock at seeing her, and lets him enter. She closes the door after him.

Gwen sits in her usual chair, but the fire is not burning, and the place is bare of all its knick-knacks. She gasps when she sees him, and wipes away the tears that Tom imagines have not left her cheeks since Anne's arrest.

'Mr Oliver.' She smiles with difficulty. 'I must apologise for the state of us here.'

'You have nothing to apologise for, Gwen.' His voice is too loud, too energetic in the space. 'I have come to see how you are all ... coping?'

'We are as best as we can be.'

'And the villagers? I hope no one is treating you unkindly?'

Gwen shakes her head. 'We are treated well, sir. I am afraid I cannot offer you anything to drink. We have everything packed on the cart now.'

They are moving, but he does not know where they are going. He will not ask. He retrieves the letter from his pocket and places it on the empty table, red wax-seal bright in the gloom. 'A letter of recommendation for you all.'

Gwen wipes her nose on her handkerchief. 'That is awfully kind of you, sir.'

Tom shrugs. Indeed, it is kind of him – too kind after what their daughter has done to Liz. But in the pit of his stomach, he knows he is not innocent in all of this. He moulded Anne, after all. He just never knew what exactly he was moulding her into.

'May I ask, how is Miss Oliver?' Gwen says.

'She is much better now, thank you. She wishes you all the best for the ... future. She is sorry for what has happened.'

Gwen laughs, though it is short and mirthless. 'She has no need to apologise. It is us ... It is ...' but she cannot finish her sentence.

Grace coughs at her mother. Gwen looks up with wide eyes, but she is too late. Mr Witmore looms in the doorway.

'Mr Oliver has come to give us this.' Gwen grits her teeth in a smile. 'A letter of recommendation for us. That's kind of him, isn't it, John?'

Mr Witmore says nothing.

'Right.' Tom rubs his hands together. 'I should leave you in peace.'

'Why did you have to come?' Mr Witmore's voice is soft. It does not match his expression. 'Why did you have to come to us? Why did you have to choose her?'

'John.' Gwen sounds weary as if she has heard her husband speak of these matters too many times already.

'Out of all the other girls you could have chosen, why her? She had no experience for Christ's sake!'

'John! Don't say such things.'

'Do you think I believe in God anymore?' Mr Witmore laughs. 'When a devil stands in my house.'

'I am sorry.' Tom bows his head and attempts to leave, but as he does so, Mr Witmore pins him against the wall.

'You have killed her!' He cries, and tears surge down his

ruddy cheeks and into his stubble. 'It should be you in that noose. It should be you swinging. You have killed my little girl!'

Tom shoves Mr Witmore against the opposite wall. 'Your daughter tried to kill Liz. Do not forget it!'

Mr Witmore crumbles under Tom, his strength dissolved. 'Do you think I ever will?'

Tom lets go of the man, takes a breath, and straightens his hat.

'Get out,' Mr Witmore whispers.

Tom does not object. He does not look back at the agony that lies behind him. He shuts the door and tries to smile at the villagers whom he passes as he makes his way back to Floreat, forcing Mr Witmore's words out of his head.

THE HOUSE IS a gallery of ghosts. Every item of large furniture is draped with white sheets. Every small thing has been packaged up and moved to the lumber room. Liz doesn't like the feel of the place. It is like the eyes of the portraits and the animals are looking at her through the holes in their coverings as she wanders, alone.

Tom left a while ago. She couldn't understand why he should want to see the Witmores after everything that has happened. She knows he will get a cold reception. She is worried in case Mr Witmore is too harsh, in case Mrs Witmore's apologies are too strong, in case they will persuade him of Anne's innocence.

She sneezes. In all the upheaval, the dust has been disturbed, and fine particles of it dance in the sunlight and tickle her nose. She needs some air.

She summons Will and orders him to ready her pony.

THE LITTLE WHITE pony is pristine and pompous, as she always has been. Liz strokes her velvet muzzle as she chomps on a carrot before mounting.

'Shall you be all right, miss?' Will says as he helps Liz into the saddle. 'Would you like someone to accompany you?'

She gazes down at the young lad, just a few inches below her while she sits on the pony. His face is so open, so innocent, so concerned. These last weeks have been dreadful for him, and tears still wet his eyes even now – he has blamed himself for Anne's execution, so Mrs Beacham has told her.

'You are a good boy, Will.'

She gestures for him to come closer and kisses him on the cheek. She feels his blush through her lips, and so that she does not embarrass him further, she taps the pony's flanks and trots away.

The breeze is like angels' wings stroking her face, freeing her hair into loose curls that ripple over her shoulders. She enjoys the movement in her hips, the grip of the reins in her hands, the jolt of her body as the pony's hooves hit the ground.

She grins at the vast sky before her as the trot turns into an easy gallop over the lawn and out towards the sea. She does not know where she and the pony are heading. She lets the little creature decide their destination for them both.

The pony makes for the sea. Soon, the vast expanse of water dominates their view. She will have to pull on the reins, come to a halt, and turn the animal around, but as her fingers tighten on the leather, the pony rears up on its haunches and throws her from the saddle. The view of the sea slides out of her vision, and she crashes into the earth.

She tries to lift her head but winces as pain shoots above her right eye. She raises her hand to the spot and finds blood there. Rolling onto her hands and knees as best she can, she forces air into her lungs and blinks away the black dots that swim in her vision. She can just make out the diminishing figure of her pony cantering away in the distance before she hears that dreadful sound – the puffing laughter she has always despised.

'I hear you are leaving. Going to Venice. How nice that will be for you both.'

Liz gathers her skirts and, groaning with the effort, rises to her feet, although the ground does not feel as sturdy as the last time she stood upon it. 'You were told to stay away, Charlotte.'

'You cannot keep me from him.'

'He doesn't want you.' How many times must the woman be told? Honestly, it is pitiful.

Charlotte casts her gaze out upon the sea. Liz can get a real look at her now. How she has changed! No one would recognise her from the beauty that she used to be.

'I won't let you take him from me.' The words are so softly spoken that Liz takes a moment to understand them.

'You lost him the first moment he saw me.'

Charlotte bares her teeth. Her black hair flies back as she lunges at Liz's neck and tackles her to the ground. Her legs straddle Liz's bodice as her hands tighten around Liz's throat.

For a moment, Liz has the image of Anne in her mind again. The thick, heavy rope secure around Anne's white neck, her red curls blowing in the breeze, her feet dangling above the ground. For a moment, Liz is just like Anne. They share the same fate. It is fitting, after all. It is justice.

The image fades, and Charlotte's puce face comes back to the fore. Liz's hands, which have been uselessly pulling on Charlotte's wrists to try to free herself, now fall away. Charlotte's strength intensifies, but Liz still has fight within her.

She remembers Tom teaching her how to punch when she was eleven years old. He had told her about a dirty trick

229

of raising one knuckle to target the softest, weakest part of the opponent. A skill he had learnt at school, out of necessity.

With his words in her ear, she punches Charlotte, pushing her knuckle into one soft eye socket, and the woman stumbles back, screaming. The diamond ring has helped, for when Charlotte looks up, Liz can see her face is cut and bleeding.

The two of them gather themselves. Liz rolls onto her front, choking down fresh air, while Charlotte staggers to her feet, swaying with the effort.

Charlotte pants for breath. 'I will kill you.' Again, she lunges, but her movements are too predictable and clumsy now, and Liz dodges her as she flounders to the ground.

'Anne should have finished you.'

'Anne?' Liz laughs. 'Come Charlotte, you do not believe that Anne could have killed anyone, do you?'

Charlotte drags herself up and spits at the floor. 'Mary.'

Liz sighs, shakes her head, looks at the blue above. It really is a beautiful day. She smiles. 'And you always thought I was the stupid one.'

'What do you mean?' Realisation dawns on Charlotte's face. 'You poisoned Mary? You poisoned yourself? You are not capable.'

'You have no idea what I am capable of.'

Charlotte reels, horrified. 'Anne hanged.'

'You helped to put the noose around her neck. I must thank you, I suppose – the blame is not all mine. Why would you care for her anyway?' Liz steps closer to Charlotte, who steps back in turn. 'You have never cared about what you have done to people before.'

'You are evil.'

'I am what you made me!' Liz erupts. Her words bounce back at her from the cliffs just feet away. The sea crashes upon the rocks below for the tide is coming in.

Charlotte glances in the direction of Floreat. 'Tom will know what you are.' She picks up her skirts and begins to run, but Liz catches her hair and tugs her back.

'You think he will care?' she whispers into Charlotte's ear. 'He has seen me fuck the men you brought to me. He has seen me as nothing but skin and bone and dirt after you sent me to the workhouse. I have birthed a stranger's child, and still, after all that, he loves me more than he's ever loved you. Don't you understand, Charlotte? Everything you have done to hurt us, to separate us, has only brought us together.'

'He does not know you are a murderer.'

'He has thought me a murderer since the day you and your house went up in flames.'

Charlotte turns to her slowly. 'You did this to me?'

Liz holds her stare. 'You did this to yourself.'

'You are a devil!'

Liz nods, for Charlotte is right. She was lost to the darkness years ago.

'You know, I almost ended it. Tom was at work. I'd been on my own for so long … The baby was all I could think about. I had a knife on my wrist.' She recalls the whiteness of her skin, the thick blue vein pulsing, the slice which brought a pool of scarlet to the surface.

'What stopped you?'

Liz sees the blade fall to the filthy floor of their rented room, a drop of blood splattering beside it. 'I saw you from the window, your black shadow lurking, as always. I promised myself at that moment, I wouldn't let you win.'

The sound of the sea roars between them. Charlotte whitens, anger flaring in her eyes as Liz smiles calmly.

'And I kept my promise.'

Charlotte snarls, her voice thrashes out of her. 'I will always haunt you, Lizzie! As will they. You think about them at night, don't you?' A smile splits her face into monstrous shadows. 'What they did to you – what I made them do to you?'

'Be quiet, Charlotte.'

'And the baby.' Charlotte puckers her lips, tuts. 'Still, better dead than to have a mother like you.'

Liz takes it like a thump to the guts. She will not cry. She chews the side of her tongue, welcomes the pain as a distraction, but it is too late. A tear falls.

'Did you really think getting rid of Mary and Anne would help you forget? You are cursed, Lizzie.'

Liz's throat is strangled. She must clear it before she can speak again. 'Perhaps.' She snatches the tear from her cheek, lifts her chin. 'But I will have the only thing you have ever loved.'

Liz grabs Charlotte's blouse, and pulls hard. The material rips at the seams as Charlotte shrieks, but Liz has stable footing and rage has given her strength.

'I will have your son.'

Liz heaves Charlotte to the cliff edge and then, with all her power, shoves Charlotte's chest. The woman tumbles towards the sea, her skirts fluttering around her like a black butterfly, until her body breaks on the rocks below.

Liz hears nothing but the pounding of her pulse as she stares at the scene. Charlotte's arms are at odd angles. Her gown has risen to reveal two thin legs, one broken, the white bone splintering up through a mass of red flesh. Blood oozes from her mouth, nostrils, and eyes. For a few seconds, her body twitches as the water washes over it. Then it stops and is still.

TOM FINDS Mrs Beacham and the twins busy preparing lunch in the kitchen as he comes through the back door. He watches them for as long as he can without being noticed. It soothes his nerves seeing a hive of women busy at work, but then Mrs Beacham discovers him and puts down her porcelain bowl. The twins, too, stop to brush their aprons clean.

'I was hoping I could speak to all of you down here. Where is Chipman and Will?'

Mrs Beacham tells him they are polishing the silver for lunch, so Cate retrieves them. The five staff members stand formally on one side of the kitchen table with Tom on the other.

'I just wanted to thank you all for your service. I know it hasn't been long.' Tom's fingers slide through his hair. 'Liz and I wanted you to know that we shall miss you once we have left and that we wish you all the very best for your futures.'

The speech feels inadequate. He had never had any intention of keeping the staff on for long, for he'd had no intention of staying at Floreat, but now he finds he has grown attached to them, their steadfastness and loyalty. They have never suspected him of anything.

'It has been a pleasure, sir,' Chipman says on behalf of the congregation and bows his head.

'As you know, we shall be leaving tomorrow. I understand there is still much work to do, but Liz and I would like it if you would join us for drinks after dinner tonight.'

That cheers them slightly, and a faint murmur of excitement rumbles through the room.

'Good.' Tom claps his hands together. 'I shall leave you to it and find out what Liz is doing.' He turns his back when Will speaks.

'She's gone out, sir. She's taken the pony.'

Tom pauses. Liz has not ridden for months – she has not even left the house for weeks. A feeling of dread steals over him. 'Where was she going?'

'I don't know, sir. I saw them heading off towards the sea.'

'Ready my horse, Will. I shall join her.'

He forces a smile to his lips as Chipman finds his riding boots. They are just coming around to the front of the stables when something catches Tom's eye. The little white pony is galloping in their direction over the lawn, without a rider on her back.

'Will! My horse!'

In a minute, Tom is cantering for the cliffs. Behind him, people are shouting, and glancing back he sees Chipman riding the white pony with Will sprinting in his wake.

The lawn merges into rolling fields as he gallops, and the sea looms ahead. Just one more gentle slope and the cliffs will be before him. He almost does not want to see what awaits him. He has images of Liz's hands clinging to the earth, slipping out of his grasp just as he reaches her. He imagines Liz badly thrown from her pony, back broken, neck snapped. He pictures her at the bottom of the cliffs, a heap of skin and bone, blood and skirts.

He chokes on his tears as the reality of the situation reveals itself, and he finds Liz sitting on the grass, a few safe feet away from the cliff edge. He slows his horse and slides off while it is still moving.

Her eyes are wide in shock. There is a deep cut on her temple, and the blood has trickled over her face, like tree roots over the earth. Her hair has mud and grass in it and bruises form on her neck.

'Liz,' he whispers, gently bringing her back into consciousness. 'It's all right.' He checks the hill to make sure that no one has come yet. It is clear, so he takes her delicate head in his hands and kisses her lips. 'It's all right, my love. I'm here. Are you hurt?'

Liz shakes her head.

'Did you fall? What happened?'

Liz points at the sea.

He kisses her again, quickly this time for he can hear hooves and sure enough, seconds later Chipman canters towards him. 'Chipman, have you a coat?'

Once dismounted, Chipman removes his jacket and wraps it around Liz.

Tom leaves her in Chipman's care for a moment and walks to the cliff edge. Below him, his mother's body sways underneath the sea's current. He closes his eyes, remembers her as she was for a second, but that memory belongs to another boy – Thomas Jacob Carter, who disappeared a long time ago. He turns his back on her for the last time.

'We must send for Inspector Edwards,' Tom says, as Will staggers towards them, scarlet-faced and breathing hard. 'That witch has tried to kill Liz.'

Inspector Edwards came as soon as he could with Doctor Kershaw in tow. He took Liz into Tom's study and asked her about what had happened as the doctor checked her pulse and cleaned her wounds. Liz said Charlotte had scared her pony, causing her to fall and cut her head on a loose rock. Charlotte had called Liz a devil, then tried to strangle her. Liz had managed to free herself, and when the woman had lunged at her again, she had dodged out of the way, and Charlotte had fallen to her death.

Inspector Edwards apologised for what had happened, berating himself for not taking Charlotte to trial in the first place, for he thought her nothing more than a harmless fantasist. Liz assured him she did not blame him for it. She said what a pity it was that some people were so ill in the mind.

Now, dressed in her nightgown, Liz stands before the fire in her chamber. She has kissed Little Tom goodnight and left him in the safe hands of Mrs Jeffries for the last time. She revels in the thought that tomorrow night, Tom, the baby, and she, will be alone in their first-class cabin, as a proper family.

Tom enters, still dressed in his dinner suit, and yawns as he makes his way to her side. She turns her face to him and lets his lips linger on her own. How she has missed those lips!

'Come to bed,' he whispers as he begins to remove his clothes.

She is impatient for him too, but there is something she must do first. She pulls out a wooden box from underneath her bed. Tom watches her, amused and curious. She opens the wooden lid and lifts the doll out of its makeshift coffin, the note still in its grip.

Tom's amusement vanishes, but she shushes his concerns. She unfolds the paper, rereads it, then throws it onto the fire. The words, *he will never be yours*, turn to ash in the grate.

'What did it say?'

'Lies.' She smiles as Tom comes beside her, then throws the doll into the flames.

They stand together, arms wrapped around each other's waists, Liz's head resting on Tom's shoulder, and watch the doll burn.

EPILOGUE

*N*ovember 1855

ON THE CORNER OF A STREET, a street filled with pigeon, dog, and horse dung, where the old brick walls sweat with human urine and gas leaks into the air, sits a little girl, no more than six years old.

Her green, saucer eyes reflect the leaden sky, which is barely visible between the roofs of the houses. Her milky skin is dusted with grime, and her lips part to reveal a toothy hole. Her hair is a tangle of white-blonde, like a spider's nest wrapped around her little head and propped on top of a bony neck. Her skinny frame is hard to determine, swathed in stained blankets, with only her shabby feet poking out from underneath the fabric in worn-out, too-big shoes.

She sits, shivering, as the pure-collectors hobble past her. A dog sniffs at her, trying to determine whether she is edible, but as soon as she moves, it scampers away. She only wishes to pet it. Vermin it may be, but then, so is she.

The little girl waits alone for her mother to return, as she does every day. Her mother's presence is fleeting.

A scabby hand comes into the child's vision offering a lump of bread. The child grabs it, stuffs it into her parched mouth, chews as best she can, and swallows with all her might. The hand holds out a glass bottle with a clear liquid in it, and the child drinks three big gulps.

'It's a cold 'un, Liz.' The figure bends to shove the girl's icy feet under the blanket, then moves a few nearby wooden crates in front of the child to hide her.

'We'll be back inside for Christmas,' the figure whispers and leans forward to stroke the child's head. Her cough is hard and wet, and she wipes her mouth on her sleeve.

'A fuck for a shillin'?' she calls into the gloom, and disappears again.

TIME PASSES SLOWLY, gazing between the walls and into the smoggy sky. Two nights have passed without the presence of a reassuring hand, and the little girl's stomach cries out for her mother. Dawn breaks, and as labourers emerge from the shadows to make their way to work, her hunger forces her to look around herself and search for food.

The broken wooden crates still encircle her, giving her a layer of protection. She peers through the splintered, damp wood for anything that she could put in her mouth, but there is nothing. The alley swirls with ragged skirts and ripped trousers, and boots that slop through the slime. Bent and blind old women beg opposite her or else shuffle along with their foul-smelling buckets towards the tanning yard.

In the distance, she can see a costermonger. The thought of food sets her dry mouth running with saliva.

But she should not move. Her mother has told her to

wait. Always wait until I come for you, that's what her mother says.

There are bad people out there, Liz, and not just the ones with knives in their pockets.

But her mother has never been away for this long before. Has one of the bad people taken her? Liz has often heard women crying for their babies when they have been taken, or crying for their men, who have disappeared.

Has her mother vanished? Is she all alone in the world? And if so, does she still have to stay where her mother told her to?

A bitter gust of wind slaps her left cheek and carries the salty smell of oysters into her nostrils. She pulls herself up on the wall as her legs threaten to buckle. For a moment, she cannot see; it is as if night has fallen. But slowly, her vision returns, and the glottal slang of her fellow street people fills her head as they move around her.

Her numb feet carry her closer to the cart, and she can see the pile of grey-black shells and the gleaming white flesh of the oysters. She is so close! Her stomach barks an order at her to reach up, reach for one silver shell, take it into her tiny palm, then tip it back into her mouth and swallow the sweet flesh inside.

She reaches up, her arm quivering with the effort, and she is just about to touch one when a sharp pain slices into her forehead and sends her reeling backwards into the street.

'Piss off, you filthy cunt.'

Quickly, before any more harm can be done to her, she gets to her feet, only to fall again with the effort. As she pulls herself up once more, she notices the oyster shell just a few feet away from her, the cause of the pain in her head. She dares a look at the cart. The costermonger glares at her, threatening her with another shell in his hand. She will not get any food here.

She stumbles away. The throbbing in her head worsens as she reaches the end of the alley and emerges into a wide street. She leans on the corner of a wall and breathes until the ground steadies.

She should go back to her hiding place, but she does not want to walk past the oyster seller again. Perhaps she should just sit here and wait. But her stomach cries and she knows she must find food, somehow.

TOM GRINS as great lumps of meat and gravy slop about his chops. He opens his lips and sucks up the air to cool the steaming contents and soothe his red gums. He chews and chews and smiles and sucks and doesn't bother mopping up the juices that slip down his chin.

Mr Brown tuts but can't help smiling. He pours Tom – who reminds him of his own son before he left for the war and never came back – a small cup of ale.

When Tom finishes, he wipes his mouth with the back of his sleeve, puts his hand to his stomach, pats it, and sighs. 'That'll do me for today,' he says. 'Thank you, Mr Brown. I'll be seeing you.' He slips his coins across the counter and strolls out like the little gentleman he thinks he is.

What to do with the rest of the day? His money jingles in his pocket, and already he is thinking about where he might find a sausage stall or someone selling sugar mice.

He dawdles for a while, looking at nothing and everything. Girls of all kinds saunter past him. On the corner of one street, a shoeblack pummels away at a gentleman's feet. The gentleman has his nose in a newspaper and takes no notice of the girls that walk by.

The streets Tom roams are well and truly alive with the hustle and bustle of the city. Omnibuses whirr past him, carrying little plump ladies or fellows with untidy facial hair and smears of paint on their dour faces. He kicks his heels, wondering what shop he might explore today, or whether he should spend his money on an omnibus to the park and run around in the bleak November sunshine. He has just about made up his mind to do so when a glimmer of white catches his eye.

He pushes through the throng of black trousers and around the bustle of dark skirts until he comes upon something the like of which he has never seen before. A globe of silver hair hangs over a hidden face, and one white stick of an arm protrudes through a filthy brown rag.

He inches towards the strange creature and touches the blanket. The creature is startled, and an ashen face looks up at him. A scarlet gash on the girl's forehead glistens in the daylight and blood seeps towards eyes of such a piercing green that Tom feels he has seen them somewhere before. Her whitened, cracked lips part and close and part again, and Tom is dumbstruck until he notices the arm reach out, open palmed, in his direction.

'Are you all right?' he says, and for the first time in his whole life, he blushes as he realises he has said something stupid.

A whine escapes from her throat. Her tongue brushes her lips with the barest of saliva.

'Here.' He pushes his flask towards her. He has to tip it into her mouth for she is too weak to do it herself.

She sips as if scared at first, but as the liquor trickles into her mouth, it brings life. Soon, she grasps the flask and guzzles until it is drained. She gasps for breath and blinks as if awakening.

'Food,' she says.

TOM BUYS A DOZEN OYSTERS. They find an empty recess in a wall and sit there.

'Here.' Tom hands her two. 'Eat them slow though, else you'll be sick.'

He watches her as she eats, the effort clear in her face. She swallows hard, then asks for another. Tom gives it to her.

'What's your name?'

'Liz.'

'Where do you live, Liz?'

Liz's gaze wanders from the oyster shell to the sky. She does not answer.

'Do you have a mother?'

Her lower lip trembles. 'I don't know where she is.'

Tom doesn't know what to say to this. People go missing all the time, he knows that. He's never thought about what it would be like to lose anyone – his mother is always in the same place. Then suddenly, he has an idea.

'Come on.' He hops to his feet and holds out his hand.

'Where we going?'

'Home. You can come with me. I'll take care of you.'

The girl hesitates, glances around her.

'I've looked after you today, ain't I?'

She nods.

'I'll always look after you,' he says. 'Come on.'

Still, she is hesitant.

'Do you trust me?'

The question lingers between them for a moment, then Liz slips her tiny hand into his, and their fate is sealed.

AN ORDINARY DOOR in an ordinary street, where the low-to-middling kind of folk tend to pass through, opens before her. Inside, it is dark once the front door is shut. She tries to adjust her eyes to the mint-striped wallpaper and the thinning carpet, but she is pulled through a narrow corridor and into another room. Before she has chance to notice the state of the shabby furniture and the grand piano in the corner, she is stunned by the presence of a beautiful woman draped on a scarlet velvet chair, reading a book.

'Mother, I …' Tom says but does not manage to distract the woman from her book. 'I found something. Someone. Mother, I found a girl.'

Awoken from her trance, the woman peels her eyes from the pages and casts them upon the waif stood in the shadow of her son. Liz squirms under the penetration and wonders if she should run.

'A girl? Does she have a name?'

Tom takes a breath, but his mother holds up one long finger to stop him.

'Can she not speak for herself?'

'Liz.'

'Is that what your mother calls you?'

Liz nods.

'Where is your mother?'

'Lost,' Tom says. 'She says she's been gone the longest ever. I said we could help.'

'Did you?'

His mother raises a black eyebrow but continues to look at the girl. Then she rises to her feet, slinks towards the child and kneels so that their beautiful faces are parallel. This close, Liz is transfixed.

'I'm very sorry, child, but I fear your mother is dead.'

The sweet scent of the woman's breath lingers in Liz's nostrils, the music of her voice dances in her ears, and the meaning of her words is lost in the hypnotism of her eyes.

'But do not worry, now, little Lizzie. We will take good care of you.'

The woman comes closer, so close that Liz can see the

pulse under her sharp jawline when she kisses Liz on the forehead.

'You can call me Mother now.'

AFTERWORD

Thank you for taking the time to read *The Promise Keeper,* and for taking a chance on a new author. I hope you will consider leaving a review online as it truly helps authors to get their work into the hands of those who will love it.

Although the second novel in the collection, *The Promise Keeper* was the first book I wrote after finishing my degree. It has been a labour of love and has gone through countless revisions. Liz and Tom have to be two of my favourite characters, and I feel a very strong connection with them and their story. Perhaps one day I will write the tale of their troubled and heartbreaking past – you, reader, will have to let me know if you would like to read that. In the meantime, think of them in Venice, listening to the water lapping peacefully through their opened casement window, and watching Little Tom growing into a young man. (That is how I imagine them, at least.)

If you would like to hear more about my work and get a **FREE** standalone novella, *The Butcher's Wife* – which is part of the *Convenient Women* collection – then please join my mailing list via my website:

www.delphinewoods.com

The third novel in the *Convenient Women* collection, *The Button Maker*, is released October 2019.

ACKNOWLEDGMENTS

Once again, thank you, reader, for taking a chance on a new author. It means a lot!

I would also like to thank my family for being so supportive and encouraging me to follow my dreams. Thank you to my mother for always being there with constructive criticism and for being the first to read my work. Thank you to my father for all his technical support. Thank you to my fiance for believing in me completely.

Thank you to Kate and Victoria for giving such detailed feedback and helping to improve this piece of work, and to Nicola Simcock for the first ever edit of this manuscript. To my writer friends, who share their troubles and dreams and make life as a writer less lonely – thank you! And a big thanks to the online Indie community, who share their knowledge and expertise and continue to fill our world with wonderful new books.

ABOUT THE AUTHOR

Delphine Woods graduated with a First from The Open University in 2016, where she studied for an Open Degree, specialising in Creative Writing.

After a busy couple of years writing her collection of Victorian mystery-thrillers, she released her debut novella, *The Butcher's Wife,* in July 2019. *The Promise Keeper* is the second full-length novel in the *Convenient Women* collection. These books are all set in Victorian England and have been inspired by nursery rhymes.

She lives with her fiance in Shropshire where she writes in her spare room, her dog by her feet to keep her warm. You can keep up to date with her news and get in touch with her via her newsletter and social media platforms.

For more information, visit her website:

www.delphinewoods.com

ALSO BY DELPHINE WOODS

The Butcher's Wife: Convenient Women Collection Novella

A proposition of murder. A chance for freedom. But at what price?

Wolverhampton, 1862, and Nettie's husband is drunk. Again. With rent unpaid, food scarce, and money-lenders on the prowl, professional slaughterer, Russell Taylor, offers to help. But what does his devilish plan involve, and who is watching from the shadows?

As she fights for survival, Nettie must discover the real cost of life, death, truth, and lies.

The Butcher's Wife is a Victorian gothic thriller novella, part of the *Convenient Women* collection, and is available exclusively to the Delphine Woods Reader's List. It is inspired by the nursery rhyme, *Pop! Goes the Weasel,* and contains mature themes.

Available via www.delphinewoods.com

The Cradle Breaker: Convenient Women Collection Book One

A familiar face. A guilty secret. Vengeance is coming.

Summer, 1865, and Bonnie Hearn thinks she's seen the stranger outside her window somewhere before.

All Luella Blyth has ever wanted was the truth. Tracking down the woman she thinks holds the answers, Luella is determined to find the murderer who sent her father to the gallows and wreak her revenge.

As Bonnie struggles to keep her secrets and Luella battles to reveal them, who will survive this game of deception?

The Cradle Breaker is a standalone Victorian gothic mystery-thriller novel, book one of the *Convenient Women* collection, and is available on Amazon. It is inspired by the nursery rhyme, *Rock-a-bye Baby,* and contains mature themes.

The Button Maker: Convenient Women Collection Book Three

A helpless stranger. A hidden past. A future worth killing for.

Autumn, 1853, and Cat Davies is drowning. On the brink of death, Osbourne Tomkins saves her from her murderer and offers her a new life at his country estate, Wallingham Hall.

But both of them have pasts which threaten their current idyll.

As suspicion turns to paranoia, and love is blinded by mistrust, Cat must fight for her life and the future she has always dreamed of.

The Button Maker is a standalone Victorian mystery-thriller, book three of the *Convenient Women* collection, and is available on Amazon from October 2019. It is inspired by the nursery rhyme, *Ding Dong Bell*, and contains mature themes.

Made in United States
North Haven, CT
28 October 2023